FIT
TO BE
DEAD

Books by Nancy G. West

Psychological Suspense

Nine Days to Evil

Second Edition 2020

Aggie Mundeen Mystery Series

Fit to Be Dead 2014

Dang Near Dead 2014

Smart, But Dead 2015

River City Dead 2017

Aggie Mundeen Lake Mystery

The Plunge 2018

A novella

Praise for the Aggie Mundeen Mystery Series

FIT TO BE DEAD

"West's fine writing and clever plot reveal her mad sense of humor...She has produced a beautifully written book, brimming with wry humor and a cleverly woven mystery. Highly recommended! I am very pleased to see there is a follow-up Aggie Mundeen novel, *Dang Near Dead*."

– Diana Hockley,
Australian Mystery Novelist and International Reviewer for
NetGalley and *Kings River Life* Magazine

"West's main characters' histories suggest they could fill a series. I hope so. I love this book!"

– Rollo K. Newsom PhD,
Professor Emeritus, Texas State University,
and an editor of *Lone Star Sleuths*

"*Fit to Be Dead* has it all: intriguing characters that point to romance, an engrossing plot, a compelling puzzle and well-disguised clues—a fun read."

– L. C. Hayden,
Award-Winning Author of the Harry Bronson Mystery Series

"Aggie Mundeen's wry observations on life, death, and the struggle to whip mind and body into shape make *Fit to Be Dead* delightful. Joining a health club has never been so dangerous...or so amusing."

– Karen McCullough,
Author of *Wired for Murder*

"*Fit to be Dead* is a satisfying read with powerful characterization, plot twists and a feisty believable protagonist."

– *Midwest Book Review*

FIT TO BE DEAD

An Aggie Mundeen Mystery

Nancy G. West

FIT TO BE DEAD
An Aggie Mundeen Mystery
First Edition 2014

Revised Second Edition
September 2019

Trade Paperback Second Edition
July 2020

Southwest Publications

This is a work of fiction. Any references to historical events, real people, or real locales are used fictitiously. Other names, characters, places, and incidents are the product of the author's imagination, and any resemblance to actual events or locales or persons, living or dead, is entirely coincidental.

ISBN-13: 978-1-7341175-0-9

Printed in the United States of America

ACKNOWLEDGMENTS

No writer completes a book without help. I am grateful for gifts of time and information from the following people.

- California publisher Terry R. Cooper, whose enthusiasm for this book spurred me on

- Richard Hawk, who explained the work of the San Antonio Testing Lab

- Dr. D.P. Lyle, physician and mystery writer who shared his knowledge of forensic medicine

- Dr. Michael Wooley, San Antonio pulmonologist who clarified the effects of inhaling toxic gas and who epitomizes the caring physician

None of my books would exist without Donald West, who sustains me and procures nourishment so I can stop writing only to eat. Any errors that exist in the novel are mine.

I do not, however, accept responsibility for whatever Aggie Mundeen might do.

One

Shaping up at my age can be murder. My Wagoneer station wagon, Albatross, chugged toward Fit and Firm Health Club. Just thinking about trying to operate the machines packed inside that club made me shudder. I'm mechanically inept. My condition may be genetic.

Before anyone figured out it was me who wrote the "Stay Young With Aggie" column, I had to get in shape. Once I decided to ditch banking in Chicago and move to San Antonio to start over, I was past thirty, overweight, devoid of muscle tone and terrified by the prospect of middle age. Naturally, my readers must never know these things.

I had already enrolled in graduate school for the 1997 spring semester at University of the Holy Trinity and signed up for the class Aspects of Aging. Now it was time to investigate physical improvement.

I called my graduate school friend, Meredith Laughlin, for support and heard her hesitate on the other end of the line. She's only twenty-four.

"That's great, Aggie," Meredith said. "I don't have much time between studying and clearing out Conrad's office, but I really should exercise."

Conrad's her ex-husband. Meredith's practical nature probably resulted from being spawned by a successful southern couple. Having virtually raised myself in Chicago, I plunged into situations headlong—unless the situation involved any form of exercise which might require physical agility.

In addition to redesigning my body, I wanted to jumpstart my social life: break out, encounter people. Not people—men. I'd been confined in that bank in Chicago like a squirrel counting nuts for too long. There had to be a good man around somewhere, a trustworthy person like Detective Sam Vanderhoven, my friend at SAPD who left Chicago the year before I did.

"Who knows? I might meet somebody at the health club," I told Meredith. Chances were slim I'd find the right man at graduate school. "Students are fledglings, and professors stagnate. Getting tenured can petrify a teacher's brain."

She chuckled. "Have fun at the health club, Aggie. I think sitting and studying expands our sitters faster than our minds."

I had written in my column about the pitfalls of inactivity: people who watched four or more hours of TV daily were 80% more likely to die of heart disease. Inactivity could result from occupying a desk at work, sitting at one's home computer surfing the net or writing a book. One writer said every book was worth fifteen pounds. Once he finished writing it, he spent the next six months getting the weight off. Dear Aggie's solution for sitters was to get up every hour to walk or do calisthenics. In addition to their daily exercise routine. Assuming they had one.

Meredith's remark spurred me into action. When I stopped at North New Braunfels Avenue and waited for the light to change, I fixated on my nails: tomato red did not match the wine trim on my warm-up suit. Okay, I was stalling.

When I veered right onto the Austin Highway, I spotted the health club: a four-story armory with convex windows that bulged out over a grassy knoll like a fat stomach over jeans. What kind of crazy people paid money to enter that unappealing edifice and exercise?

The parking garage for inmates was on the other side of the building. I rolled by the asylum, contemplating alternatives. With people living past one hundred, middle age struck around fifty. Perhaps laboratories could genetically test every person who reached ninety-nine, drug companies could synthesize their genes into pills, and pharmacists could sell them like vitamins. Until those procedures were initiated, I supposed everybody pushing forty had to rely on maintenance.

With my heart dancing a tango, I settled Albatross in Fit and Firm's garage. What if I was too klutzy to master the machines? If that were the case, I'd need an alternative plan to spark my social life. Personal ads. Thank goodness I knew how to write. I snatched my yellow Big Chief tablet off the seat. "Single white female. Intelligent. Curious. Interested in everything. Desires to meet intriguing man." I ripped off the sheet—I'd polish the ad later—and tossed the tablet on the seat.

Inhaling a liter of air, I pried myself from the car and pointed my body toward the club, hoping I wasn't about to kill myself on some peculiar apparatus. I crossed the garage exit and was approaching the entrance when a shaggy arm flew up in front of me and blocked the door. Hairy fingers gripped the sheet I'd torn from the tablet. He grinned down through hair flopping on massive shoulders.

"You must have dropped this." He devoured me with close-set eyes. "'Interested in everything,' huh? Me, too. We should get together."

Chills tumbled down my spine into my socks. My feet froze.

"I'm not interested in everything," I stammered. "Actually, I'm not interested in anything, (cough) since I'm about to throw up."

When he dropped his wooly arm, I lunged through the door. He didn't follow. Head down, I crossed the stuffy foyer and approached the girl at the desk.

"Is it all right if I look around?"

"Sure." She smacked her gum. "Sign this form and I'll issue you a guest pass. Good for today only." I glanced outside and didn't spot the primitive, but I was sweating from a case of nerves. This health club was stifling. Heat rising from sweaty bodies on upper floors must have sunk to ground level. I unzipped my jacket, exposing my T-shirt with Garfield the Cat hoisting his barbell. A magnificent blond creature with Caribbean eyes swaggered up from nowhere. He smiled at me as if I were Sandra Bullock. I'd never felt so gorgeous in a jogging suit. This hunk would never feel the need to write to Dear Aggie.

He blinked at Garfield on the front of my shirt. "Hey, I'm Pete Reeves." He extended a bronzed hand.

"Aggie Mundeen." He beat everything I'd seen at any financial institution or graduate school. He stood over six feet tall, a blond lifeguard type. After toiling days at the bank and dragging my body to night classes to earn a BBA, I felt skittish about meeting hunks— but eager to catch up.

"Would you like to tour our fabulous club?"

Only a corpse wouldn't tour with Pete. "Okay." I prepared myself to view a universe of flawless specimens. Maybe I could interview them for my column. I felt Pete's hand on my shoulder. He squeezed me around the entrance desk and pointed to the establishment on the left.

"There's Tofu Temptations Grill. Beyond the grill are men and women's locker rooms. The swimming pool is behind the locker rooms." He irradiated me with a smile. "Olympic-sized, indoor pool. Heated to a satisfying temperature."

I cleared my throat. Thinking about being in the water made me suddenly desperate to use the bathroom.

"Would you like to see the pool?"

"No, thanks." I'd remembered to stuff a swimsuit in my purse, but I didn't need extra steam along with the heat Pete was generating. I was suffocating. "I'll catch you later after I check out the ladies' room."

His smile vanished. Before he could speak, I crabbed sideways into the women's locker room, smiled at him and crashed into a towel depository inside the door.

The din of high-pitched voices ceased. I righted the metal container, smiled agreeably, and plunged through a variety of fragrances toward the farthest lockers. Chatter resumed above the racket of showers and hairdryers. Assorted women in various stages of undress robed and disrobed. I had discovered a nudist colony of magpies.

I grabbed a towel and found an empty locker. Two women flanked my space. Monica, a naked, pencil-thin woman with doorknob breasts, introduced herself. I was pretty sure she'd always been thin. She probably had trouble gaining weight or building muscle no matter what she ate or how much she exercised. Definitely an ectomorph.

Her friend Mindy, a heaving Mason-jar woman, toweled her substantial body on my other side, her curly red hair flapping around her jowls. She had the opposite body type: endomorph. She probably ate half what Monica did and gained weight. I was researching how people should eat and exercise depending upon their body type. I'd seen a few mesomorphs around, lucky people who could gain muscle and lose fat if they simply ate and exercised moderately. They were rare.

After peeling off my warm-up T-shirt and tights, I wrenched my cheap turquoise swimsuit on over sticky skin and envisioned the hunky-but-dependable man I'd find in the pool. He and I would slide like arrows through rippling water. I was not seeking thrills or emotional involvement, just safe companionship. I knew how to swim, so gliding through water seemed like the safest way to exercise. I could access the pool from the back of the locker room without having to traverse the lobby.

I flip-flopped my K-mart thongs to the entrance and gaped at the Olympic pool, a rectangular jewel set in an oblong room. This pool would look perfect nestled into a Greek hillside overlooking the Aegean Sea. Eight lanes were painted with black stripes that ribboned the bottom of the pool.

Inhaling the purifying odor of chlorine, I scanned the pool for swimmers and spotted a woman at the far end. Backing down the nearest steps, I luxuriated in water lapping against my body and bounced toward her to begin my workout with a chat.

Despite my splashing, she ignored me. She floated face down, didn't have snorkel gear and wasn't coming up for air. My heart pumped faster. I started running with the water dragging against me. The pool seemed twice as big as before. Despite being totally out of shape, I had to reach her. I ignored the fleeting memory of my earlier leaps into situations that had proved disastrous. Gulping a breath, I plunged in, ripped water with my arms and kicked hard.

I finally reached her, grasped her shoulders and flipped her face up. The water wasn't too deep for me to stand. Panting from exertion, I leaned over her. "Are you okay? Can you hear me?"

She was little more than a girl. Unconscious. With blue lips.

"Help! Help!" I whipped my head around, desperate to find somebody, anybody, near the pool. My cry reverberated through cavernous space. Cradling her chin with one hand, I grabbed her hair with my other hand and tugged her toward the ladder. I backed up the first rung, struggling to hoist her up. She looked small, but she felt like the Titanic. She turned bluer. I put my ear to her nose and mouth. Her silence terrified me. Time was running out.

"Give me her arms." Blond curls loomed above us, bobbing over a red shirt and white shorts—the club uniform. I was never so glad to see another human being. With remarkable strength, the staffer pulled the girl up the ladder while I shoved her from below.

She pulled the victim from the water and shook her gently, calling, "Are you all right?" I scurried out of the pool after the unconscious girl. The instructor initiated standard CPR procedures. Frozen, I waited for the girl to respond. She remained limp. Since the girl made no response, the instructor placed her on her back, tilted her head back to open her airway and listened for breathing. She swept a finger down her throat to clear any obstruction and placed two fingers on the girl's carotid artery. "She has a pulse!" Pinching the girl's nose closed, she covered her mouth with her own.

When she blew in two breaths, the girl's chest rose. "The color's coming back to her face," I said.

She felt the girl's neck again. "Her pulse is stronger." The instructor crouched over and blew air into the girl every five seconds until she sputtered. By then I had stopped breathing. The girl started coughing up water.

"Whew." The blonde settled on her haunches. "She's reviving quickly. We still have to call nine-one-one." She strode to the women's locker room door, yanked it open and powered through it toward the phone. "Somebody swallowed pool water," she called out.

I snapped my eyes back to the girl. She coughed, struggling to clear water from her lungs. She sat up and started to cry.

"What happened? I could have drowned..."

I didn't know what to say. When the blond savior came trotting back, I felt like somebody had lifted a freight car off my shoulders. "You're great at CPR," I told the trainer.

She smiled. "I've had to use it a couple of times. We're required to learn CPR to work here." She bent down to touch the girl's shoulder. "You're Annie, uh, Cindy, right? I'm Sarah Savoy. We talked after aerobics, remember?"

The girl squinted at her rescuer and at the pool, eyes fluttering. "It's Holly. Holly Holmgreen. Was it only this morning I went to your class? I hoped I could still do aerobics. You were so nice to me."

Holly seemed fine to me. She was thinking and remembering. My breathing returned to normal.

With flawless features in a doll-like face, ringlets plastered against her soaked head, and huge eyes with bushy lashes, she exuded a helpless appearance. She glanced down, embarrassed. "The doctor said swimming might help. I've been so depressed." She shook her head. "I'm sorry to cause this trouble."

Poor thing. She could have drowned. Now she felt ashamed of being depressed. A few more seconds in the water might have depressed her permanently. The horrible possibility made my heart ache.

If Sarah Savoy knew what had upset Holly before she entered the pool, she didn't disclose it.

Holly glanced at me. Distressed at revealing her misery to a stranger, she averted her eyes.

I heard the EMS siren and chattered to relieve the tension.

"I'm Aggie Mundeen. I'm new here. When I got into the pool, I swam over to say 'hi' and realized you were unconscious. Do you remember what happened?" My feet started to itch. The phenomenon occurs when my curiosity is aroused.

The girl squeezed her eyes shut. "I'm not sure. I felt a buzz...a vibration." Her eyes opened wide. "It felt like...like electricity in the water. A shock. I don't remember any more after that."

I crawfished back from the pool. Sarah Savoy nudged Holly away from the water's edge, straightened to her considerable height and scouted the pool's perimeter. "Nobody uses electric equipment in here."

Following Sarah's gaze around the pool's border, I spotted a dark object on the far side under the water. A tail attached to the blurry article snaked out of the pool toward the window that rose to the domed ceiling. We hurried around the edge and discovered a radio/tape player submerged beneath the water, not far from where Holly had floated. Somebody had plugged it into the outlet under the window. The player appeared to have fallen in.

Sarah's face reddened. "I can't believe this. Management never allows appliances near the pool. Locker room signs warn people not to bring them in. Maintenance men have to get the manager's permission to schedule repairs at slack times." She reached for the radio.

"Wait, it might shock you. Unplug it and drag it out by the cord." My barking command surprised me. Maybe I'd acquired the habit from Sam. His delivery used to be authoritative, like most law enforcement officers. After his family died, though, his words developed a sharper edge.

Obviously, the pool was no longer electrified, or I'd be recovering by the pool next to Holly. Even so, I was relieved to see Sarah unplug the radio and draw it out, cord first.

"I'm taking this gadget to the manager. He'll know how to handle this." She wrapped the cord around the radio and set it inside the ladies' locker room. We heard EMS sirens roaring closer to the club.

Holly watched Sarah walk back toward her. "Somebody used a radio by the pool? Who would do that? They could have killed me."

Sarah bent and patted her shoulder. "It's okay. You were the victim of a stupid accident. Thank God, you're all right. Sounds like EMS is here. We'll wait here with you, Holly, then I'll report this to the manager. He'll probably close the pool. I hear the EMS crew in the lobby. I'll go get them. Aggie, will you wait here with Holly? Warn anybody who comes in to stay out of the water. I'll be right back."

"Sure." Sarah probably forgot I was experiencing my first day at Fit and Firm. She rushed back through the women's locker room, a bundle of efficiency.

I sucked in a lung full of air for the first time in twenty minutes. What happened to the electrical charge when I entered the water? If I'd slipped in minutes earlier, would Holly and I be floating corpses? What would the manager do? An electrical surge could have changed Fit and Firm to Fit but Dead. Not good advertising for a health club. I'd become punchy with relief. I wasn't thrilled with getting older, but it beat being a corpse.

I didn't mind staying with Holly. She'd expelled the water from her lungs, and I didn't think her health was compromised. Besides, only she could answer questions bouncing inside my head. I had to talk fast.

"I guess you didn't see anybody else in the pool area?" I glanced around. Besides entrances to the men's and women's locker rooms, I saw one other closed door. I rubbed my feet together.

"No. Nobody was here. I wanted to join water aerobics, but class had ended. I'm a strong swimmer, so I wasn't afraid to swim alone."

"Did something upset you?" I couldn't help it. I tingled with curiosity.

"Yes. I took Valium earlier. If only I hadn't..." She began to sob.

My eyes started to fill. "I'm sorry. I shouldn't have asked."

"It's okay. I didn't keep it a secret. I'm not married. I got pregnant and gave up the baby."

My stomach flipped. Girls were so casual about unplanned pregnancies. A few years ago, unwed mothers kept silent, ashamed. Youth made people do dumb things. Age did have a few advantages. I didn't want Holly Holmgreen to reveal any more. I'd joined Fit and Firm for self-improvement, and my fitness plan hadn't included solving somebody else's problems. I used my problem-solving energy to help people who wrote to Dear Aggie. Yet I couldn't help but feel empathy for this girl.

We sat motionless, except for my patting her hand when she sniffled. My queasy stomach churned from the agony I knew she felt. If only I could do something to help her.

Sarah returned with three EMS men carrying a stretcher and a load of equipment. While they approached Holly, Sarah taped "Pool Closed for Repairs" signs on the women's locker room door and pool ladders. She returned and knelt by Holly. The techs took Holly's blood pressure and asked her questions.

Sarah gave us a report. "The signs are temporary," she said. "The manager will lock entrances to the pool while he investigates what happened." I had a sudden urge to talk to the club manager.

Holly insisted on standing. The men reluctantly helped the shaky girl to her feet.

"I'm fine," she announced. "I'm not going to the hospital. I've been there too much lately."

"They'll need to check you out," a technician said.

"I'm refusing treatment," Holly said.

"We'll have to give you a form to sign that you're refusing services," the technician said.

"Sure."

He brought her the paper and pen, and she signed it. I noticed her hand was steady. She thanked the men. "I'm ready to go," she said.

She walked slowly toward the women's locker room, resolute. I caught up alongside her in case she stumbled. Sarah was on our heels.

"You'll have to sign another paper saying you don't fault the club for your accident," Sarah said. "I'll have to make a report. It's a club requirement."

"That's fine," Holly said.

While Sarah ran to get a release form, Holly and I sat in chairs in the ladies' locker room.

She turned to me. "I'll take my time getting dressed and make sure I feel perfect before I drive home. I'm sick of hospitals."

Sarah   reappeared with the release document and Holly signed.

"We don't want to frighten the other members," Sarah said. "If we tell everybody about this, the manager says he'll have to close the club. You'll lose your exercise place, and we won't have jobs."

Despite my urge to go size up the manager, I offered to walk Holly to her car. "That would be nice," Holly said.

Sarah appeared skeptical. "Okay...if you're sure..." She studied Holly.

"I'm fine. I'm okay to drive home." She smiled at Sarah and me, but her smile was sad. "You two saved my life."

Maybe I was too suspicious. Maybe somebody wanted to shorten Holly's life.

Two

After Holly drove off, I went back through the ladies' locker room to the pool. I wanted to see the "Pool Closed" signs and glance around, make sure no one was about to get in and that no electrical cords were submerged.

A man in red swim trunks emerged from the men's side accompanied by a male instructor decked out in the club uniform. While the trainer posted another "Pool Closed" sign, I calculated Red Shorts was a six-foot-three mesomorph with a stomach like a washboard. He would never need anti-aging tips.

Aware of his scrutiny but too unnerved to attempt southern chitchat, I called over my shoulder, "Don't get in the pool. It might be electrified." I tromped toward the women's room.

Red Shorts followed. "Hey! Wait a minute. What's goin' on?"

I wheeled around. Determined not to stare at his fully revealed six-pack, I studied his face. Except for his black curly hair and purple eyes, his resemblance to Tom Selleck was startling.

"They're closing the pool for repairs." I fingered my dripping hair. "Something about electricity."

"That's right up my line. I run an electrical bidness."

Did he say bidness? I must have appeared puzzled.

He leaned forward and squeezed my hand. "I started the company out in West Texas before I came to the big city." His eyes penetrated mine. "Mickey Shannon. Glad to know you."

"Uh, same here. Aga...Aggie Mundeen." Why didn't my Irish mother bless me with a lyrical name like Emily or Beverly? Mickey Shannon ambled closer, his gaze washing down to my feet and back to my flushing face. I'd picked a lousy time to wear my ratty blue-green swimsuit.

"What's the problem with the electricity?" When he leaned toward me and grinned impishly, I knew I was about to endure an Aggie joke. When I came to San Antonio, I had no idea what Aggies were. Everybody called Texas A&M University's students and graduates "Aggies," so my name spawned a barrage of jokes. But Aggie was preferable to being called Agatha, which sounded like somebody gagging.

"Did you hear about the professor who asked the Aggie what would happen if we didn't have electricity?" He looked eager. "The Aggie said we'd be watching TV by candlelight." He exploded with laughter.

I might have snickered if we hadn't just hauled Holly from the water. My face tightened.

"Somebody left a radio by the pool, and it fell in. They need to check the electricity before allowing anyone in the water. They're going to block access to the pool."

"Well, now, that sounds reasonable." He winked. "Wouldn't want a bunch of fritter-fried members, would we?"

Fritter-fried? His cavalier attitude irritated me. Then I realized he didn't know a girl had almost drowned or that somebody might have caused her accident.

I produced a southern-sweet smile calculated to induce him to share superior knowledge. "Since you own an electrical company, where do you think the circuit box is for the pool?"

He evaluated my face. "They probably installed it in an equipment storage room around here. Maybe over yonder."

Wherever that was. Was that how they gave directions in West Texas? He pointed to the closed door near the women's locker room.

"Since you're an expert, why don't we check it out?" I strode toward the door.

"Well, now, wait. My company doesn't service this club. The manager should be the one to…"

He hesitated, but curiosity propelled me toward the door. I grabbed the knob and strained to turn it, but the fixture wouldn't budge. Somebody had locked the room.

"Well, see? It's not something for us to get into. The club will handle the problem just fine."

"I suppose so." My urge to meet the manager escalated. The accident, if it was one, was a serious error. "If someone dropped a radio into the water, could the current electrocute a swimmer?"

"Shouldn't. Not if everything works right. Outlets installed near water have GFCIs, built-in shutoffs. When an electrical charge hits the water, the circuit breaks."

"No electricity would go through the appliance?"

"Right."

"Could a small amount of electricity pass through, enough to stun a person unconscious before the circuit broke?"

"It's possible. Especially if a person was close to the electrical source. Or there might be a short somewhere."

"A short. What would cause that?"

"Faulty wiring, maybe. But that's pretty unlikely. They take a ton of precautions in a club like this. You goin' to the weight room? I could show you how to use the machines."

Was my mechanical incompetence that obvious? Pain shot up my leg into my right bun, the result of churning through water at mach speed. I wished this man would stop grinning like Tom Selleck.

"Maybe tomorrow," I said.

"I'll look for you. You work out the same time every day?"

My schedule was growing more definite by the minute. "I might come in the morning." I smiled and bustled toward the women's locker room before Mickey Shannon's violet eyes could pierce my Ross Dress-For-Less swimsuit.

I yanked open my locker, peeled off the damp tube and tossed the flimsy garment into the trash. I sprayed sticky deodorant under my arms. Most of the members had cleared out. The only person left, Monica-with-the-doorknobs, reclined nude in the glass-enclosed steam room with one arm stretched ballerina fashion over her head, knobs pointed skyward. Obviously an arranged pose. My giggle erupted before I could squelch it. I didn't think Knobs heard me from inside her bubble, but Mason Jar jiggled through the room and gave me a dirty look for cackling at her friend.

She tapped on Knob's glass cage. "Here's the hair spray you wanted. I got it from the janitor." Knobs waved thanks, and Mason Jar set the bottle on a vanity shelf. As she left, I fingered Mason Jar a wave to make peace.

Back in my T-shirt and tights, I felt bedraggled. I knew my chin-length hair lay flat and dripping and my cheeks were flushed. With the turquoise suit gone, my saucer eyes probably vacillated between blue and green. If I weren't so disheveled, some might find me pretty. Actually, I was closer to interesting. During my frantic years at the bank, I spent time working my way up, not dwelling on my appearance. After work, I'd rush home, throw the nearest edible morsel down my throat and freshen up for a stimulating night class featuring accounting or statistics so I could earn my BBA. After class, I'd trek home, read letters to Dear Aggie and think up ways to help readers (and myself) avoid aging.

Somehow, I'd managed to blast my way from eighteen to way past thirty without taking stock. Now that I didn't have to work— thanks to my wildly appreciating bank stock—I could focus on personal improvement. I eased in front of the mirror. Everything on my five-foot-four-inch body seemed proportional. With a few pounds gone and some muscle tone, I might look presentable. I might even discover I had mesomorphic tendencies.

As for aging, I would count on my professor at University of the Holy Trinity to provide some answers. Even before I left Chicago to start over, I, Aggie Mundeen, had decided that thirty-something was old enough. The prospect of catapulting into middle age decrepitude terrified me. I knew I was obsessing about approaching forty, but the milestone signified my diminishing chance at happiness.

To get my mind on a more pleasant subject, I thought about

my friend Sam Vanderhoven. He wouldn't gape at me like Mickey had, although Sam's benevolent eyes never missed anything from behind his tortoise shell frames. He might gawk at the rare sight of me in a swimsuit, but then the corners of his mouth would turn up, and his salt- and-pepper hair would flop toward his glasses. He was slim and six to eight inches taller than me. He said a detective needed to stay in shape, but I couldn't picture him in workout clothes. I hadn't decided about his body type. He wore khaki shirts and slacks and garish ties splattered with random patterns. By age forty-five, his taste in clothes was, unfortunately, pretty well established.

Since my heart had stopped slamming against my ribs, I decided to peruse the facility. When I emerged from the locker room, Pete Reeves was leaning against a wall six feet away. He was apparently determined not to let a prospective member escape. His smile curved around teeth gleaming like a whitewashed fence.

"Ready to take the tour?"

"Sure."

"Then let's stroll upstairs." As he hopped up to level two, I tried to keep pace and not trip. He led me by handball courts, administrative offices, and past a basketball court toward the weight room. I dissuaded him from showing me how to operate the equipment.

We hiked up another flight to level three. What was I, Aggie Mundeen, former vice-president of a Chicago bank, doing in sneakers, tights, and a teenybopper T-shirt, scaling stairs to exercise? By the time we reached the third floor, I'd counted forty-four steps, was breathless and my leg muscles were in spasm. I wasn't about to complain.

"We have every machine imaginable for your cardiovascular workout: treadmills, stationary bikes, rowing machines, Body Treks, mountain climbers..." He made the contraptions sound like nirvana. I gulped air while exercisers bounced around on alien equipment and beamed at Pete. Everybody appeared young, but some had skin that looked a little tucked up. At least they weren't perfect.

My nose twitched at the odor of healthy sweat. The motion of people and machines reminded me how inactive I'd been, physically and emotionally. I doubted I could conquer the devices, but the muscles rippling across Pete's spandex boosted my enthusiasm.

"You can warm up here." His voice was seductive. "Then stretch before going to the weight room." He unveiled his teeth.

I was thoroughly warm, and a room jam packed with weight machines was definitely out. Pete said aerobics classes met on level four, but I wasn't eager to scale more steps to start jiggle jumping. I wasn't sure I could do strenuous aerobics.

"Why don't you stroll around for a while?" He grinned. "I'll be downstairs near the front desk if you decide to join."

What confidence he had. His leaving gave me a chance to conclude I couldn't tackle a mechanical contrivance before tripping downstairs to fill out membership papers. I was signing my check at the desk when Pete waved at me and vaporized. He was probably scurrying to the business office to apply for his commission.

Having written a substantial check, I decided to return to level three and attempt to exercise. A few people padded on treadmills in front of the TV, watching soap operas. Throbbing music reverberated overhead, boosting their exercise frenzy. A news anchor railed about the obesity epidemic. Fit and Firm's clients sweated toward perfection, oblivious to the fact that an almost-fatal accident had recently occurred on the premises.

The Body Trek machines looked safe. Next to a springy-haired girl, a machine identical to hers was unoccupied. I studied her contraption. The foot pedals moved back and forth at variable speeds, handgrips pumped her arms, and she could grab the stationary rail if she panicked. I had no reason to feel jittery, even though my total life experience at the bank and at school had been mental, not physical. *Just get on the Body Trek, next to the waif who looks somewhere between pubescent and twenty-nine, and act nice.*

She appraised me. "Do you come to the club often?"

"This is my first time. I'm supposed to work up to four days a week." *In my next life.*

"I do three days of cardio and two days in the weight room. I'm Patricia Drexel."

Patricia had a perfect figure, flawless skin, and auburn hair that shone with every bounce. Despite the obvious benefits of the weight room, I doubted I'd set foot in it.

"Pleased to meet you. I'm Aggie Mundeen."

"So, are you an Aggie? We have a slew of them around here."

"So I've heard."

I arranged my noodle-flat feet on the pedals, eyed the computer display and forged a death grip on the rail. The board flashed various options. The "Cardio Workout" button reminded me of rehab patients, so I punched it and grasped the handles. The foot pedals revolved slowly.

Every couple of minutes, the speed increased. The pedals whirled faster and faster. When the handles started yanking my arms forward and back, forward and back, I morphed into a praying mantis. Patricia might have giggled. I didn't have time to check. Hoping my feet wouldn't slip off the pedals, I lunged for the stationary bar. The display board flashed and beeped, oblivious to my terror. With my knuckles white from gripping the bar, I concentrated on slowing my legs until I could stand almost straight.

Patricia had reduced her speed and was surveying the far end of the room. I determined I was able to turn my neck and followed her gaze to a man in red shorts popping up the stairs. I recognized Mickey Shannon and turned away, too agitated to flirt.

Patricia hopped off the Body Trek and swished her hand at me. "That's enough cardio. Time to do weights. See you later." She streaked toward Mickey, caught up to him, bumped him accidentally and beamed up a beguiling smile. He gazed down, obviously enjoying his good fortune. They bobbed downstairs together, probably to the weight room.

Fit and Firm might be the perfect place to meet people, but I didn't fit in with these specimens. I needed time to master the machines without disabling myself and more time to study southern etiquette. My flirting arsenal had rusted. Plus, I had either witnessed a careless accident or an attempted murder. All in all, not a good start.

If Sam were around, he could quiz Mickey about the electrical system and accompany me to meet the manager. When Sarah took him the radio, did the manager call the police? Or did he play down the incident, intending to root out the culprit himself so he could keep the club open?

Thankful that I hadn't shattered a bone, I slipped off the Body Trek, quaked to the water fountain and slurped. The muscles in my legs and derriere contracted like they'd been poked with a cattle prod.

Even a health club held secrets. Holly's secrets were painful. Her revelations might be dangerous to the resilient psyche I'd primed to match my soon-to-be-buff body. I'd prepaid for a three-month membership, so I'd have a hard time avoiding Holly since the pool incident linked us together. And I might be the one person who could help her.

My watch showed 1:00 p.m. The manager was probably back from lunch. I could pay him a visit and have plenty of time to get to my 3:00 p.m. class. I freshened up. I'd fought enough machinery for one day. My itchy feet were trapped in socks and Adidas. This was the perfect time to meet him.

Three

I lumbered down to level two, aimed for the corridor of offices and knocked on the door that read, "Club Manager, Harold Thorne." A box-like man in gym shorts filled the door frame. I felt like a boot camp rookie shoved before the drill sergeant. He looked older than forty. The instant I passed thirty, I sprouted a previously dormant antenna that honed in on sagging skin and body bulges. The picket-fence crew cut on his scalp ran almost to the sides of his square head. He scrutinized me and offered a paw.

"Harry Thorne."

"Aggie Mundeen."

His beady eyes opened wide, which lifted his brow and pushed his ears out. "You're the woman who found Holly Holmgreen in the pool and helped Sarah get her out."

"That's me." Word traveled fast.

"I wanted to talk to you...Sarah's so ditsy...to get your version of the accident." His eyes narrowed.

I slipped past him into the office while I described what happened. "You concluded the incident was accidental?"

"Sure it was." He crossed muscle-bound arms. "I caught those maintenance guys playing their boom box before while they worked at the pool. I told 'em if it happened again, they were history. When Sarah brought me the radio, I knew it belonged to them. They denied taking it near the pool, but I knew they were lying. I fired 'em."

Harry Thorne didn't waste time contemplating options. Whatever his motives, he intended to keep the mishap under wraps and not involve the police. Wasn't he supposed to notify the club's insurance company so they could file a report with OSHA? Had other accidents occurred at Fit and Firm? If Harry reported this one, maybe he'd lose his job.

It was his call; he was the manager. But as the second potential victim of electrocution, I intended to probe further. I molded my face into a pleasant countenance.

"Do you use the biggest electrical contractor in San Antonio...the one with the huge ads?" I knew zip about San Antonio contractors.

Harry rocked back on his heels, leaned forward, re-crossed his arms and planted his feet. His red socks above spit-and-polish tennis shoes looked silly at the end of his hairy legs. He furrowed his brow.

"We use Stanton Electric. They're a good little firm."

I produced a quizzical look and blinked. "I guess it's hard to find enough competent employees when you run a big place like this?"

"You bet. Maintenance guys are the least of my problems. I have to find muscled-up trainers so amateur body builders respect 'em." He grimaced. Harry didn't appear to hold much regard for amateurs. "I gotta get pretty boys for the women. Sheesh." He rolled his eyes. I thought about Pete Reeves.

"I gotta hire female trainers. I get all kinds in that group."

"Sarah Savoy seems to do a good job."

"I gotta hire those good-looking babes, even if they're airheads. They get guys' hormones raging around here. Pretty soon, the blockheads are chasing every girl in sight."

"You mean young girls like Holly Holmgreen?"

"Yeah. Like Holly. But I don't think her bad luck had anything to do with guys chasing her. Stupid accidents happen. We'll keep an eye on her."

Once Harry had learned all I knew, he was ready to dismiss me. My curiosity percolated, so I scanned his office, trying to get a sense of what lay behind his self-assured toughness. On his desk sat a photo of two men boxing in a ring while a referee shouted at them and a crowd egged them on. I saw my opening to initiate a friendlier conversation. "Were you a boxer?"

"I boxed some. My dad wanted me to go professional. He owned the gym. Smelly old place. Nothing but sweat, blows and blood. I couldn't wait to get out of there. I did learn how to bring order to a crummy place. Say, you wanna sit down?" He flipped his mitt toward a chair and whipped behind his desk. He yanked the center drawer open, tossed in the offending photograph, muscled back his swivel chair and surveyed his domain. He seemed to be warming up a bit. I smiled and glanced around, sharing his enjoyment.

"I decided someday I'd manage a club with class, like this one. They say it takes three generations to rise above your family's status. I did it in two." He clenched his jaw as if expecting me to dispute his assessment. I kept quiet and pasted congeniality on my face. I'd also heard it took three generations for offspring to squander the fortune of the person who created it. I kept my thoughts on generational advancement and decline to myself.

"I was determined to manage a clean facility and run the place right. It wouldn't be no dump like my dad's boxing gym. I'd have a club where people could get in shape without a lot of riffraff mucking up the place—where girls could come exercise without being treated like meat."

The tops of Harry's prominent ears turned red. Had someone mistreated a girl in his family? I thought Harry would be fiercely protective of his wife and daughters. "Does your family exercise here?"

"I'm divorced. My wife was one of them featherbrained babes. Couldn't tell a jewel from a ball of mud. We never had kids."

Harry deflated in his chair, possibly regretting his lack of children. He must fancy himself the "jewel" his wife didn't appreciate, which was a hard concept to reconcile with his steamroller appearance. I felt sorry for him. It must be frustrating to project an image to the world so different from your perception of yourself. I glanced at the other photograph on his desk. He followed my gaze.

"That's my brother, Billy. He was a year younger than me. Died in Vietnam at twenty-two. One of the last soldiers killed when we evacuated Saigon."

"I'm so sorry." I wished I hadn't focused on his brother's picture. Yet, he seemed relieved to share his grief. He shook his head as though he still couldn't believe his brother had died. Head down, he remained quiet a few seconds.

Then he peered up at me and wormed his brows together. I think he was beginning to wonder why I was perched in his office. The last thing I wanted to do was rile Harry Thorne.

Our chummy chat had ended. I stood and offered my hand, a significant gesture in Texas. "It sure is nice to meet you, Harry. I'm glad Holly wasn't injured. She's a sweet girl. It's nice to know you're keeping everything under control. You operate a wonderful club here."

He didn't smile, but he seemed complacent when I stepped into the hall.

My brain throbbed. The headache had materialized when I held my breath waiting for Holly to spurt pool water. The pain increased when I realized we both could have been electrocuted. Clinging to the Body Trek had exhausted me. My tension grew while I sat in Harry's office wondering whether he'd eject me. I didn't think he'd told me all he knew. Trying to decipher answers without having all the facts drained the last of my energy. It was time to go home.

When I started down the steps, something made me glance back. From his office doorway, Harry glowered at me. When our eyes met, he whipped inside.

Four

I staggered out of the club with my head pounding. The air was crisp with the sun shining. Driving home, I perched forward on the seat to take pressure off my contracting derriere muscles. I eased Albatross into the garage, swung my aching legs from the Wagoneer and clomped through the kitchen door into my bungalow. Except for my rigid posterior, I felt rubbery. To gain stamina for my 3:00 p.m. class, I tried to eat. The food stuck in my throat and I upchucked the measly breakfast I'd consumed hours earlier. I'd registered for Aspects of Aging to learn how to avoid decrepitude. Now I was too debilitated to attend class.

After brushing my teeth, I summoned enough energy to retrieve mail from the floor, where it had landed when the postal carrier sailed it through the slot in my door. There were a couple of bills, lots of junk, and a letter to Dear Aggie. I tore it open.

Dear Aggie,

Since you said the first step to avoid aging is getting in shape, I bought "slim-with-no-gym" workout clothes from a catalog to rein in my bulges so I'd look good enough to join the health club. The "shaper" tunic and pants have built-in spandex liners. These suckers are tight. Should I send them back and forget it?

Miserable in Milwaukee

Despite my current state of weakness, I picked up a pen.

Dear Miserable,

If you can't breathe, you can't exercise. At the health club or anyplace else. That spandex probably cost as much as a month's fitness-club membership. Send those pinchers back, join the nearest club, wear whatever decent workout clothes you have lying around and don't worry about other people. They're worried about themselves.

Agonizing with you,
Aggie

I didn't have more letters to answer so I decided I might as well hit the books. I actually enjoyed studying. I was pathologically curious—about everything except banking. For my Dear Aggie column, I researched every aspect of how to avoid aging. To house my research, I'd bought the perfect antique cabinet at Broadway Antique Auction and kept it in my bedroom.

For years, I'd wanted to study liberal arts. Even though I'd missed my first class, I could keep up if I mastered the material. After waiting so long to attend graduate school, I wasn't about to fail. I picked up the notebook that Dr. Carmody, my professor for Aspects of Aging, had compiled for us and plodded to the sofa. His syllabus said we'd start by studying normal aging in disease-free individuals. Perfect. I could learn how to stay young and share the information with my readers.

The first section discussed maximum life span: "In the absence of disease, maximum life span is one hundred twenty years—the longest, documented time anyone has lived." Fantastic. I had time to get my body in shape and scout for a good man. If nobody electrocuted me in the pool.

"Even without disease, genetics and lifestyle affect aging." I leaned back and gazed at the ceiling. They forgot to mention life experience. Club Manager Harry Thorne was probably under fifty, but weighty pockets under his eyes made him look older. His body was in phenomenal shape, but losing his brother had aged him. Maybe he had a gene for baggy eyes. Or maybe he was stressed out from trying to hide an attempted murder.

I watched winter light seep through the front window and make pale dots on the living room wall. I wished I knew something about my genetics. After my parents died when I was a baby, Aunt Novena and Uncle Fred raised me in Chicago. I lifted their photograph from the coffee table. We never discussed genetics; nobody wanted to suggest our piecemeal family wasn't perfect. Fred and Novena looked so dear, huddling together, their hair gray by the time I turned twelve. Their moral principles still supported me. I returned their photo to its place of honor.

As far as I knew, I was healthy. I felt good and was optimistic and inquisitive—some might say nosy. Despite pain, I was exercising. I craned to see my reflection in the window across the room. I looked younger already.

Flipping through the notebook, I discovered information about biomarkers. When pinpointed, these key biological signs could measure an organism's aging status better than chronological age. I was going to love this course. Being way past thirty didn't matter. I could hardly wait to tell Meredith and Sam they had biomarkers.

My sixty-year-old neighbor, Grace Livermore, must have indestructible biomarkers. Whenever I had a petty concern or felt old, I visited her. Even though I didn't know much about her, I sensed she was wise and could help me put things in perspective.

A sound jerked me from my musings. The knob on my back door rattled. I strained to listen. When I came home and parked Albatross in the garage, I had pulled down the overhead door and come into the house through the kitchen. Once the garage door was down, no one could see me enter the house. Was someone trying to break into a house they thought was empty?

The phone was on the other side of the room. I could sprint to it and hope nobody shot me as I leaped across open space to dial nine-one-one. Or I could scream. My throat tightened just as my legs froze, so I perched and listened. When the knob rattled again, I screamed so loud I scared myself. I thought I heard footsteps pound away outside. Paralyzed, I pondered what to do while I waited for my heartbeat to return to normal. Did the footsteps outside have something to do with the incident at the pool?

If I called SAPD now, Sam would find out about the pool incident. I wasn't ready to discuss what had occurred there.

Unable to think of anything else to do, I creaked to a standing position, slithered along the wall and tiptoed toward the kitchen. Nothing looked different. I flipped off the ceiling light and crept toward the back door. It remained locked, thank goodness. The outside light was on. Peeking through the top half of the door, I peered down at the concrete landing. I saw no mud, no footprints, nothing but dried grass flattened around the stoop.

Trekking to every window in the house, I peeped out. Everything looked normal. Locks fortified my windows and chains secured my doors. I padded back to the living room, reasoning with myself. Somebody had tried to loot an empty house, heard me scream and took off to find an easier target.

Grabbing the phone from its cradle, I set the handset on the coffee table within arm's reach and sank onto the sofa. Having the phone close by calmed me. Despite witnessing a scary pool accident and having a burglar rattle my door, I absolutely had to study.

Curling into the cushions, I picked up the binder and found the next section, "Organs and Organ Systems." Organs declined at different rates, I learned, even within a single individual. Today's events undoubtedly aged some of my organs. I forced myself to focus: this was the perfect opportunity to assess the status of my innards.

"Heart: Grows slightly larger with age, but cardiac output stays almost the same because the heart pumps more efficiently." This was encouraging since mine had just skipped a few beats. I wished I could watch somebody's heart inside their body. Did Sam's heart atrophy from suffering when his wife and daughter died?

Could it ever recover? When I lost my child and my faith wavered, my heart felt hammered, then bruised. Did it shrink? When I was near people who had suffered loss, I felt my heart expand.

"Lungs: Maximum breathing capacity declines forty percent between ages twenty and seventy." I grabbed a pencil. My calculations showed my breathing capacity had already declined thirteen percent. Peachy. I held my breath to expand my lung volume.

"Brain: Loses cells with age but adapts by increasing connections between cells—synapses—and by re-growing branch-like extensions that carry messages in the brain." If my gray matter kept working, even with modifications, I should be all right. My oversupply of curiosity probably stimulated my brain. I chewed on my pencil. I sure didn't relish the thought of losing brain cells while my fat cells lived forever. Maybe I could shrink them with exercise. Then annihilate them. Overall, my physical condition appeared satisfactory.

"Personality: After about age thirty, personality is stable. Sudden changes in personality can suggest disease." Sam, although saddened, seemed basically the same as when I knew him in Chicago. He evaluated situations before plunging in. He was even-tempered except when grief overcame him. He'd maintained his sense of humor and was trustworthy. His critical traits seemed intact.

When I picked up the photograph of him with his family, tears pooled behind my eyes. They were so beautiful. Despite Sam's calm exterior, I feared that, without them, he must have changed. I put down my pencil, closed the notebook and vowed not to tell him what had happened at the pool. Connecting him to another young girl's suffering would cause him more pain. I had less reason to mention the minor, inconsequential rattling of my doorknob.

I scratched my foot. What I needed to do was return to the club, find out who knew Holly Holmgreen and inconspicuously snoop around.

Five

I pried myself off the couch. Even though I'd managed to study, my mind kept wandering to Holly Holmgreen's blue face. I needed the comfort of visiting Grace. I didn't know a lot about her except that she'd been widowed several times. I sensed that experience had made her wise. After what had happened, I needed her wisdom. She was definitely an expert at enjoying life—a good study for my plan to avoid aging.

I wobbled to my front porch, eased sore legs down to round concrete stones that led to my driveway and walked across the asphalt to her yard. Grace had the only emerald green lawn on our street. She hated the sickly yellow grass that marked San Antonio's winters and had her yardman throw out rye grass seed every fall. The instant I knocked on her door, Boffo started barking.

"Grace, it's Aggie."

"Come on in. I locked Boffo in the bathroom."

Boffo and I had not bonded. I was glad she'd trapped the yippy mutt. A rat terrior/dauschund mix, Boffo was just tall enough to sniff my ankles and plop his body over my shoe so he could chew my laces. Grace needed him for a watchdog. Unfortunately, he viewed my feet as prey.

She stood in her kitchen over a wrought-iron table. Her cheeks were pink. White strands poked out from her graying hair. Her hands, which usually fluttered like hummingbirds, were encased in rubber gloves smeared with concrete the consistency of peanut butter. She held them up like a surgeon poised to operate.

"I'm going to grout this table. I mix the grout with water and have to let the mixture set for ten minutes. Boffo gets bored and tries to climb into the grout bucket. I'm afraid the concrete might dry on him before I can get him out."

The cur yelped from the bathroom. I appreciated Muttface's problem with boredom, but I enjoyed the thought of his being weighted down with concrete so he couldn't jump on my feet. His short legs kept him from bounding very high.

I didn't understand pets, never having owned one. They sensed my ineptitude. I considered boning up on dog handling. I could walk Boffo for Grace and loosen my derriere muscles. The mutt and I might even become friends.

She grabbed a float, scooped grout from the bucket and pressed the implement between tiles. Before she covered the whole surface, I examined her design. Concentrating on her work would keep me from thinking about Holly.

In the center of her table, she'd created a winsome dove with white tiles. Alongside the dove, she'd placed curving rows of creamier tiles, line after line, with each row darker than the last. Musky pewter tiles rimmed the outside of the table.

"It's beautiful."

"I intended to give this table to one of my daughters, but I'll have a hard time giving it up." She waved her glove toward a photo on the kitchen bar of two dark-haired girls who looked almost identical.

"They're Charlie's and my children. Linda was fourteen in that picture, in her dramatic period. She called herself Linda Lovelace, Linda Lamoure—some movie star name. She thought Linda Livermore sounded like a cut from the meat market. Kim, twelve, teased her, chanting, 'Smelly Livermore, Smelly Livermore.'"

I giggled before I saw sadness skitter across Grace's face. She pushed grout into crevices with a trowel and pressed hard. "They were happy then, before their dad died."

"I'm so sorry."

"Charlie was thirty-nine. He was an alcoholic, but we weren't ready to lose him." She sighed and bent over her table. "Pull up a chair while I finish this."

Grace was twenty years older than I was. Yet I felt comfortable sitting while she worked. She'd filled her house with tile tables. She'd probably tile the piano bench if she didn't sit there so often.

The bathroom door squeaked. When Boffo poked his head through, his teeth were clamped on a cellophane bag of bath crystals.

"Uh-oh. I thought I locked the door. He drags out things I haven't seen in years. I can't grab him with these gloves on. Get a doggy treat from the counter and wag it to tempt him. Then pop it in his mouth so you can yank that bag away."

I flipped him the treat, snatched the bag and got a whiff of his breath. That hybrid vigor could knock you over. I darted toward my chair, racing to sit and fold my feet up before the mutt could devour his treat and attack. I reached the chair, but that mongrel was fast. Before I could hoist my feet, he pounced on my tennis shoe and snapped his teeth on the laces. Grace laughed so hard, she stopped grouting. He chewed a while, then panted a dog grin.

"Meredith talked me into joining a health club."

She smirked at me over metal-framed glasses. "Did a gorgeous hunk give you a tour?"

"Well, Pete Reeves, the guide for prospective members, is a bronze statue with ocean blue eyes who poses as a person. Another guy, Mickey Shannon, looks like Tom Selleck, but his drawl bothers me."

"Those southern drawls come and go, depending on who they're talking to." She moved around her table.

"No kidding?"

"Yep. Welcome to Texas. The good-old-boy thing is used to advantage."

Grace had lived in Texas most of her life, if you didn't count working in New York and St. Louis as an advertising executive and traveling to Europe with three husbands, all of whom, I'd heard, had died.

I bent to pet Boffo, but he growled and kept slobbering on my shoe. I watched him chew my laces while Grace smoothed grout between her tiles.

"Some men are just too good-looking," she said. "Girls flock around them like a covey of quail. When a man thinks he's irreplaceable, the attention doesn't take long to ruin him. He concludes he doesn't need to talk or even think much. Charlie was like that—a real hunk. When we married, I was twenty and he was twenty-two."

I was eighteen when I fell for Lester the Louse. Grace scooped grout from the bucket and studied the next section of her table. "Moderately handsome guys are better. Men forced to take stock of themselves are more worthy."

Sam's face flashed across my mind. I classified him as moderately handsome. His nose was ordinary. His mouth tripled in size when he laughed. If a thirty-five-dollar barber slicked his hair back, he might look distinguished. When his hair scattered haphazardly above his forehead, he looked genuine. Nothing was phony about him. When we met again in San Antonio after we'd both left Chicago, he seemed glad to see me.

Thinking about Charlie Livermore, I inadvertently shifted to curl up my other leg. Boffo crouched to attack. I lowered my leg, and he resumed grinding my laces into soggy strings. I sighed. "What happened to Charlie?"

"He lived hard, partied hard, and drank hard. We had a great time, but he overdid everything. He drank too much one night, came home and parked in the garage. He was apparently listening to the radio and passed out. His cigarette caught fire and the car burned up."

"How horrible."

"I don't think he knew what happened. The girls really suffered. I had taken Kim to a birthday party, so Charlie and Linda went out to dinner. We came home, parked in front like we always did, and found Linda inside talking on the phone. We smelled smoke, ran to the garage and found Charlie. I'll say this for him: he squeezed seventy years of living into thirty-nine." She looked up. "I guess I sound callous about his death. It's just that he drank so much, I felt like we'd already lost him." She resumed working on her table.

Imagine, Charlie dead at thirty-nine. Having lived for eons inside an emotionally sterile bank, I was way past thirty and just now poking out of my shell.

Grace had suffered real tragedy in her life, yet she seemed more hopeful than embittered. I sensed there was more to Charlie's story than she revealed—pockets of her past she kept buried. I didn't know what had happened to her other husbands, but I was astonished she'd lost all three. How sad and unusual. Like the incident at the pool.

She troweled grout over the remaining tiles, evaluated her work, swiped off excess grout and flipped rubbery globs into the garbage can. She picked up a moist sponge and began to caress residual grout off glowing tiles. It was like watching diamonds rise from ashes.

The beauty of her table moved me to blurt out what had happened. "A young girl named Holly Holmgreen almost drowned from being electrocuted in the health club's swimming pool. Just before I got into the water."

She stopped sponging and pinned me with steel blue eyes. "Did somebody try to kill that girl, and you got in the way?"

I hate it when people say things I don't want to think about. "It's possible."

"Your detective friend, did you tell him about it?"

"I didn't want to worry him over an accident." Grace was apparently too distracted by her table to challenge me. I changed the subject to Aspects of Aging and told her about the man who had lived one hundred twenty years.

"That's great news. I just bought ten sheets of piano music and my guitar lessons start next week. I could use sixty more years." She washed her tools in a water-filled bucket. "I need to tile more tables for the back porch."

She loved what I told her about biomarkers, how scientists might be able to pinpoint triggers of aging and disarm them. We joked about what sparked our triggers and forgot about everybody who'd died or almost died.

Grace hauled her rinse bucket outside and grabbed a hose to squirt concrete off her gloves. She left the back door open, and Boffo bounded after her, yipping at the water. His high-pitched bark set my teeth on edge. At least he detached himself from my shoelaces. I was liberated.

"Want a sandwich?" she called, peeling off her gloves. "Peanut butter and mayonnaise? With a pickle?" She ate strange food at odd intervals when she took a break from a project.

"No, thanks. Let's go to Las Tapitas later this week." I sneaked away from my chair, hoping Boffo wouldn't notice.

"I'll wear the broom skirt and serape I bought at the Mexican Market," she said.

I knew Boffo would get bored with the water hose. He probably blamed me for his incarceration in the bathroom. Chatting time was over. I streaked toward Grace's front door. "I'll call you."

Boffo drew a bead on me and lowered his head to charge. Before I flew halfway across the living room, he caught up and pounced. I limped to the front door, dragging one foot with Muttface sprawled over it. I reached the porch and was just about to high kick him through the nearest goal post, when Grace stopped chortling long enough to call him.

I yanked her door closed and heard him screech to a stop on the other side, yelping. That dog needed to run a thousand laps. If I wanted to visit Grace, I'd have to devise an exercise plan for the obstreperous mutt. Maybe I could sic him on the creep who put the radio by the pool or on the idiot who tried to break into my house.

I needed to concentrate. Tomorrow, I hoped Mickey would show up in the weight room so I could pump him for information about the electrical system. Why didn't the current zap me when I entered the pool? If electricity had knocked Holly unconscious, what had neutralized the charge? Maybe the safety mechanism kicked in, like Mickey'd said it would. Or something else might have interrupted the current. My curiosity was hard-wired.

Walking home, I was still clutching Boffo's bath crystals. I tossed them on the sofa and mulled over ways to harness the mutt's aggression.

I hopped in my car and whipped down to Walgreen's on Broadway to buy shoelaces and 409 to clean dog slobber off my shoes.

On the drive home, I mused about Mickey Shannon. What kind of man was he, this Tom Selleck clone who seemed more interested in Aggie jokes and in my less-than-perfect body than in a near-fatal electrocution?

If Grace's instincts were right, and somebody had tried to kill Holly, I had to help this girl. I knew how she felt. She had suffered the same pain I endured. I couldn't let her suffer even more.

Six

When my feet hit Saltillo tile Tuesday morning, my body had petrified. Stiffness upon rising was a definite sign of aging. I clomped across the bedroom floor to reach my warm bathroom rug. At least the queasiness I'd felt sitting by the pool with Holly was gone. I chalked it up to trauma.

When I peered in the mirror, I was astonished how perky I looked. My eyes, clear and sharp, looked green from their proximity to Garfield's emerald orbs on my sleep shirt. My hair was lopsided, so I re-parted it and blew upward to fluff the strands. I regretted missing Dr. Carmody's Monday class. I might have missed important information.

I slipped into Mohair slides and ambled toward the kitchen. If I drank enough coffee, maybe I could go exercise before my body discovered what I was doing. I wanted to crack Mickey Shannon's reticence. He knew more than he was saying.

On the other hand, I could enjoy the solitude of my suburban Alamo Heights bungalow soothed by strains of Debussy. The throbbing music at Fit and Firm combined with members' obsessions with physicality wore a person out. How much trauma could I endure to get in shape? Did I really want to struggle through the rigors of exercise and flirting? It if kept me young and attractive, I could handle it.

I jumped when the mailman shoved mail through the brass slot. Did somebody need to share their pain with Dear Aggie? Sure enough, there was a letter.

Dear Aggie,

I started exercising at a club two days ago. Pain and inflammation rule my body. I've seen ads about Thermatone Pills that promote gentle healing with fifteen ingredients including antioxidants to flush toxins from my aching joints and muscles. What do you think?

Pained in Peoria.

Dear Pained,

Have you torn something or merely stretched a tendon beyond usefulness? If you're not better in two days, call your doctor. Those Thermatone Pills could have been smuggled from Hongotovia. They probably cost more than your health club membership. I took something like that once. I was oblivious to pain but suffered mental confusion and peed a lot. Stick with aspirin.

Your partner in pain,
Aggie

I filled my coffee mug, smoothed a smidgen of peanut butter on dry toast and slipped back to the sofa. With great care, I set my mug on the mahogany table centered between my facing sofas so as not to spill coffee on my Tabriz rug. This masterpiece covered pockmarks in my wood plank floors, a unique condition that had helped me afford the house. I padded to the armoire I'd captured at Broadway Antique Auction, stuck a CD in the player perched on top and plopped on the sofa to absorb "Claire D'Lune."

For the first time in my life, I was relieved of responsibility and financially secure enough to do what I wanted. When the conglomerate consumed the bank where I worked, and the stock I'd purchased annually from age eighteen multiplied a thousand fold, my security catapulted from zero to comfortable. I tongued peanut butter around my mouth. Naturally, I ditched my bank job, kept my columnist job, flew to San Antonio where the weather was warm, and embraced my new career as a graduate student.

I polished off the toast and smiled at the turquoise, orange and purple Serape-striped fabric on my sofas. My couches were oddly captivating, like people at Fit and Firm. Maybe—if the radio dropped in the pool turned out to be an isolated incident—I'd invite new friends from the club over to show off my Spanish-style bungalow.

I flopped lengthwise on the sofa. If I wasn't going to exercise, I should study. Dr. Carmody's class met at 3:00 p.m. Monday through Thursday, so I had the whole day free before class. I grabbed the binder and flipped to the section on average life spans.

I learned that from 1900 to 1990, U.S. life spans increased from forty-seven years to seventy-five years, thanks to antibiotics, better medical care, improved sanitation, and lifestyle changes. By making headway against cancer and heart disease, some scientists thought life span could be extended even further. Fantastic. I stretched my arms over my head, ready to live forever.

A Japanese man, Shirechiyo Izumi, reached one hundred twenty years before he died. I could work with that: I'd have two-thirds of my life yet to go. I closed my eyes and assimilated Debussy. If Izumi hadn't died from pneumonia, could he have lived even longer? I popped up, leaned over the notebook and scanned the text: scientists debating his longevity used two separate theories of aging. This looked like technical reading, which made me antsy to escape my nest.

I plumped my sofa pillows and traipsed across the living room to peer out the window. The sun was shining. I wished I were younger and enjoyed the love of a good man, but except for being alone, my horizon looked promising.

I felt so good, I even wanted to exercise. If I went to the weight room, I might meet somebody who knew Holly. I could also check out dating prospects. I jumped into workout clothes, hopped into

Albatross and sailed down Burr Road to Harry Wurzbach to maneuver my way toward the Austin Highway.

After squeezing into a parking slot in Fit and Firm's garage, I bounced into the club wearing my snappy new waist-length T-shirt. The shoulders had small pads sewn in—a ploy to visually narrow my hips. Why should workout clothes look frumpy? Guilt slipped over me for advising *Miserable in Milwaukee* to throw on whatever she had. I planned to appear appetizing in case I got the chance to quiz Mickey Shannon.

I checked in, aimed for the stairs and climbed the first step. I was admiring my clingy tights when my right quadriceps went into spasm. A wave of nausea passed through me from peanut butter I'd scarfed down for breakfast. The next shock came when my right calf muscle cramped. Climbing one measly step had hardened it to stone. Gritting my teeth, I drew my left foot onto the step. My left quad muscle shrieked. At least the quad burn balanced the pain soaring through my right calf. I ground upward, step by miserable step. Club members sprang past me. I was too old for this torture.

I staggered to the second-floor landing, spread my palms and leaned on the wall to stretch my calves. When the knots loosened to rubbery globs, I tottered around the edge of the basketball court and peered into the weight room, looking for Mickey. A bank of metal and rubber machines lined the room's periphery. More odd-looking devices crisscrossed the center. For a mechanically challenged person like me, this room crammed with equipment was scary.

Off the main room in the far right corner was a smaller room with a sign on the door that read, "Pilates." I had no clue what the word meant. Maybe the manager hired a Greek instructor. When I peeked in, two women lay face down on thick mats with their knees drawn up under them in fetal positions and their noses pressed into the mats. The female instructor leering over them, arms crossed, looked more German than Greek. Was she Mrs. Pilates? Mr. Pilates' assistant? I couldn't tell if the women on the mats were praying or cringing from the trainer. The class did not look appealing.

I returned to the main room and studied the first machine near the entrance. The chair looked sturdy, and the handgrips were immobile. A metal roller covered with spongy material jutted out eighteen inches below the seat. I eased down and squinted at obtuse instructions pasted on the contraption. "Leg extension. Place feet under roller. Straighten legs, keeping feet flexed. Do two sets of ten repetitions. Weight: 50 pounds." I slipped my ankles under the roller and strained to lift my feet. My legs didn't budge, but my back kinked.

"Ouch."

The man on the adjacent thingamabob was sympathetic. "Each machine has to be set to your height and the weights to your strength before you can use it. Let me help you."

His smile made me want to know more. His mother had probably hated to cut those brown curls. I stood quietly while he adjusted my machine. He reeked of potential. He was a couple of inches taller than me and had probably just used the leg lift. He adjusted the bar only a single notch. That was okay by me. His height seemed dictated by a short knee-to-foot bone, which positioned the trunk of his body lower than usual. I didn't want to stare. I could research leg bones online. He wore red socks like the club trainers.

I didn't intend to flirt with every man at the health club. But after Lester ran off when I told him I was pregnant, and I stumbled through umpteen miserable years of not dating anybody, I found the male species newly interesting.

"I'm Ned Barclay. I work out here all the time, mostly weights. I can show you how to use every machine. Go ahead. Try it."

Noting his delectable muscles, I perched as he instructed with my stomach muscles tight and back glued to the chair. I hefted the rubber-covered bar up and down with my legs until the fronts of my thighs burned. People entering the room circled wide around my legs as if they expected the bar to fly off and hit them. I know I have a strange effect on mechanical equipment, but geez.

"Shall we try a couple more leg muscle machines?"

"Sure." I loved his encouraging smile. Maybe he knew Holly Holmgreen.

The second machine had an identical extension. You placed your feet above the bar and pressed your legs downward. With ten repetitions, you could cause equal injury to the backs of both thighs.

"Do you know Holly Holmgreen?"

"Let's try the leg press."

This apparatus looked safe enough. The seat had a back support and large footrest. I relaxed and gazed at Ned's liquid brown eyes. "I met Holly yesterday at the pool, on my first day here."

"Let's move the seat back farther from the foot-rest so your legs are nearly straight. Put your feet on the platform, bend your knees and ease the platform toward you. Now, push your legs straight out."

I pushed. This footrest was not designed for relaxing. Ned told me to shove the torture tray out twelve times, at which point my thighs began to spasm. Oblivious to my quivering hams, he enumerated the benefits of the machine. "The leg press works your quadriceps, hamstrings, gluteus maximus..."

I didn't know the names of my body parts, but I'd discovered where they were. It was difficult to concentrate on Ned's anatomical treatise with my legs twitching.

"I know Holly Holmgreen. In fact, I used to date her." He squeezed his words through thin lips, but he had a good vocabulary and great diction. I'm a sucker for men who speak well. Even my Aspects of Aging professor probably couldn't rattle off muscles extemporaneously the way Ned did. I decided not to press him about Holly. Their relationship must be over.

"Let's move to the inner and outer thigh machine." He took my hand and pulled me off the seat. I wobbled to the next chair and plopped down. "For outer thighs, put the pads outside your legs and push out."

After ten repetitions, he repositioned my legs outside the pads and said to squeeze my legs together umpteen times, which successfully damaged my thighs all the way around. How many women, too weak to remove their quivering thighs from this vise, had perished here?

"Let's give your legs a rest and work on your upper body. We'll try 'the row.'"

Since the row worked every fiber in my arm muscles, Ned had me do two sets of ten repetitions. His knowledge of anatomy impressed me, but he apparently didn't realize how inactive I'd been. I was determined to get in shape and wanted to be agreeable, but my muscles were sprung. If we ever completed this tortuous circuit, it would be afternoon, and Ned would have to summon a caretaker to wheel me from the facility.

Fortunately, Mickey sauntered in, ablaze with red attire and a boyish smile. He walked toward us. Ned peered up at him, about two feet up, and understood that he was not Alpha Male. Weight rooms resurrected animal instincts. Ned slinked away, as though Mickey had thrashed him and I'd rejected him. Ned Barclay was a super guy. I resolved to find him later.

"Did you hear anything about what happened at the pool?" I whispered to Mickey.

"They conducted a quiet investigation of the electrical circuitry. It's on a separate system from the rest of the place." He leaned close, smirking. "Talkin' about water, did you hear about the Aggie who drove his pickup into the lake? While he was trying to get the tailgate down, his dog drowned."

He exploded with laughter before I could get him back on track. "Mickey, what about the radio?"

"Nobody's talking about it."

"Is the pool open?"

"Yeah. They must have fixed the problem."

Harry Thorne had managed to keep the incident quiet. Mickey, focused on working out, seemed totally disinterested in the pool's electrical system. I'd try to learn more later. He led me from one machine to the next, talking and laughing. When we got to arm-strengthening devices, I discovered my rare medical condition: muscle fiber deficiency. Twenty reps on the row had critically stressed my arms. I tried to ignore my misery by focusing on which one of Mickey's muscles would bulge next.

From across the room, Patricia Drexel eyeballed Mickey. I had to admit her legs looked great, even in the stupid red socks worn by club regulars. Red socks spoke volumes: "Unlike you, I work out regularly and am in really good shape." When she wasn't gaping at Mickey, she shot daggers at me, apparently convinced that her bump-and-smile routine indicated ownership. I stared back. Without thinking, I wrinkled my nose. If Patricia were seriously jealous, she might be capable of violence.

We'd nearly completed the machine circuit. I'd startled every muscle in my hibernating body when I realized it was time to meet Meredith. I'd gotten her a two-week guest pass, although I doubted she'd join the club because of her time crunch. Since we'd registered for different classes at the university, exercising together would give us a chance to compare notes. We'd agreed to do a quick cardio workout before lunch. I wanted her opinion about what had happened to Holly.

"Got to go," I said. "I'm meeting a friend."

Mickey looked stricken.

"Girl friend."

He pumped iron, gazing around for a lucky woman who needed help, and spotted Patricia Drexel basking in Pete Reeves's electric eyes. He straightened to the top centimeter of six foot three, clenched his fists and strode toward them with a Neanderthal gait. He stopped with his face three inches from Pete. Blue Eyes shrugged and shuffled away, relinquishing Patricia.

Weight room protocol mimicked the law of the jungle. Health clubs were supposed to enhance everybody's life, but I sensed that beneath this veneer of healthy living, repressed fury was biding its time.

I hadn't retrieved a shred of data from Mickey about the club's investigation. Ned was obviously reluctant to talk about Holly. If

Mickey hadn't chased him off, I might have learned more. Conversing with Patricia did not appear promising.

I had to devise a better way to obtain information.

Seven

On my way out of Machine Mecca, I glanced toward Mr. Pilate's room to check on the women crouched on mats. They were gone, but two others were flopped over gigantic two-foot-diameter balls. The women looked like enormous bugs that had captured mountains of food too huge to eat. What kind of exercise was that? Hopefully, Mr. Pilates would appear and show them what to do. I wished I had time to watch.

When I reached the third floor, Meredith was already on a treadmill. During our first semester of graduate school, we took Shakespeare's Tragedies and Abnormal Psychology—courses that intrigued me like accounting never had. I thought Aspects of Aging would prove riveting.

Tall, elegantly slim and blonde, Meredith had sad eyes. Grief over Conrad's tragedy still plagued her. I tried to acknowledge her loss without naming him.

"How's everything going?" I climbed on the adjacent machine.

"All right, I guess. Losing Conrad hits me off and on. Keeping busy helps." She pushed a button to increase her speed.

I thought about Lester the Louse. Although it was painful at the time, sometimes it was better when people parted ways. Some guys weren't worth the trauma. They left you with a tendency to mistrust men.

I pushed "Slow Start," 2 mph. "Aspects of Aging looks interesting. How are your classes?"

"I love American and British Lit, but the profs assign a pile of reading."

I couldn't hold back my news another second. "You'll never guess what happened my first day here." I told her about the pool, Holly, Sarah, the radio and Mickey's take on the electricity, throwing in his likeness to Tom Selleck.

She seemed excited, but not about Selleck. She walked faster.

"Did Holly intend to electrocute herself? Could she have put the radio in the pool, thinking she'd have a quick, painless death?"

Meredith read too many novels. I increased my speed to 2.5 mph. "She was depressed, but I doubt she was trying to kill herself. She was very grateful when Sarah and I got her out."

"Thank God you didn't get in sooner. Was it a dumb accident, or did somebody purposely submerge the radio?"

While I considered what she'd said, I peered over to check the settings on her machine. She sped up to 3.5 mph.

Meredith's logical mind pursued all possibilities, but I couldn't imagine who could want to kill Holly. She radiated sweetness and seemed too young to have collected many enemies. The question of timing nagged me. I had overheard somebody say swimmers waited impatiently for water aerobics to end so they could swim laps. Slipping in to submerge a radio during the brief interval between aerobics and lap swimming would be risky, although someone coming through the locker rooms or equipment room could accomplish it.

"Probably an accident." I tried to ignore my itching feet.

"She's lucky you arrived when you did."

I supported Meredith after her husband disappeared. I could help because I had just met her and wasn't emotionally involved in her dilemma. This situation was different: Holly Holmgreen had given up her child.

When I looked over again, Meredith had increased her treadmill speed to 3.7 and started jogging. "Why don't you call Sam? We could get him a guest pass and tell him what happened. Let him check around."

I nodded noncommittally. When he came to San Antonio, Sam had to apply to SAPD like a newbie, even though he'd been a Chicago homicide detective. After going through the San Antonio Police Academy, riding with field training officers and working a patrol beat, he scored high enough on the detective investigation test to request a slot on the murder team in the Homicide Division.

He led the search for Meredith's missing husband. That was a whole other story.

Once Meredith's crisis ended, we rarely saw Sam. Back in Chicago, he and his wife Katy had been my best friends. He was the only man I'd trusted for years. Reconnecting with me in San Antonio probably reminded him of Chicago. He needed time to heal before I could even begin to gauge how he felt about me.

He was the last person I wanted around Holly Holmgreen. Being a detective, he would automatically suspect attempted murder. When he learned Holly had relinquished her child, he'd research the adoption. Having lost his adopted daughter along with his wife, this case would be painful for him to investigate. My right foot slipped off the conveyor belt. I grabbed the rail.

"Are you okay?"

I blinked back tears. "My muscles are tight from walking yesterday. I've had enough of this treadmill. Let's try lunch at Tofu Temptations Grill. Maybe you'll meet the people I told you about."

We showered and dressed, me for afternoon class and Meredith for Conrad's office, where she would help his ex-patients find other doctors. With the morning rush over, I secured my favorite primping station in the dressing area where the angle of triple mirrors provided privacy. I felt pampered using the club's luxurious facilities. My station was stocked with a hair dryer, curling iron, Q-tips, and cotton balls. Deodorant, hair spray and body lotion filled the club's signature opaque pump bottles. Tiny elegant script labeled each bottle's contents. I inhaled the lemony scent. Showers and toilets were located in a secluded alcove with lockers standing off to one side. A plush place.

"Yuck," Meredith blurted. "I almost sprayed hair spray under my arms." We pondered how many women had confused the bottles and spent the rest of the day with their arms stuck to their sides.

On our way to Tofu Temptations, Meredith said she asked Sam to join us. Sure enough, he sat at a chrome table on a red and orange vinyl chair, frowning at the sandwich on his plate. He looked up and grinned. Tufts of hair bounced toward his glasses. We motioned for him to stay seated and got in line to order.

Behind me, a lanky fellow with a ruddy face and bug eyes peered over me at the oversized menu on the wall. "Vegetable Sauté," he read reverently, "served over brown rice..." He gazed down at us. "I'm an anti-fat, anti-sugar vegetarian," he announced, as though his revelation ranked right up there with a call to the priesthood. Meredith flashed him a definitely-not-interested glance, so he concentrated on me. "I'm Sheldon Snodgrass."

Gad. His name was worse than mine. "Aggie Mundeen. Pleased to meet you." That was apparently enough chitchat for Sheldon.

"They sauté vegetables in soy sauce, mustard vinaigrette, olive oil or water." He eyed me expectantly, waiting to see which delicacy I'd choose.

If they ruined vegetables by nesting them in brown rice, I didn't think any kind of liquid would help. If I wanted soy sauce, I'd find a Chinese restaurant. I felt obliged to make a healthy choice and scoured the menu for something edible.

"How about the Garden Vegetable Sandwich?" Underneath, he read, "Vegan," which seemed to please him immensely.

Wasn't that some character in Star Wars? The description of the sandwich read "with carrots, red onion, sprouts, avocado and a peanut butter miso spread on whole wheat bread." What a horrible way to ruin peanut butter. I kept searching until I found a chicken salad sandwich with actual mustard and mayonnaise. "Sandwiches look good."

"Yes. I'm going for the tofu eggless salad sandwich on whole wheat with sprouts." He looked ecstatic.

I ordered tuna and cheese with light mayonnaise on Parmesan bread and chose fruit instead of fries. Their fries were probably brown rice spliced with tofu. Sheldon didn't appear impressed with my selection, but he padded behind me toward our table. We introduced him to Sam, who had a ham and cheese sandwich on his plate. He wore civvies, his usual khaki pants and shirt, and a brown tie splotched with a Rorschach orange-and-purple pattern. For undercover work, I hoped he stashed it.

In the midst of vigorous chewing, Sheldon issued an invitation. "I'm having a little get-together at my house Thursday night. Light refreshments...you know, healthy gourmet fare. If you're not busy, I'd love for you all to come."

We were noncommittal. Sheldon seemed awfully eager. Sam scratched his cheek and scrutinized him as if he'd recently beamed down from a distant planet. When Sarah and Holly pulled up chairs, Sam gave them his detective's perusal, then kicked back, stretched his legs and eyed Sarah's thick hair and great figure. I almost blurted out that Holly was the one who deserved his attention, having nearly drowned.

Ned Barclay entered the grill, and I waved him over. He produced his beautiful shy smile, saw me flanked by Sam and Sheldon, turned beet red and carried his food to the other side of the room.

When I glanced over later, he snapped his gaze away, stone-faced. I supposed I embarrassed him by calling to him while I sat between two men. Ned Barclay seemed easily hurt.

Sheldon and Sarah did most of the talking. She was into health and nutrition, which sent Sheldon into an orbit of statistical revelations. When they progressed to exotic cuisine, I felt queasy.

I had little to say about anything outside of institutional settings like banks and colleges. Socializing for its own sake was a new experience for me, but I enjoyed listening and felt cozy and warm sitting with Sam and Meredith. We had each suffered loss and survived.

"Meredith, how are your courses going?" Sam asked. Having

watched her lose her husband, he appeared to be measuring her psychological condition.

"They're good. I'm taking Twentieth Century American Lit, beginning with Hemingway and Fitzgerald."

"I'll bet they're a relief after the flowery prose of earlier writers." Sam had majored in English before he went to law school. When he and Katy married, he joined the FBI. After his family died in the automobile accident, he switched to police work. He said he preferred catching criminals to yapping about them in court. I surmised that, somehow, he found police work less stressful than work for the FBI.

"In British Lit, we're reading Shakespeare's plays," Meredith said.

The three of us loved Shakespeare's work. Apparently satisfied that Meredith was recovering, Sam leaned companionably toward me. "What are you taking, Agatha?"

Holly and Sarah jerked their heads up. Sheldon looked puzzled. To them, I was "Aggie," which sounded like a person closer to their age.

"Aspects of Aging."

The corner of Sam's mouth turned up as though he found my choice amusing.

"My first class met yesterday, but I missed it. Some sort of stomach bug."

"Are you all right?"

"Oh, sure. I'm fine." Actually, my stomach felt unsettled, but I was glad to see Sam and ignored my discomfort. Since Meredith had enticed him to the club, I considered getting him another guest pass to take advantage of his investigative knowledge. Katy used to brag about cases he'd solved in Chicago. He could determine whether I'd witnessed an accident or an attempted murder.

I concluded it was better to keep things casual. "How's your work going?" I asked him.

"Everything's pretty quiet right now, which is good since several guys are on vacation."

I felt my face relax. "I'm glad to hear it." With Sam's division understaffed, the department would dispatch officers from another team if word about the pool incident leaked out. Nestled in my brain was the notion that if I managed to successfully solve a crime, Sam would be impressed.

After lunch, Sam returned to headquarters. Meredith left to disperse medical records from Conrad's empty office. Sarah, who taught land and water aerobics, needed to tape music for her classes.

Sheldon, having wound down from discussing the content of our food, went to his office to lay out feature articles for *Food, Fitness, and Euphoria*, the magazine he edited. I didn't ask if I could subscribe. Holly and I were the only two left.

As the others filed out, Pete Reeves strolled in for a late lunch and dazzled us with a smile before turning sea blue eyes toward the oversized menu behind the counter. I tried not to gawk. Holly lingered at our table, apparently wanting to talk. I wasn't sure I could stand up anyway. My legs had turned to stone. I hope they'd revive in time to carry me to my afternoon class.

"My stomach's a little queasy." My revelation didn't seem to faze Holly.

"Yesterday at the pool, I felt like you understood. About the baby, I mean." She planted her elbows on the table. "Can we talk about it?"

Sometimes, one had to listen. I ignored my stomach.

"The baby's father denied paternity. With him totally disinterested in being a father, DNA testing seemed useless." She clouded up. "I chose to give up the baby without ever knowing where the infant went or who would raise the child. I made a terrible mistake." Her tears spilled over. "He gave me...I took lots of Valium before I got in the pool."

Despite increasing nausea, I managed to pat her hand. I checked the foyer to estimate how fast I could jet to the locker room on fossilized legs. The housekeeper was pushing a double-decker tray of toiletries and cleaning supplies from the men's locker room to ours. I didn't want to charge into the bathroom, sick, with her there.

I forced my attention on Holly and tried to comfort her. "Try not to blame yourself. You did what you thought was best at the time." I stretched my back against the chair to give my stomach room to expand.

My heart ached for Holly, but I couldn't pass up the opportunity to delve into events the day of the accident. "What happened before you came to the pool?"

"I tried Sarah's aerobics class. By the time class ended, I was pretty despondent, having just signed final adoption papers. With Valium slowing me down, aerobics was just too hard. Sarah was sympathetic, but I didn't want to give up exercise completely, so I went to the pool." Her eyes were moist.

"Water aerobics was over," she said. "Nobody was swimming laps. The pool was deserted, and I got in. You know the rest."

Holly looked emotionally whipped, but I didn't think she'd attempted suicide.

"I'm ready to go home," she said. "My car's parked in the garage. Are you leaving? Walk over with me."

Sheldon was right about the hazards of greasy food. Either that or Tofu Temptations' food was contaminated. I felt terrible.

Having stashed my curling iron in a locker—a better curler than the club provided—I wanted to retrieve it before somebody else did. "You go ahead. I need to stop by the locker room. I'll see you tomorrow."

I barely reached the bathroom. The janitor had abandoned her cart and left. After losing my breakfast and lunch, I debated whether I was too shaky to drive home. I should have heeded Sheldon's advice and gone for the (gag) tofu eggless sandwich.

At 2:00 p.m., Fit and Firm was deserted. Contrasted with the feverish bustle of the morning, the facility was ominously still. The cleaning lady had supplied new spray bottles for primping stations and had tossed empties to the bottom of her cart. I wanted to leave before she returned.

I retrieved my curling iron and was splashing my face with cold water when I heard screams.

Forgetting my stiffness, I charged out of the locker room past the entrance desk and followed the cries outside. Members and staff had poured onto the sidewalk and were racing to the farthest exit of the parking garage. When I caught up to them and pushed my way through the crowd, I saw a girl lying across the concrete exit, closer to the street than the garage. A car must have hit her.

Her head swiveled away from me. Blood seeped from it. Her legs were bent unnaturally. I saw black smudges on her thigh. Her left shin appeared to be broken. The contents of her gym bag, including a pair of red socks, were scattered from the force of impact. I was afraid she was dead.

Her blue warm-up looked sickeningly familiar. I strained forward. My hands flew to my face when I recognized the sad little face of Holly Holmgreen.

Eight

People murmured to each other, trying to make sense of what they saw.

"I heard a scream, tires screeching and a thud."

"Somebody called nine-one-one."

I whirled away with my hand covering my mouth and acid rising from my stomach and leaned against a concrete pillar. If only I'd walked out with Holly. Whenever I walked past garage entrances, I scanned both directions, leery of cars zooming in and out. Drivers raced in, eager to begin workouts, or they'd finished exercising and were dashing out to start their day. Holly, in her depressed state, must have been oblivious to the danger. I might have seen the car coming and saved her from being hit.

Because I worried about a lousy curling iron and begrudged ten minutes of my valuable time, this girl could be horribly injured. Or dead. Even though I felt sick, I should have walked her to her car or asked her to wait until I felt better. How deeply had I buried everything Aunt Novena had taught me?

I tried to remember where I'd parked my Wagoneer. With tears streaming down my face, I trudged into the parking garage, away from the voices. I knew I should stay. I longed to help Holly, but I panicked. I could still hear voices of people around her.

"Who hit her?"

"Did you see a car leave?"

"No."

"Me neither."

Just as I reached Albatross, I heard the wail of a police siren. I cringed inside my car. As soon as somebody called 911, SAPD would dispatch patrol officers to the scene to secure the area. Nobody would be leaving until they interviewed potential witnesses. I backed Albatross out of its parking space and rolled quietly toward the garage's second exit. Except for her assailant and the girl at the entrance desk, I might have been the last person to see Holly. The police would want to ask me a lot of questions. I didn't have the courage to stay.

As I cleared the exit, I saw a police car swing in and an EMS ambulance screech to a stop near Holly. EMS technicians flew from the van and flocked around her, checking vital signs. Squinting in my rear view mirror, I thought they'd found a pulse because they whisked her into the ambulance and squealed away. They'd make heroic attempts to save her as they raced to the nearest hospital's emergency room. I prayed for their success.

Driving at a crawl, I saw a second police car and van arrive. An officer, probably from Traffic Investigation Detail, sprang from the car. A team of officers burst from the van carrying cameras, measuring tapes and collection bags. The first patrol officer must have seen the black tire marks on Holly's thigh, suspected a hit and run and radioed for the evidence team.

With my heart racing, I turned Albatross away from the garage and forced myself to drive slowly so I wouldn't attract attention. Noises and smells from countless hours I'd spent years before at Chicago's police station assaulted my memory.

I remembered wild utterances from people whose brains were scrambled from drugs, the rank odor of unwashed bodies, and officers shouting and cajoling over the din as they tried to salvage order from chaos.

When Katy and Lee Vanderhoven died, the only thing that kept me from drowning in grief was hanging around Chicago PD and learning about traffic investigations. Since I'd been a friend of Detective Sam Vanderhoven's family and Aunt Aggie to his daughter, Lee, the officers put up with me when I loitered at the station asking questions I couldn't ask Sam. They told me the brakes in Sam's old Mustang hadn't held on Chicago's icy roads. Katy and Lee slid into a tree and died instantly.

I couldn't face another tragedy.

At home, I pulled into my driveway and sequestered myself in the garage. When I pictured Holly on the pavement, a shiver rose up my neck. Once the medical team put her in the ambulance, technicians would swarm the area where she'd lain. I envisioned them shooting photos, gathering fibers, glass, metal and other bits of evidence. Detectives from Traffic Investigation would measure the distance from where she landed to stationary landmarks like the curb to determine the force of impact and probable damage to the hit-and-run car. They'd look for skid marks: Did the driver swerve, brake or accelerate? Did Holly's shoes mark the concrete at the place where she left the ground? The car that hit her was probably gone, but officers would search the garage for cars with signs of damage.

I got out of my car and forced my legs to carry me into the kitchen. How would the police know whether a careless driver had screeched from the garage, hit Holly, panicked and driven off? Or whether someone heard Holly say she was leaving, waited until she stepped across the exit and raced toward her at full speed before she could reach the other side? Was this another accident? The day after Holly was nearly electrocuted? I didn't think so.

Throwing my workout bag onto the dining table, I sank into a chair. If EMS couldn't save Holly, the emergency room physician would pronounce her dead. The hospital would notify the Bexar County Medical Examiner. Because of Holly's age and the circumstances, he'd order an autopsy to verify the cause and manner of her death. Everything was so clinical. So tragic. So final. In minutes, a girl full of life would be reduced to an object of study.

Stumbling to the sofa, I collapsed. I'd lost so many people I loved: Lester. Aunt Novena and Uncle Fred. My baby girl. Then Katy and Lee. When Sam fled Chicago to escape the pain of their death, I lost him, too.

I'd grieved silently with Holly over the loss of her child. And the loss of my child. No wonder protecting Holly meant so much to me. I was also protecting myself. And she might be gone. She wouldn't even have the opportunity to grow old.

My sculpture of bronze runners stood poised on the coffee table. They were strong, free and leaping forward, the way I wanted to live. Instead, I felt like Grace's shattered tiles, immobilized by grief, waiting for passersby to step on me and crush me into smaller bits.

Pushing myself off the couch, I wandered aimlessly and gazed at my paintings, the impressionistic watercolors I loved. Now they looked amorphous—littered with broken bonds like the formless path of my life. I felt such sadness for Holly, for Sam's misery, for aborted relationships, for my own weaknesses. I peered through the window at cars cruising up and down Burr Road. Golfers played on Ft. Sam Houston's course, even in January. How odd that life continued on, unaware.

Thankfully, SAPD wouldn't send Sam to investigate this crime. Sam's Murder Squad in Homicide didn't handle traffic investigations. When someone discovered a body other than a traffic fatality, SAPD assigned Sam's unit to investigate. Murder was so alien to Sam's nature, I supposed he could deal with it objectively. But it would be agonizing for him to deal with this young girl's death. Fortunately, a detective from Traffic Investigation would work the case. I peered through the window and gazed down the street, amazed at how normal everything looked.

Although officers had questioned people at the scene, tomorrow they would interrogate the club's staff and members, trying to determine what time Holly exercised and who her friends were. I dreaded the interview. It was bad enough to have helped save Holly from drowning only to see her lying still on the concrete. The police would require me to relive every detail.

I raced to my bathroom and lost the last of my lunch. I'd eaten very little breakfast. After Sheldon's dissertation, I'd only picked at my sandwich. After I brushed my teeth, I trudged to the front door, made myself scrape the mail off the floor and opened a letter.

Dear Aggie,

My adorable baby is a year old. I, however, am not adorable, having gained thirty pounds since he was born. The fatter I get, the more depressed I become. The more depressed I become, the more I eat. Can you help me?

Fat in Pflugerville

It was hard to think, but I started writing.

Dearest Mom in Pflugerville,

You're not alone. One study showed 14-25% of women are at least eleven pounds heavier one year after delivery. Postpartum depression is common (10-15%) and this can act as a barrier to weight loss...

I put the letter aside. Stats wouldn't help. Pflugerville Mom knew she was depressed and overweight. I was in no condition to give advice.

I staggered to bed for a nap. My last thought before falling asleep was that, having missed Dr. Carmody's second class, I'd probably fail Aspects of Aging and chalk up an F.

Nine

When I woke an hour later, I lay on my leopard bedspread and gazed at streaks the afternoon sun cast on my ceiling. The fading light made me think of Chicago's winters.

After Aunt Novena and Uncle Fred died, I was on my own. Lester and I had planned to marry, but when I got pregnant, he skipped out. I was eighteen, penniless and alone. The one flimsy barrier between me and starvation was the bank job I'd recently secured. How could I care for a baby? My bank didn't provide childcare at work. I managed to transfer to a branch bank in the suburbs where I worked until my daughter was born. Then I placed her for adoption.

I rose and paced the room, my heart aching again from giving her up. When she was fifteen, I learned she'd died in a freak accident. Clutching the windowsill, I blinked wet eyes at the disappearing sun. I'd done my best for my baby girl, giving her life and sacrificing my heart to place her in a loving environment. But I'd never see her again. I banged my fist against the sill.

Holly had suffered a senseless catastrophe. I couldn't blame myself for her or my daughter's tragedies, but what happened to them made me look hard at my life. I tried to help Dear Aggie's readers stay healthy and young, but was that enough? I criticized egocentric club members, but hadn't I been totally consumed with improving my own body? My motivation to help others grew largely out of my fear of growing old.

I flopped on the edge of my bed. Maybe I should stop dwelling on myself. Aunt Novena would have reminded me that focusing on my shortcomings led nowhere.

Curiosity usually got me into trouble, but maybe I could put my inquiring mind to good use. Wasn't seeking truth a higher calling than helping people stay young? Wasn't seeking truth the same as sleuthing? With a little snooping, maybe I could find out who wanted Holly dead.

My feet itched. With my determination rising like floodwater, I clomped to the bathroom and scoured my teeth. I would find out who'd wanted to kill Holly Holmgreen. If I had to socialize with perfect women and egotistical men and punish my body on metal machines to smoke out the person who wanted to kill that girl, my agony would be worth it.

I marched to the living room and paced around the sofas. Holly had suffered more than enough. If I could unmask her attacker and uncover his motive, I could find redemption for the sad girl who made questionable choices but harbored no malice. Exposing Holly's enemy would be therapy for me. My monument to my daughter. The quest might even revive my faith.

I felt ready to help the depressed mom who'd written me.

Dearest Pflugerville Mom,

Tell your favorite doctor you're depressed. They have great medicines for postpartum depression that increase the efficiency of the chemical messenger, serotonin, in your brain. These meds lift your mood. You'll feel hopeful enough to begin exercising. A side effect of exercise is WEIGHT LOSS. You go girl!

Been there,
Aggie

Writing Pflugerville Mom made me feel better. Before I could concentrate on sniffing out Holly's killer I had to get my mind off my grief. I was too distraught to attend class, but I simply couldn't fail Aspects of Aging. Grad school was my chance to start over. I had to study.

I plopped on the sofa, yanked the binder from the coffee table and flipped to Theories of Aging regarding Mr. Izumi's 120-year lifespan. If he hadn't succumbed to illness, could he have lived longer? Or had he approached some built-in, biological limit?

Scientists split into two camps: Programmed Theorists believed Izumi had a biological limit. His cells either stopped dividing and died, or his immune system or hormones declined, leaving him susceptible to disease and death.

I was already worried about my hormones. I cuddled the sofa's throw pillows. Maybe the other group of scientists had a cheerier outlook. I straightened up and leafed through pages.

Error Theorists thought people aged from wear and tear on vital parts of their cells and tissues. Quitting my bank job had undoubtedly helped me avoid wear and tear.

These scientists also said that the faster an organism used oxygen, the shorter its life span. So I stood, inhaled and walked around breathing slowly to regulate my oxygen consumption. I grew bored and floated back to the couch.

Error Theorists worried about cross-linked proteins and genetic mutations. Poor Mr. Izumi: his cells were subject to a variety of glitches. None of the scientists understood how he reached 120 years, but once he did, they agreed something was bound to get him.

Maybe he'd planned to live 119 years and take a year to repent.

Sinking back into the sofa, I flipped listlessly through the notebook, searching for keys to delay aging, and stopped at antioxidants. Some researchers thought vitamins C, E and beta-carotene fought oxidative damage, which hardened people's arteries and led to heart disease. But other studies showed that when antioxidant vitamins invaded cells, cells stopped producing their own antioxidants, leaving free radical levels unchanged. Cells were stubborn. I might as well forget about taking antioxidants and stick to eating decent food.

Ten

Focusing on my studies had helped ease the shock of Holly's being hit by a car, but I suddenly realized I was famished. Grace and I had discussed going to Las Tapitas. Living in San Antonio taught me nothing was more therapeutic than Mexican food and Margaritas. I called her to confirm and stood on her porch within the hour.

"Come on in while I put Boffo in the backyard. The yardman filled his escape hole." I peeked in and watched the pooch follow her out the kitchen door. Maybe the mutt would bark the whole time we were gone and be too pooped to attack me when we returned. If I got lucky, he'd abscond permanently. Grace came back, apparently read my expression and put her hands on her hips.

"Terriers and dachshunds were bred to hunt vermin in their native lands—to chase fox, otter, weasel, badger and rats out of earth dens. Your feet remind him of vermin, so he's inclined to attack them. He can't help it."

"I think I heard him in my yard last night."

"Really? Let's check your side of the fence." We traipsed outside her fence line to see where he'd escaped, while he howled from inside her yard. About six feet over in my yard we found a round hole where Muttface had probably surfaced.

"He actually dug all the way through that tunnel into my yard?"

"Looks like it. There must be a varmint in the tunnel, probably a rat. People who own this breed actually hold Earthdog competitions where dogs chase rats through tunnels and rout them out."

Boffo was a pest, but his digging prowess was amazing. With Earthdog training, this mutt might be a leading competitor.

"His opening is blocked. I doubt he can get back in the tunnel. Next time Ernesto comes, I'll ask him to fill the hole in your yard."

"No hurry." This dog possessed incredible talent. How many dogs burrowed through tunnels? Grace could rent him out to prisoners trying to escape. I wished I could train him to root out the weasel who hit Holly.

Once we'd finished dealing with Boffo, I noticed Grace's red two-inch heels and ankle-length skirt. It had vertical stripes of red, orange, purple and fuchsia and reminded me of a porch umbrella, but I liked the bright colors. To ward off our 45-degree Texas winter, she wore a red turtleneck and purple woolen shawl, a Mexican serape. I wore my navy blue turtleneck with matching pants, a red boiled-wool jacket and navy boots with one-inch heels in case Chicago's winter blasted south.

Grace had smoothed her hair. White streaks threaded back to her bun like marshmallow tendrils. Her skin looked moist. She wore blush, shiny lipstick and plenty of black mascara. She was ready to party.

We took Hildebrand across Highway 281 to McCullough, turned south and drove past abandoned buildings toward town. Businesses still operating had bars on the windows. When we reached Main Street, Las Tapitas greeted us like a beacon, defying the odds against neighborhood decay. Grace said a new restaurant owner had bought the establishment a while back, restored it and added a lighted patio on the back.

I let her out and parked in the lot across the street. When I entered the restaurant, she was perched at a table by a window overlooking the patio, sipping one of the Margaritas she'd ordered.

Outside the window, two levels of patio decking surrounded the trunk of a huge oak. Fans on down rods hung from the tree's mighty branches. Grace said customers enjoyed the patio all summer, even when temperatures skyrocketed to over a hundred degrees. Now the fans were off, and the owner had placed vertical heaters around the patio.

Having embarked on a healthy eating regimen, I ordered chicken fajitas and a guacamole salad. Grace ordered three Tex-Mex cheese enchiladas with sour cream and chili and asked the waitress to leave the menu so she could study the desserts. I doubted I could interest her in whatever I learned about diet and nutrition. I couldn't tell my Dear Aggie readers how to order healthy Mexican food, either. The revelation might give them a clue to my location.

I wanted Grace to talk and distract me from thinking about Holly. "How's your tile work going?"

"Good. I'm at the imagination stage. I spread tile pieces on the back porch coffee table, rearrange them, play the piano for thirty minutes and go back to reposition the tiles. Once they fall into a pattern that appeals to me, I start gluing and grouting. I love the permanence of tiles."

Permanence would hold strong appeal for a woman who'd lost three husbands. I thought about Charlie Livermore dying so young. After I downed half my Margarita, my curiosity about Grace's other husbands bubbled up.

"After Charlie died, how did you manage with your girls?"

"I went back into advertising. Charlie believed in life insurance, which helped. When I turned forty-one, I met George Ball. He was forty-five and had two boys, Patrick and Michael. When George and I married, we created a conglomerate." She retrieved a photograph from her purse and handed it to me. "Here's a picture of the six of us." She stood smiling at George Ball and his teenage boys, flanked by her dark haired girls, Linda and Kim. Our food arrived and she dived into her enchiladas.

"The children all got along?" I spread guacamole on my fajitas. Her food looked better.

"Oh, sure. Linda was nineteen and had switched from theatrics to science. She completed her basics at San Antonio Community

College and was reading scientific books to get into UT Austin's Pharmacy School. She helped Kim with chemistry. By seventeen, Kim had morphed into our resident Martha Stewart. She loved fashion design and managed to get Linda interested in fabrics. They both fussed over George's boys, which made him happy." She paused. "As soon as we married, George really settled in." She gazed outside. "Look at that sunset. The patio lights will come on soon."

I blinked outside at the dropping fireball and recognized the man ascending the steps to the patio. Harry Thorne. It seemed strange he'd go out to eat, alone, so soon after a tragic event occurred at his club. I remembered his angry scowl after I left his office and didn't relish facing him again. Slumping in my chair, I picked up the menu and blocked my face in case he glanced our way. "That sun is really bright. Too much light for my eyes."

She stirred her drink and peered into the liquid. "My girls babysat the infant of a neighbor girl. Her grandparents were helping their son raise this girl and her sister, but raising yet another generation, their great-grandchild, would be hard on them. After the girl delivered the infant, my girls grew so fond of her baby, they begged George and me to adopt her."

"Hmmm." I turned slightly toward the patio. "So many people long for babies. So many others give them up."

With the eye not covered by the menu, I searched for Harry Thorne. He sauntered between tables, pausing near space heaters, like he was looking for somebody. A waitress walked toward him, and they chatted. She gestured toward our dining room, probably telling him he needed to come through the front entrance to secure a table.

"I wasn't totally against raising the girl's baby, but George decided we were too old. He did seem old. Every night after dinner, he'd plop in his recliner to watch TV and fall asleep."

Even now, Grace seemed too young for that ritual. Shielding part of my face with the menu, I watched cheese ooze from her enchiladas. My healthy fajitas were dehydrated.

I sipped my Margarita and willed the sun to set. Once the patio lights came on, diners outside could see each other instead of being drawn to watch diners inside. We were lit up like targets. Harry might have entered through the patio so he could peruse people in the dining room without being noticed. I hoped he wasn't looking for me.

"After Charlie, weren't you, well ... bored?"

"Sometimes. Then George would perform an admirable act, a deed that reflected his kind nature, and I'd get physically stirred up." She tented her hands and rested her elbows on the table. "We women heat up slowly, you know, like water put on to boil. Sex is mostly in our heads. At least, that's where it starts."

I crunched a tortilla chip.

She leaned forward conspiratorially. "You know how men turn on like flashlights? Respond quickly to any hint of sexuality?"

I nodded, although I didn't really know that much about men. When Lester left me, I was barely eighteen. Years passed before I wanted to date anybody. Then I got picky. I wanted somebody stable who would care for his family and value his work, somebody without conceit who had a keen sense of humor. Somebody like Sam.

"Anyway" she said, "I'd get hungry for George, but he'd conk out in front of the TV. Fortunately, the four children kept me so busy I usually collapsed by nightfall." She put down her fork and leaned back in her chair. "You know, we never expected instant or prolonged happiness. We believed we earned our happiness." She sighed. "George and I enjoyed three years together. He was forty-eight when he died."

I gasped. "What happened to him?"

"His blood pressure was high and his heartbeat was irregular. He went on a weekend hunting trip with some old college friends. They did a lot of walking. George wounded a deer and got excited. They tracked it. His buddies said he just keeled over. After so many years of being sedentary, I guess the excitement was too much for him."

Imagine. She'd lost two husbands before she was fifty, one from alcohol and one from inactivity. I was glad Sam stayed in shape. I was still debating about whether to subject myself to further indignities in the weight room. If I could just persevere, I'd have more to tell my readers.

The sun finally set. Lights strung through massive oaks twinkled to life above tiled patio tables. Harry Thorne sat facing our dining room. He'd apparently talked the waitress into seating him outside.

Someone dimmed our overhead lights. The waitress glided over and lighted the candle on our table. I blew it out.

"Let's enjoy the darkness. We'll have a clearer view of the patio."

"Tell me about your second day at the health club," she said.

"It was terrible. A hit-and-run driver smashed into one of the members walking into the parking garage."

"No!" She dropped her fork.

"It was Holly Holmgreen, the girl shocked unconscious in the pool just before I got in the day before."

"Somebody tried to kill her!"

I gulped water. I wasn't absolutely sure, but I couldn't deny it.

"You got in the pool only minutes behind her." We swigged Margaritas.

"You've got to be careful at that club. You shouldn't go back. As close as you were to the murder attempt, the killer might think you saw something. Did you?"

"No."

We sipped.

Harry Thorne kept staring in our direction. Our table was dark, but when we rose to leave, he might spot us.

"You called the detective, right? Sam, isn't it?"

"Well, actually ..."

She put down her drink and folded her hands on the table. "What are you trying to do, Aggie?"

"Nothing. It's just that Sam still grieves from losing his family.

He'll suffer even more if he has to solve this girl's murder."

"Then who's going to solve her murder? You?"

"No. SAPD will send other investigators. Besides, the officer who works with Sam is on vacation."

She pinned me with level eyes. "Tell me about this detective. Tell me about Sam."

I shrugged. "I knew him in Chicago. He and his family were my best friends. I attended a banking convention here and told them about the climate, the slow pace, the river. Six months after he lost them in an auto accident, he moved here."

She waited.

"When I quit my bank job and was free to live anywhere, I realized he was the only person I knew outside Chicago.

"Um-hmm."

"He's a good man. Smart. He's a lawyer who likes detective work. He's a Shakespeare fan. Reads a lot."

She gazed at the patio. I hoped Harry didn't think she was staring at him. He would focus on us.

I got her attention. "Are you going to have dessert?" I wanted to get the check so we could leave, but she ordered another Margarita.

"Sam sounds like Ray, my third husband."

"What was he like?"

"He read a lot, too. He was smart ... inquisitive ... observant. He liked to tell me about ideas or incidents that intrigued him. By the time I met Ray, George's sons, Patrick and Michael, were at USC. Patrick was about to graduate. My daughter Kim had married and moved to Oklahoma. She and Steven had their first baby girl." She smiled. "Kim decorated their house and everybody else's house right down to soaps for the bathrooms."

"Linda went to pharmacy school?" I searched for the waitress.

"No. She still read science books, but after George died, she seemed to lose her motivation. When Patrick and Michael left for California, Linda quit school and opened a health food store near USC. She gave the boys jobs and a stake in her business. I think she wanted to hold our family together."

I caught the waitress's eye and motioned for the check. Grace had nearly finished her drink. As we rose to leave, I thought about all the joy and pain she'd experienced—how her life contrasted with my life at the bank where I was merely marking time.

"Do you get to see your children?"

"Not often. They came home when Ray died two years ago. My girls adored him, but none of them could stay long. Kim and Steve had three children by then and needed to return to Oklahoma. I see them more often than I see Linda and the boys, since Oklahoma is closer than California."

I didn't ask her how Ray died. As soon as we paid the check, I speed-walked to the front door of the restaurant, slipped through waiting customers and peeked out front before crossing the street to my car. Grace followed. We climbed into my Wagoneer, and I drove out of the lot as fast as I could without squealing the tires. As we turned north on Main, I peered in the rearview mirror.

Harry Thorne burst out of Las Tapitas and ran for the parking lot. He wouldn't recognize my car. Fortunately, my windows were tinted. I set my jaw and drove to Highway 281, pushing the speed limit. "Tell me about Ray."

"Are you sure? You seem nervous."

"Go ahead. Tell me about him."

"With the children grown, we spent a lot of time together. We noticed the same things. It was eerie, as though our thoughts moved around together. I was forty-eight when we married. Ray was fifty-two. He found good executives to run his insurance company, which gave us time to talk about our earlier lives, read the same books, travel. We were soul mates. Ray filled the holes from my other losses. We enjoyed ten wonderful years together. He's been gone for two."

"Losing him must have been really hard."

"Sometimes, when I notice something, I know exactly what Ray would say about it. It's comforting, as though he's still here. When I see him again, I think we'll be pretty caught up on things."

"You mean in heaven?"

"Yes."

I hadn't thought a lot about heaven, although I believed it existed. I was always too busy groping my way through this life. I looked in the rearview mirror and didn't see Harry's car.

Grace giggled. "I guess I haven't told you ... I have a suitor."

"A suitor. You mean a tailor...someone who makes your clothes?"

She burst out laughing. "I guess 'suitor' is an antiquated term. It's a man who chases you, who wants to date you."

"No kidding. Who is he?"

"His name is Elmore Mosley. I met him at church and he called me. He's sixty-four, a widower."

"Do you actually date him? I mean, do you want to?"

"Not particularly. But he's called so many times, I guess I'll go out with him. I can't leave the phone off the hook or the contraption makes that buzzing sound. At my age, if you don't answer, the phone company dispatches EMS to your house." She grinned.

"Does Elmore drive?"

"Sure. We'll go someplace to eat ... maybe to a movie at The Quarry. He's a nice fellow. I'm just not interested in a relationship."

I tried to picture their relationship. "You don't want to marry again?"

She sighed. "I adjusted my life for three men, and I lost them. I'm not sure I want to adapt to anybody else."

"Don't you get lonely?" Margaritas made me nosy.

"Sometimes. I met the men at different stages in my life. I was blessed with wonderful husbands, and I grew with each one. Now I have so many things to think about that my loneliness doesn't last long. I do think about Ray...how he would view something."

"You really loved him, didn't you?"

"Yes. And you know what? Love never stops." Sam's face flashed across my mind. I reminded myself that a liaison had to begin before it could continue into eternity. The prospect of anything more than friendship developing between Sam and his daughter's Aunt Aggie was remote.

We were driving up my driveway before I realized that Harry Thorne had looked pale—haunted—not at all like the burly manager that I remembered.

It occurred to me that Dr. Carmody might have discussed more recent studies in class. I checked my watch. It wasn't 10:00 p.m. yet. He was probably still up and happy to assist a student in need. I decided to give him a call and explain my absence.

"Professor Carmody, this is Aggie Mundeen. M-U-N-D-E-E-N. I'm in your afternoon Aspects of Aging class .... Yes, I did miss class today ... that is correct. I actually missed the first two sessions. It's my stomach. I think I contracted a bug at Fit and Firm .... Fit and Firm is the health club where I exercise. Yes, the name of the club is intimidating .... You think I should try exercising my brain? That's what I'm doing. I've been studying your material on antioxidants. If I could borrow your notes for the last couple of classes..."

It could have been a faulty connection, but I think he hung up.

Eleven

Wednesday morning I forced myself to return to Fit and Firm. When I wheeled into the parking garage, I was glad to see that no crime scene tape marked the far entrance where the car had hit Holly. Police must have finished gathering evidence. Club employees must be relieved law enforcement wasn't highlighting the tragedy. As I walked from the garage to the building, I slowed my gait, my skin prickling from anxiety that I was about to have my worst fears confirmed. I queried the girl at the entrance desk

"Holly Holmgreen," she whispered, "the girl hit by the car, died."

My eyes filled. I felt dizzy. Blinking my eyes to regain control, I silently vowed to find Holly's killer.

I scrutinized the club layout. Beyond the entrance foyer, the ground floor included Tofu Temptations Grill, locker rooms and the swimming pool. Holly's killer had attacked on the ground floor of the parking garage and in the pool, areas that provided easy access and escape. I searched for additional entrances and exits but didn't see any. As I ascended the first flight of stairs, I realized the killer could be working out somewhere in the club.

Level two housed administrative offices, basketball and handball courts and the weight room. As far as I knew, no crimes had been committed there. When I reached level three with the cardio equipment, exercisers were sweating on mountain climbing machines and scaling revolving steps that didn't go anywhere. If my legs ever stopped shaking after climbing ordinary stairs, I might tackle those moving steps. In a year or two.

Maybe I could firm up my arms by pulling bars on the rowing machine. Men weren't excited by bat wings. But the rowers were pretty far from the TV, and my arms were pitifully weak. I searched for machines I could operate and surveyed the area for people who looked capable of murder. None of the members appeared suspicious. Nobody even glanced at me.

I spotted Meredith on a Body Trek. Delighted to see her using her guest pass, I grabbed the machine next to hers and set the device to "Manual, Slow." Nobody was close enough to hear us, so I got to the point.

"I guess you heard about Holly."

"It's just horrible. Who would hit that poor girl? Makes the pool accident appear less accidental, doesn't it?

"Yep."

She pushed buttons to increase her speed. "Aggie, you've got to call Sam. I know he's not in Traffic Investigation, but murder is murder."

"I'm sure he knows about it. I don't need to call."

Meredith glanced over with one eyebrow raised as if she suspected me of contriving something. I changed the subject. "Did the police interview you?"

"No," she said, "but they asked me to stick around. When we ate together at Tofu Temptations, somebody must have surmised we were Holly's closest friends."

"Maybe we were, at least here at the club." Without thinking, I blurted, "Holly reminded me of myself at her age." I bit my lip, not about to divulge why. "After I saw her poor lifeless body in the street, I barely made it home before vomiting." I saw no reason to mention that nausea had plagued me long before I heard screams that drew me outside.

She studied me. "Maybe you should see a doctor."

"The shock of seeing Holly upset my stomach. Besides, at my age, getting in shape takes a toll." Meredith looked skeptical, but she hated to challenge an old, sick person.

A man in street clothes materialized at the top of the stairs. His stance was rigid, his stomach was flat and he had short hair whacked by a cheap barber. He swept level three with piercing eyes. I pegged him for a cop. He strode toward us.

"I'm Detective Steve Garrett." He showed us his badge and ID. "You ladies knew Holly Holmgreen?" Smiling, he took out his pad and asked for our names and addresses.

My stomach clenched from dread at discussing details of Holly's death.

"Mrs. Laughlin, I'd like to speak with you about the deceased. The club set up a room for us downstairs." Garrett helped Meredith gently off the machine. Texas police officers are so courteous. Talking with this man might not be so terrible.

He turned to me, "Where can I find you, Ms. Mundeen, in fifteen or twenty minutes?"

"I'll be in the weight room, Detective." Machine Mecca was the last place I wanted to go, but if I was ever going to get in shape, I needed to step it up. I had actually scheduled a trainer.

I followed Meredith and Detective Garrett down the stairs, and they peeled off toward the administrative offices. As I trudged toward Machine Mania, Mickey Shannon sidled up real close and strolled step-by-step beside me.

"Hey," he grinned intimately, "we need to work out together."

When we approached an alcove where the wall jutted out, Mickey eased me into the crevice. He put his arm up on the extension and grinned close to my face, blocking my exit. "Did you hear about the Aggie who went hunting and shot two deer? The taxidermist asked if he wanted them mounted. 'No,' said the Aggie. 'Kissing will be fine.'"

I couldn't help but chuckle until I saw Mickey's hand aiming for my chest. I squirmed to wiggle out from underneath his arm. I refused to be one of his health club conquests and was not in the mood for his antics. "I paid for a trainer, Mickey. He's probably waiting for me. I didn't know when you'd be in the weight room."

He dropped his arm and stopped smiling. He'd designated

himself physical fitness expert and unofficial flirt for all unattached women. I'm sure it hurt not to be appreciated. "Well, sure, if that's what you want." The warmth left his eyes.

Practicing my southern belle response, I smiled sweetly and patted his arm. "Next time, Mickey, I want you to help me." He exhaled and seemed to feel better. I feared I'd implied more than I intended. By the time we entered the weight room, he strode jauntily beside me.

His spectacular face unexpectedly molded into concern. "You hear what happened to that poor little thing...what's her name?"

"Holly. Holly Holmgreen."

"Terrible." He shook his head. "Just terrible."

"Yes. It was."

Ned Barclay was exercising across the room, facing the other way.

I peeked into Mr. Pilates' room. Four women lay face up on mats with their legs stretched out and feet perched on top of huge balls. They lifted their backs remarkably high off the floor. It must be a terrible strain to maintain those positions. The female sergeant leered over them. If she worked for Mr. Pilates, he must be a terror. I would avoid that class.

Since I'm genetically endowed with mechanical ineptitude, the weight room still looked scary. I'd even had confrontations with kitchen appliances. The day I made coffee to celebrate the first morning in my San Antonio home, I forgot to put water in Aunt Novena's coffee pot. I was standing in my living room when I heard the blast. I thought some Texan had fired a gun. With no water in the percolator, the pressure had built up high enough to shoot those grounds right to the ceiling. The brown stain never did come off. Fortunately, people who came to my house never looked up.

I was just about to bolt from Machine Mania when Pete Reeves, my scheduled trainer, sauntered over. When Mickey saw he still outsized Pete by three inches and twenty pounds, his charm returned. "We'll sure plan on working out together, Aggie." He winked at me and spun around to scan the room for prospects.

Pete, long, lean and lifeguard gorgeous, immobilized me with his incredible eyes. "We'll start with your upper body, using machines that work your arms and back."

I imagined him massaging my shoulders.

"I'll instruct you on each machine and prepare a chart describing each exercise and listing the number of repetitions." He radiated a smile.

"Okay, Coach."

We stopped at the seated bench press. He said to hold the grips at the sides of my chest, keep my elbows pointed out away from my body and press forward to a straight-arm position. I pressed. The grips didn't budge.

Pete rolled his eyes. "Keep trying."

Elbows out, I strained against the grips. Nothing.

He glanced around, his smile plastered on. "Try not to grunt." He probably longed for one of the young, gorgeous specimens he usually coached. He lowered the weights to thirty pounds. I tried again and managed to shove the grips forward five times. He added five repetitions.

"Your face is red." He rolled his eyes up. "Let's see if we can manage the rope grip extension."

Exuding displeasure, he backed me up to a pulley with a handle on the end. He told me to grasp the handle behind my head, point my elbows toward the ceiling and extend my arms up straight. When I pulled, the handle went up three inches. In spite of my obvious inability to control the device, he made me wrench the blasted handle up twelve more times. How did this sadist ever get to be a trainer?

I spotted Ned Barclay across the room and yearned for his patient approach to exercise.

"Let's try some standing bicep curls," Pete groused.

With my arms twitching, I followed him to the next station. The handle for this apparatus was on a pulley attached to the floor. At least I could see what I was doing.

"Grab the handle. From a straight arm position, curl the bar to your chest." I struggled through twelve repetitions, and he added eight more. My arm muscles quivered so much, I didn't think I could hold a toothbrush. If only God had made me thin, I wouldn't have to endure this torture.

"You'll like the next one." Pete unveiled perfect teeth. "You get to lie down on the floor."

The thought of reclining was delicious. As soon as I lay down, he handed me a heavy iron bar, told me to place the rod across my chest and push it straight up. After I shoved the bar up five times, he put weights on both ends. I insisted I simply could not lift it. My arms were mush. If I managed to lift the pole and dropped it, the bar would land on my nose, my chin or my boobs.

Pete said he had an appointment. "Forget the other arm strengthening machines. You can finish with leg extensions." He flipped his hand toward the machine that Ned Barclay had chivalrously repositioned for me. When he removed the torture bar from my chest. I wondered how long it would take me to get up off the floor.

Having endured the longest thirty minutes of my life, I scraped myself up, dragged my body to the leg extension machine and slumped in the chair, not bothering to check the settings. I gazed to a faraway place outside the building and pondered how my abused limbs could possibly lift one more frigging bar.

I held my breath and hoisted my legs with all my strength. They flew up like twin rockets. Ned Barclay, bending over me, was about to speak, but it was too late. My foot hit him full force between the legs.

His smile contorted into a grimace, then to fury. He stumbled away in reverse, cradling his crotch behind a towel. He bobbled backwards across the gymnasium, straining to keep his knees from buckling. His face was crimson. Every person in the weight room and basketball court gaped at him. His eyes were fixed on me in horror. I wondered if he'd ever walk normally again.

Twelve

How, in a split second of self-absorption, had I managed to alienate, and perhaps injure, a really nice man? My full-force upswing in a short vertical space could be disastrous. Did I rupture the poor fellow? Change his voice? Shorten his life span?

Of all the people I could have walloped, Ned Barclay would take it hardest. He'd never believe my blow was accidental, not after Mickey practically chased him out of the weight room, and I did nothing to prevent it. Not after I made him blush by calling to him in the lunchroom when I sat perched between two guys. After the lunch incident, I'd intended to find Ned and apologize, but I never did. Considering what I'd just done, an apology wouldn't cut it. My best option was to flee. Slipping off the seat, I slinked at top speed, head down, across the other side of the basketball court.

Once Detective Garrett found out I'd skedaddled from the weight room, he would probably elevate me to number one suspect as Holly's killer. I needed to work on my social skills. If I irritated every man at the club, including the investigator, how could I work undercover to solve Holly's murder?

Detective Garrett would have to wait. My immediate problem was reaching the women's locker room without running into Ned. With him writhing in pain and thoroughly embarrassed, this wasn't an opportune time for us to meet. If he turned out to have a horrible temper, I could be facing an abbreviated life span.

Instead of creaking down the stairs, I opted to jump into the rarely used elevator. I pressed "one" and cringed in the corner. A pair of red socks stepped into the elevator cage. Fortunately, they weren't attached to Ned Barclay. They belonged to Sheldon Snodgrass, the picky eater who'd latched on to us at Tofu Temptations Grill. His eyes bulged above his Ichabod-Crane smile. The mere sight of him made me long for something soaked in butter.

With no food signs in the elevator, Sheldon focused his attention on me. He inspected me from top to bottom. His eyes lighted on my Lycra pants and bugged out. "You know the party I'm having? The one Thursday night?"

He slithered over, blocked me in the corner and smiled down at my T-shirt. He wasn't issuing a general invitation a person could avoid by remaining silent. For a vegetarian, he looked downright carnivorous. When the elevator door opened, I considered screaming until I realized he was handing me a card. I had the distinct impression he wouldn't let me escape until I read it.

Food, Fitness and Euphoria

Sheldon Snodgrass, Editor-in-Chief

The printed card included his address and the party's date and time. He waved his arms. "This is *Euphoria's* party of the year. All the food buffs come—restaurant owners, chefs, the press—it's a big bash."

There are times when one must lose gracefully. Who knew? I might discover a savory, life-prolonging new dish to describe in my column. I might even pick up clues about Holly's murder.

I tried to match his excitement. "You're so kind to invite me." I nearly gagged on my southern inflection. "I'll remind Meredith Laughlin of your invitation. She'll be delighted to come."

No way would I enter Snodgrass's healthy habitat alone. "Sam Vanderhoven might like to come, too. He's a good friend of ours." Without mentioning Sam was a detective, I let Sheldon know we had a male protector.

At least, unlike Ned, Sheldon didn't view me as evil incarnate. Elated by my acceptance, he didn't seem to notice how fast I slipped around him, skittered off the elevator and raced for the locker room.

As I zoomed past the steam room, I saw Doorknobs reclining with her nubs pointed skyward. I'd read about some group that erected triangular tents to capture atmospheric energy waves for their bodies. Maybe Doorknobs had a unique way of making contact with energy waves.

Since I hadn't perspired much in the weight room—probably a lot less than Ned—I only freshened up, helping myself to dollops of the club's creams and sprays. Maybe I could catch Meredith before she left to find out what the police had asked her. I could learn whether Sam was involved in the investigation. Even though I was getting hungry, I decided not to eat at Tofu Temptations Grill. Their food was contaminated. I'd talk to Meredith and then eat at home.

I couldn't find her, but Detective Garrett found me. When I apologized for my absence in the weight room, he squinted. "I just missed you. I heard you left in a hurry."

Blinking at the floor, I told him I'd suffered a physical emergency that required me to leave. He didn't pursue the subject. He led me to a small room on level two that the club had provided for questioning. "How long have you known Holly Holmgreen?"

I described what happened in the pool, how Sarah and I pulled Holly out and what she'd said in the lunchroom before she left the club for the last time.

"We learned she lived alone. Do you know anything about her associates? Who she dates?"

I had no idea. Garrett's question indicated the police knew nothing about the baby she had placed for adoption. Or maybe they did know and were tracking down the father, but chose not to reveal the information.

Our interrogation room was so cramped, I could read Garrett's notepad. Under Holly's name, he'd written her address, so I memorized it. I shut my eyes and asked for forgiveness. But what better way to learn who killed Holly than to search her place?

When Garrett finished with me, I drove home with my stomach grumbling and my arms aching. How could I get into

Holly's apartment on Brees Boulevard? If she lived in the units I pictured, they were in a nice neighborhood off North New Braunfels. Residents were quiet and probably didn't meddle, at least in public. Since Garrett said Holly lived alone, I wouldn't have to worry about a husband or roommate. The police probably hadn't roped off her apartment with crime scene tape. Calling attention to the unseemly event would upset the neighbors. SAPD had undoubtedly checked her living quarters, but maybe I could find some detail they missed.

On my way home, I stopped at the Harry Wurzbach/Burr Road traffic light to stretch my arms. I definitely couldn't tell Sam what I planned to do. He'd be furious if I usurped his and Garrett's authority and ignored SAPD. If I did find something, my discovery could blight the department's reputation.

Part of Sam's suffering, I suspected, was from his inability to prevent Katy and Lee's deaths. His feelings of responsibility weren't rational, but his training included averting catastrophes. I knew he'd do everything possible to keep me from tracking down Holly's killer. To get into her apartment, I'd have to be sneaky and fast. Fortunately, my legs felt operational.

In mystery novels, sleuths picked locks with a credit card, but I didn't know how to do that. A dexterous person, I'd read, could pick a deadbolt lock by using a hairpin with the rubber tip pulled off. Being mechanically inept, I figured I'd still be probing when the cops came to haul me away.

After parking Albatross in my garage, I went into the kitchen to microwave a weenie and eat a banana. I needed sustenance to attend class and gear up for breaking and entering. Maybe I could get Holly's apartment manager to let me in. I could go just before 5:00 p.m., when the manager was about to close for the day, and conjure up something credible to tell him.

My stomach felt unsettled, but better than usual. I'd endured some pretty traumatic events. Whose stomach wouldn't rebel? Body pain also contributed to nausea. I dressed in a beige sweater and slacks with no jewelry, swiped on pale lipstick and grabbed a crushable hat to cover my hair. To sneak into Holly's apartment, I needed to be monochromatic and unmemorable.

Class didn't start for an hour. To get my mind off planning an illegal entry, I decided to visit Grace. Just as I stepped outside my bungalow, a gold tone Lincoln Continental glided up to Grace's curb. A man emerged. Grace's suitor? He wore a tweed overcoat, brown gloves and a brown felt fedora. Neatly trimmed gray sideburns inched below the hat. He looked down, so I couldn't see much of his face. I walked toward Grace's house.

"Hi. Are you visiting Grace, too?" Curiosity was a powerful motivator.

He smiled up at me with keen eyes. "Yes, we're going to a movie. You are?"

"Grace's next door neighbor, Aggie Mundeen. Behind Grace's front door, Boffo barked and growled. The mutt must have heard my voice.

"Boffo! Grace ordered. Quiet down. It's Elmore."

I considered retreating so Boffo wouldn't eat my foot before he attacked Elmore's expensive shoes. I wheeled toward my bungalow.

"Bye, Elmore. Tell Grace I'll catch her later. Enjoy the movie." Slipping inside my door, I cracked it open enough to peek though. Grace wore a long black skirt and sweater, red spike heels and makeup. She'd tied a red ribbon in her hair. Elmore hugged her while Boffo barked. Even from my house I could see that when Elmore rerleaed her, she resembled a purring cat. She leaned over to grasp Boffo's collar, and Elmore bent down to pet him. I slapped my hand over my mouth. Elmore was about to lose a finger. Boffo licked Elmore's hand and flipped onto his back so the man could rub his stomach. The scrappy mutt mushed into docility. Amazing. This suitor thing might develop into something.

Thirteen

It was time to drive to University of the Holy Trinity. Since I'd missed Dr. Carmody's Monday and Tuesday classes, and he'd hung up on me, I didn't expect a warm reception. Clad in neutral garb with no makeup except lip gloss, my strategy was to slip into class unnoticed and melt into a chair near the door.

As I tiptoed in, a dozen students, flopping around desks in various postures of disinterest, glanced up. Professor Carmody honed in on me, peering through Coke-bottle lenses. His buzzard head perched on his stuffed bear body. He sniffed, as though a bad odor had assaulted his knifelike nose.

"You are?"

"Aggie. Aggie Mundeen."

He snapped his eyes to the list on his desk, as though he hoped my name wasn't on it, and ran a fat finger down the paper. "Mundeen. Mundeen...Agatha." His voice dropped. "You missed class Monday and Tuesday."

"Yes, sir."

He frowned at me through smudged optics. "You called me at home to request my notes."

"Yes, sir."

He stretched a scrawny neck from his barrel chest and glowered through bifocals. "Is this the care and concern you usually give to academics?"

"No, sir. I suffered an unavoidable event. A family emergency." I hated kowtowing to the old stuffed bird. The situation brought back memories of acquiescing to inflated egos during night school in Chicago. But the safest approach was to limit my responses. I didn't want him to kick me out of class before I learned how to avoid aging.

"Take a seat." He indicated a chair on the first row where my angle of vision was on a level with his paunch. If I looked up, I'd see beady eyes straining through scratched glass and nose hairs.

"Let's get started." He wrinkled his beak. "Today we consider the effects of under-nutrition on health and longevity. UCLA scientists fed mice thirty to sixty percent fewer calories than normal in food containing necessary nutrients. The mice lived far beyond their normal life spans. Refer to graphs on page thirty."

Did anybody care whether the mice were happy or miserable during their prolonged lives? My stomach growled. The weenie and banana I'd consumed were proving insufficient. When I blinked, a jar of crunchy peanut butter materialized on the wall behind Buzzard's head. I struggled to focus on page thirty.

Buzzard driveled on. "Since under-nutrition increased the life spans of other organisms, researchers investigated how caloric restriction affected aging in primates, our closest animal relatives."

I had doubts our unique bodies had descended, fully formed, from animals, but it was interesting to muse over which creatures could have passed a few genes to Carmody, considering his round body and buzzard noggin. My immediate concern was lasting through the afternoon without additional nourishment. When I focused on the wall, the peanut butter vision blurred. Carmody prattled on.

"Tufts University scientists discovered that caloric restriction in mice prevented or slowed the development of every disease and all types of tumors. They wondered whether caloric restriction would similarly affect humans."

Now he was getting somewhere. I blocked out the peanut butter mirage. Carmody obviously never strove to reduce calories, but I might actually give the plan a whirl. I needed to live a long, disease-free life. I had a murder to solve.

He cited other studies supporting the value of under-nutrition. Despite his ponderous delivery, the topic was interesting. At least he hadn't dropped me from class or worse, excommunicated me from grad school. Relieved, I let my mind wander to breaking and entering. As soon as class ended at 4:00 p.m., I drove down Hildebrand to my house to grab a Coke and find a bigger banana. I had plenty of time to get to Holly's apartment on Brees Boulevard.

Once my stomach was full, I pulled a khaki baseball cap down over my hair and maneuvered Albatross down New Braunfels, past the McNay Art Museum, toward Brees. When I applied the brake, my thigh cramped. When I veered right on Holly's street, both arms ached. Getting in shape meant living with pain. I drove up the hill and turned into the block-long complex of pink brick apartments, found the manager's office and rang the bell. My monochromatic clothes were perfect for an illegal entry.

As I waited on the stoop, window blinds to my left parted and then snapped shut. Seconds later, a sour-faced woman cracked the door. Yellowish mousy hair, teased and sprayed in a 1950s style, poufed around her face. This must be beauty shop day. Her blue shirtwaist dress hung straight to her knobby knees. A toe poked through one of her furry house shoes.

"I'm sorry to bother you, but my mom sent me to my sister's apartment. Holly died unexpectedly, and Mom is devastated. She's sixty-two and bedridden. She asked me to bring her Holly's photos before they get tossed out. Isn't apartment 305 just around the corner? It'll only take a few minutes. I'll lock up." She squinted cataract-blurred eyes.

"The police already mucked around here. What happened to your sister?"

Dropping my gaze, I pictured Holly's body and sniffed. "She died in a terrible traffic accident. So unexpected." I rolled up misty eyes. "You have the key to her apartment, don't you?"

Her eyes narrowed to milky slits. "What was her last name, your sister?"

"Holmgreen. Holly Holmgreen."

"What's your name?"

"Norma. Norma Abernathy. My husband's name is Able."

"You don't look a thing like Holly. Aren't you too old to be her sister?"

I noticed the vulnerable toe sticking out of her shoe. "Mom conceived Holly during menopause. She was a big surprise. That's why Mom was so crazy about her. If I start now, you can rest and I'll be through before you get hungry for supper."

"Well, the police got what they wanted. Holly paid ahead for a month. Follow me." She grabbed keys, shuffled to 305 and let me in. She formed a yellow smile under her bulbous nose. "Do you need an apartment?"

"I have one, thanks." I smiled sweetly and closed the door, careful not to snag her toe.

Holly had decorated her habitat with pink French mini-prints on the overstuffed loveseat and chairs. White gauzy curtains hung at the windows. Boffo could destroy her fluffy rug in seconds.

Her kitchen and bath were tidy and ordinary, so I traipsed to the bedroom. A baby-blue quilted spread, with bows stitched onto buttons, topped the puffy king bed. On the nightstand lay two bodice-ripper romance novels, a couple of hair and fashion magazines and one on vegetarian cooking.

I peeked into her closet. Ruffles trimmed most of her dresses and blouses. For her tiny feet, she had at least twenty pairs of shoes with spike heels. Her flat shoes had straps across the instep. Most girls in their early twenties dressed to appear older, not younger.

The police had undoubtedly removed photographs, but a few framed pictures remained. One photo lay face down on her dresser, so I picked it up. Mickey Shannon smiled at Holly with his arm encircling her waist. His fingers spread up toward her breast. She didn't look like she objected.

I opened her top dresser drawer and poked around. The police had either overlooked a packet of pictures or considered them unimportant. I flipped through three or four photos of Holly with Ned Barclay. The sweet, handsome man apparently adored her. It looked reciprocal.

A group photo showed club members and staff at a party. Holly sat near Sheldon Snodgrass. Both were laughing. I spotted Manager Harry Thorne in the picture, looking morose.

There were more photos of Holly with Ned, Mickey and Sheldon. Did one of them father her child? Did one of them kill her?

I padded back to her closet. Captivated by the doll-like quality of a black flat with embroidery across the top, I picked up the shoe to see whether the design was glued or stitched on. A wrinkled scrap of paper was wedged in the toe. I dug out the paper and peeled it open, expecting to find a store receipt. Instead, I found a typed message: "Sorry to be possessive. I know you hate restrictions. It's just that I care."

Someone had torn the paper across the bottom, eliminating the signature. Why didn't Holly rip up the note instead of tearing off the signature and crumpling the paper in her shoe? Maybe she was glad that he cared, whoever he was, even though she didn't like restraints. Who had tried to constrain her? Mickey? Ned? Sheldon?

The typestyle on the note was common. I'd seen the same lettering on documents at the bank. Fingerprints would be on the paper, but I'd have to consult the police to learn whether they could find a match. Not an option. Sam would find out I'd been snooping.

I folded the paper into smaller and smaller squares and stuffed the wad down the front of my bra. I snatched up four framed photos and heard the front door click. When I whirled around, Sam stood at the threshold.

He stared at me, glanced at the photos, raised his eyebrows and studied my face.

"Why'd you come here, Agatha?" When he was in a jovial mood, he called me Aggie.

"I...I...was concerned about Holly."

"We're all concerned. That's why SAPD has a homicide team. That's why I'm here. I wanted to see whether anything was disturbed after Garrett and I examined the place."

Gad. Sam and Detective Garrett were working as a team: one from Homicide, one from Traffic.

His eyes focused on me like lasers. "Why are you here?"

I sensed his anger covered more than my breaking and entering. Did he think my interference suggested he was incapable of finding Holly's killer?

Maybe my intrusion made him think I blamed him somehow for his wife and daughter's deaths years before. Perhaps he thought I didn't trust him to discover the truth now because questions about their accident had never been fully answered. I'd heard talk at Chicago PD about whether some criminal who hated Sam could have planted worn brake hoses in Katy's car. Investigators never proved the cause of the crash.

Sam's hostility blanketed me like a shroud. I hated having him angry with me. I didn't want him to think I was hiding facts about Holly's murder, so I decided to come clean.

"In the lunchroom on the day she died, Holly told me she'd delivered a baby. After months of anguish, she gave her newborn up for adoption. She was depressed and took Valium before she got in the pool the day she...the day before the car hit her."

I wanted him to appreciate the difficulty of Holly's decision. He didn't need to know I'd withheld the information that she almost drowned. Having gone that far, I blurted the additional reason for her distress.

"Holly gave up the baby without knowing where the infant went or who would raise the child." My voice broke. I couldn't help it. I sniffled. "I guess I wanted to come here so that, somehow, Holly will know somebody cared."

He flushed. "So you think Holly worried about where her child went? She could have chosen open adoption with her, the child and the adoptive parents knowing each other." His teeth were clenched. His voice grew louder. "Or semi-open adoption, where she sent the child gifts on special occasions, without the adoptive parents or her child ever knowing who or where Holly was." His face took on a purple hue.

"At that point, what did it matter? Once Holly got pregnant and decided she didn't want her baby, there weren't any great options." His fury made him irrational. If he ever learned the truth about me, he'd wish I'd been run over with Holly.

He filled his lungs, blew air through his nose and spoke through a locked jaw.

"Now. What did you discover to help us find Holly's killer?" He was struggling to return to an even keel, but his eyes didn't belong to my trusted friend from Chicago.

"Here are some photographs." I lifted them, my hands shaking. "Maybe one of these men fathered her child."

He took deep breaths as he studied the photos. "We saw these photographs and others. We're questioning those men. Maybe one of them killed her. That's why you shouldn't be here, Agatha. If one of them is the killer, he might decide to track you down." He let his message sink in.

"Did you find anything else?" he asked.

"No." My heart was about to burst.

His voice softened. "Let us handle this. There's no reason to put yourself in danger. I'll tell the landlady we're through for today and follow you home."

"Don't say Agatha. I told her I'm Holly's sister, Norma Abernathy. Wife of Abel Abernathy."

Sam closed his eyes and shook his head. Before he turned and stormed out the door, I thought I saw the beginning of a smile. Maybe I just wanted to see it.

I tiptoed out of Holly's apartment. Since Sam forgot, I locked the door. When I glanced toward the parking area, I saw Harry Thorne lumber out of his Ford truck. His face looked pasty and drawn. Was he coming to Holly's place? He felt obligated to protect young girls at the club, but why would he show up at Holly's apartment after she died?

I considered hiding to see if he'd manage to get into her apartment, but I didn't relish confronting another angry male. Plus, Sam was waiting.

Slipping away from Holly's door in the opposite direction, I took a circuitous route to my car and dropped the apartment key through the landlady's door en route. I decided not to mention Harry's arrival to Sam; I wanted to think about why Harry was there. Maybe I could find a way to slip into Harry's office at the club and poke around. That would really tick Sam off.

It was a shame Sam and I carried so much emotional baggage. Not only did the burden wear us out; it complicated my efforts to find Holly's killer. Sam, Bless him, made sleuthing incredibly difficult.

Fourteen

Sam stood by my Wagoneer, waiting. "Where did you go?" His question sounded more like concern than accusation.

"Nowhere. I got lost among the buildings. These apartments go on forever."

He seemed past registering surprise at anything I said or did. "I'll follow you home and check your locks in case the killer trailed you."

I thought about Harry Thorne and glanced around.

After Sam closed my car door, I waited until he got in his vehicle to stick my key in the ignition. My hand shook. I scanned the row of cars to my right and saw Harry Thorne backing out his white Ford truck. When I eased my car into reverse and sputtered out of my space, I was trembling all over.

I crept to New Braunfels and drove south at twenty-eight mph. I feared Harry was following us, but I couldn't drive fast with Sam right behind me.

Sam probably thought I was afraid to go home, which I was. I was too rattled to face him and afraid of what I might say...of what he might say. Holly's life undoubtedly reminded him of the unknown woman who'd relinquished the child that he and Katy adopted.

He didn't know I was that unknown woman. He knew, when we lived in Chicago, that Lester and I had decided not to marry and that my bank transferred me to a satellite branch for several months. He didn't know I'd secured the bank transfer so I could secretly deliver Lester's baby. Or that I had proposed to his wife, Katy, that she and Sam adopt my daughter.

I stopped at the Austin Highway light by the McNay Art Museum and scrounged through my glove box for Kleenex. In my rearview mirror, I saw Sam's car, followed a few cars back by Harry's truck. Unlike Sam, I was well acquainted with Harry Thorne's white Ford. I managed to wipe my eyes and blow my nose before the light changed.

Since Sam and Katy couldn't have children and had decided to adopt, she and I made a pact: the most painful pact of my life. Katy's obstetrician and her attorney would arrange for the Vanderhovens to legally adopt a baby who would soon be available, my daughter Lee. Katy and the doctor swore that Sam would never learn the identity of Lee's biological parents.

Six months after my baby was born, I transferred back to the main Chicago bank and became Lee's Aunt Aggie. Sam never knew I was Lee's mother.

Barely able to drive, I grabbed more Kleenex and reminded myself I'd done my best for my baby girl by placing her in their loving home.

When I turned left on Burr Road, I spotted Sam's car behind me, but I didn't see Harry's truck. Was he navigating a back route, waiting until Sam wasn't around to protect me? Was Harry hell-bent on tying me to Holly's murder and determined to punish me?

Maybe I'd misread Sam. If he knew I gave Lee to him and Katy because I loved the baby and admired them, maybe he wouldn't hate me for deceiving him. Maybe he could still be my friend. My feelings for him went beyond friendship, but I could never let him know. How could he ever forgive me for living a lie and causing him to live one?

I drove up the hill. Sam followed me up the driveway and plodded over to open my door. Without saying a word, he took my elbow and steered me, with a light touch, to my cottage. He realized I'd been crying and brushed his finger under my eyes. "I'm glad you're home, Aggie. You've made a good life here. There's no reason for you to be snooping in a murder."

"You're right. There's no reason for me to snoop."

I considered telling tell him about Harry, how he'd scowled at me, searched for me at Las Tapitas, materialized at Holly's apartment and followed us. If I told Sam, he'd probably stay with me until he could get another officer to relieve him. He might also focus exclusively on Harry Thorne and forget about the other suspects.

Whatever I said, he'd probably delve deeper into Holly's past. His discoveries might spur him to pursue the truth about his adopted child.

From my front porch, I saw Grace peering at us through her window. Boffo panted beside her, his stubby forelegs planted on the sill. She gave me a thumbs-up sign, which I ignored. I was focused on Sam. It would be impolite to not ask him in. "Would you like a Coke?"

"No, thanks. I need to get back to work." He paused, then turned and marched into my living room. I thought he was going to check the locks.

He gave me a serious look. "There's something I need to say."

Fifteen

Sam whirled to face me.

My heart whammed against my chest. "It's about your neighbor."

"Grace?"

"Grace Livermore. Did you know she had three husbands who died?"

"She told me." We faced each other like sentries in Korea's demilitarized zone.

"Didn't that strike you as unusual?"

"I found it tragic they died so young."

"SAPD thought the circumstances were beyond unusual. They suspected the deaths might not be accidental. When I came to San Antonio, they'd decided to reopen the files."

My hand flew to my mouth. "The police kept files on Grace's husbands? They suspected she killed her husbands? That's preposterous!" I flung my arms out and marched around the living room. "Grace couldn't hurt anybody. She's warm and creative and loving." I turned to face him. "You don't know her."

He staked out a place on my sofa, leaned forward with his elbows on his knees and froze me with his eyes. "I know it's damned unusual for one woman to bury three husbands."

I couldn't deny that, but Grace Livermore was the last person in the world to commit murder. She'd loved the men. And the children. I paced. "Did they investigate the deaths when they occurred?"

"They did. The family reported Charlie Livermore took one of his daughters out to eat. When they came home, he stayed in the car to finish a cigarette and listen to music. When his car caught fire, he burned to death."

I glared at him and started pacing. "That's precisely what Grace told me. Linda was talking on the phone." I gestured like a defense attorney. "Grace and Kim came home from their party. They smelled smoke, ran to the garage and found Charlie's car in flames. Grace thinks he never knew what happened."

"I'm sure he didn't. He was an alcoholic and had probably passed out. Since he was thirty-nine, they did an autopsy so the medical examiner could determine the cause and manner of death." He leaned over the coffee table to study my family photographs.

"What did they find?" I was thinking like a sleuth. I knew Grace could never commit murder.

"Charles Livermore died of cyanide gas poisoning."

Breathless, I sank to the other sofa.

"He wore a wool and silk sport coat. When he passed out, the coat caught fire and cyanide fumes encircled his head. Plastic and foam in the car seats ignited, producing more cyanide gas. In a closed car, with Charlie in an alcoholic stupor, he inhaled more than enough cyanide to kill him. It's a common scenario when people burn in a car. The ME determined that the level of alcohol, plus the cyanide in Charlie's blood, killed him."

I sank further into the cushions. "So you're telling me Charlie Livermore's death was an accident."

"The ME deemed his death accidental. But when Grace's second husband, George Ball, died seven years later, and Grace married Ray Peters four years after that, and he died, the police decided to take a closer look at Grace Livermore." He picked up the photo of me with Aunt Novena and Uncle Fred.

I shook my head. "Grace simply couldn't do the things you say. She's still broken up over Ray's death." Sam had planted a seed of doubt, but I was determined to defend Grace. My heart told me he was wrong. This time, I would stand up for my principles. "Grace told me George Ball suffered from cardiac arrhythmia and high blood pressure. He never exercised. Then he went out and walked for three days, drank alcohol every night, tracked a deer and keeled over with a heart attack. Three men who were with him saw him fall."

He tilted toward me. "Did she tell you George had the wrong pills packed in his pill box? That instead of 100 mg tablets of Metroprolol, the Beta Blocker he took twice a day, they found ordinary aspirin? Somebody switched the pills."

My heart skipped. I was glad to be sitting down.

"The abrupt withdrawal of his medication, coupled with excitement, exertion and alcohol, could have caused his heart attack."

I felt weak. "Maybe George made the substitutions himself. By mistake."

"It's possible. His cardiologist said patients frequently take meds incorrectly. His friends said George was ecstatic about the hunting trip, but that he wouldn't be so careless with meds he knew were vital for his heart condition."

"Could someone in his family have substituted the pills? By accident?"

"The file says the family kept meds in one cabinet. Meds for George's three-day hunting trip were transferred from larger bottles to George's pillbox. Someone could have put in the wrong meds by mistake or exchanged them on purpose. Naturally, his family's prints covered the bottles. His buddies' prints were on his pillbox. They went through his things trying to find something to help him."

"I guess someone from SAPD questioned Grace and the children after George died?"

"They all seemed horrified to think somebody could have switched the pills and swore they didn't do it. Since SAPD has reopened the files, they'll interview the children again. One lives in Oklahoma and the others in California, so the investigation will take a while. Then they'll talk to Grace."

He picked up my photo of him with his family. Even though I was Lee's Aunt Aggie, I never displayed a photo of Lee by herself or with me.

It seemed like a hundred years since I'd sneaked into Holly's apartment and played amateur detective. I felt more washed out than my khakis. I never imagined sleuthing could cause such torment. Like Sam and Meredith, Grace was my friend. Since I'd lost my mother when I was young, Grace was almost like a mother to me. SAPD's suspicions about her just couldn't be true.

Sam must have realized the impact of his devastating news. He put down the photograph and joined me on the sofa.

"Did they do an autopsy on George?" I asked.

"The procedure showed he died of a heart attack. The question was, why?"

"The ME ruled Charlie's and George's deaths were accidental, right? So they have absolutely no proof Grace had anything to do with what happened to them." I didn't tell him that Grace was a little bored with George. I knew she loved him.

"There's no proof."

"So why are you telling me all this?"

He looked directly at me. "I know you spend time with Grace. I know you like her. I just want you to be careful."

He had pummeled my heart by suspecting Grace, but I couldn't be angry with him.

"I need to go," he said. But instead of leaving, he picked up his family photograph. "They were something, weren't they, Aggie?"

I swallowed. "They were special."

He lingered over Katy, then dwelled on Lee's face. Was he remembering how Katy's obstetrician called and said he had a patient who would deliver a baby girl who, as soon as she was born, could be theirs?

Surely he asked about the baby's parents. For years, he must have wondered who had abandoned Lee.

With the photo in his hand, he studied me. Fortunately, my bland clothes didn't accentuate the color of my eyes. When I wore blue or green, they adapted to the color. This was my only feature Lee shared. Otherwise, she hadn't resembled me. Her hair was curlier and lighter than mine. She had hair and features like her runaway father.

"It's hard not to look back, isn't it," he said, focusing on my eyes, "and wonder what might have been?"

I cleared my throat. "Yes. It is." How could I break his melancholy? I had to maintain our fragile friendship. If he ever suspected I was Lee's mother and had deceived him, he'd be livid. The thought of even touching me would repel him.

I needed to change the subject fast. "Thanks for bringing me home. It's been a long day for both of us."

He stood me up and clasped my arms. "Try not to worry about your friend Grace. SAPD's suspicions are probably groundless. Sometimes people have too much time on their hands. Even cops."

We needed to talk about something else. With the weight of deceit surrounding us, his closeness made me uncomfortable. Besides that, the scrap of paper I'd retrieved from Holly's shoe and stuffed down my bra itched like crazy.

Stepping back, I peered up wistfully. "Will you pick up Meredith and me for Sheldon's party tomorrow night? He's expecting us."

His jaw dropped. "Sheldon? Sheldon Snodgrass? The weird eater? We're going to his party? Why would we go to his party? We hardly know the guy." He looked like a stunned owl. His eyes were wide open.

"Meredith said she thought the event would be a blast." Dredging up my sweetest southern smile, I led him to the door. As soon as he cleared the threshold, I flipped him a wave, closed the door and scurried back into the house.

Next, I had to break the news about Sheldon's party to Meredith. Lying was getting easy. Wasn't that some kind of personality disorder?

I peeked through the curtains and saw Sam shake his head as though he was confused. He pulled away. My prospects for a relationship with him were growing dimmer. He suspected Grace of murder, and I knew she couldn't kill anyone. He would investigate Holly's adoption and, I feared, Lee's adoption. Any day now, he'd discover that the feckless mother of his beloved daughter, Lee, was me.

Overwhelmed by the urge to compose a personal ad, I grabbed my Big Chief tablet.

"Single white female. Young. Formerly a banker. Loves humor..."

Who was I kidding? Bankers didn't quit working while they were young. They loved playing with money.

A banker who loved humor? Nobody would believe that.

I had just put down my pen when the doorbell rang. Had Sam returned?

Sixteen

"It's me, Grace."

When I opened the door, she stood on my front stoop with a wide grin on her face. "Did you see me wave through the window?"

"Yep."

"That's Sam, isn't it? The detective?"

"That's Sam."

"I could tell from his khaki shirt and pants. The clothes indicate he's steady and serious, not sold on himself. His orange and yellow tie reveals a romantic streak. He's wildly appreciative of the beautiful things in life. You should watch a Texas sunset with him." She produced a big smile.

I collapsed on the sofa, laughing. "You're something else. How can you surmise all that from his clothes?"

"Experience. Three husbands, remember?"

She perched expectantly on the arm of my sofa, probably waiting for me to disclose more about Sam. I didn't have the energy to discuss him or Holly's murder. I certainly wasn't going to reveal SAPD's suspicions about her. Elmore Moseley was a better topic.

"Elmore's attractive. How was the movie?"

"We didn't go. We went to dinner at Alexander's at the Quarry. We started talking and sat in the booth for two hours. Then we came home and snuggled in front of the TV."

She saw surprise on my face.

"We only cuddled. When you're my age and you've lived alone, you appreciate the warmth of another body. Being held renews your life force. I know I sound weird. You have to experience it."

There was no way this woman could kill anybody. She rested her chin on her fist.

"Sometimes, when you spend days without speaking to anyone," she said, "your vocal chords become dormant. When you speak, your voice cracks. That's one reason I sing when I play the piano." She shrugged. "Even if nothing serious ever develops between Elmore and me, people aren't meant to be alone. At my age, you see things for what they are and count your blessings."

We heard yipping and scratching outside my front door.

"Oops. Sorry. Ernesto stopped up Boffo's hole and filled the one in your yard, but he dug out again." She withdrew a handful of doggy treats from her pocket and strode to the door. "I dropped a couple of these on the way over. I knew if he strayed into your yard, he'd smell them." She cracked the door and bent to give Boffo his treat. He panted, displaying his friendlier dachshund lineage. When I approached him, he growled. I wondered if my recent stomach problems gave me halitosis. If Grace hadn't been there, I might have coughed in his face.

I considered stocking doggy treats in case I ever had to entice Muttface off my shoes and lead him back to Grace's house. If I failed to learn how to re-channel Boffo's instincts, I'd probably regret it. He licked her and followed her away from my bungalow, waddling happily toward home.

Exhausted from my eventful day, I showered and prepared for bed, wishing I could make sense of the events. Brushing my teeth, I glanced in the mirror to see how wiped out I looked and saw a tumor in the upper part of my arm. I gaped at the lump, gripped my toothbrush, and it grew!

That's when I realized it was a muscle. I'd never had a muscle in my arm. I'd never had a visible muscle, period. I checked my other arm. Sure enough, I had a twin tumor—the glorious result of time spent in the weight room. How long would it take me to resemble Arnold Schwarzenegger? The next time I corralled Mickey and Ned to quiz them about Holly, I'd express my gratitude for their help using weights. I especially wanted to thank Pete Reeves.

I remembered mail I'd scooped from the floor after Sam left. I grabbed it from my bedside table. Somebody needed help.

Dear Aggie,

I finally incorporated cardiac exercise into my life. Now my sadistic (hunky) trainer tells me I need to add weight training. I birthed two children, have a new grandchild and just turned fifty. Why on earth do I need muscles?

Happily Round in Rochester

Dear Happily Round,

Congratulations on being a fit, young grandmother. Unfortunately, you cannot train for heart fitness and skeletal muscle strength at the same time. Muscle mass peaks between ages thirty and thirty-five and then begins a slow decline. What do you care, right? You also lose bone mass after menopause (sorry for using the "m" word) causing you (and the rest of us) to be prone to osteoporosis—weak, thinning bones. If you fall and break a bone, you'll be laid up recovering and unable to lift your grandchild. Muscle strength helps prevent that. Women ages fifty-five to seventy-two doing weight training twice a week had amazing results: one lost ten pounds without dieting. Another regained eight percent of the bone mass she lost after menopause. The third woman, a golfer, drives the ball thirty yards farther than before. Everybody had fewer bulges, not more. Stay Happy. Add the weights.

From the weight room,
Aggie

Despite having discovered two new muscles, I felt like a mass of sprung rubber bands. Before I crumpled into bed, I cracked the window to get fresh air. Grace was playing the piano and belting out a song like Ella Fitzgerald. Boffo howled accompaniment. I was glad somebody was happy.

Seventeen

Thursday morning, I phoned Meredith. "We have to talk."

"What's up?"

"Big news about Holly. I'll meet you at the treadmills in fifteen minutes."

I drove to the club like a maniac and flew past the check-in desk. I didn't know I could climb stairs so fast. My heart raced. Halfway up, my left bun went into spasm.

Meredith had commandeered machines closest to the television. I eased onto the treadmill next to hers and set the contraption to 2.5 mph, hoping my derriere muscles would relax. "I got into Holly's apartment and looked around."

"How'd you get in? Didn't the police lock it?"

"Sam was there and let me in." The lie rolled off my tongue. "I saw a photograph of Holly with Mickey Shannon."

"Really? Well, they say opposites attract. She was so delicate and he's so...indelicate."

"I know what you mean, but they seemed pretty chummy in the picture. He'd slapped his hand close to her boob, and she didn't seem unhappy about it." Mickey's words flashed across my brain. "When I saw Mickey on my way to the weight room the day after Holly died, he couldn't even remember her name."

"Unbelievable. Maybe she told him to take a hike. He wouldn't like that."

"No. Or he might have pretended he barely knew her so he wouldn't be considered a suspect."

Meredith increased her speed. "I bet Mickey could get furious if somebody rejected him."

I told her about the party photograph of club members and staff, including manager Harry Thorne.

"Hmm. You know, I didn't think much about it at the time, but Tuesday morning, around ten-thirty or eleven, I passed by the manager's office," she said. "He had the door closed, but I heard him arguing with some girl. I wonder if it was Holly."

"What did they say?"

"I heard only snatches. He sounded angry and did most of the talking, something about dating members and staff—I guess he meant her—something about the club being respectable. The girl fired back, asking how he knew anything about being respectable."

Ouch. Harry wouldn't have appreciated that.

"I heard her say, 'Leave me alone.' He boomed a response. She blasted back she'd made a mistake coming to this club. I heard her push against the door, so I hurried down the hall so they wouldn't catch me eavesdropping."

"Did you see her?"

"No, I just heard her. Since I only met Holly once at Tofu Temptations Grill, there was no logical reason to connect her with the voice I heard."

It wouldn't have occurred to me either if I hadn't seen Harry show up near Holly's apartment. My rear end started feeling pliable, so I maintained my speed.

If it was Holly who Meredith overheard, when Holly and I talked at Tofu Temptations Grill the day she died, why didn't she mention seeing Harry Thorne after Sarah's class before she went to the pool? Did some link exist between her and Harry? If so, why had she concealed it?

Meredith sped up. "I heard something else about Harry. He left Tuesday with a stomach bug. A staff member had to drive him home."

"Tuesday is the day Holly died."

"If you're the club manager," she panted, "having a murder

occur in your place would be devastating. No wonder he went home."

Harry would be especially upset if he and Holly had a connection. What kind of association did they have? Was the person who killed Holly also trying to kill Harry? Was that why he was sick? What kind of lunatic was loose at Fit and Firm? I might have to tell Sam everything I knew whether I wanted to or not.

"Did you see Harry here on Wednesday?" I asked. If Harry went home sick on Tuesday, it was odd I'd spotted him at Las Tapitas the same night. The next afternoon, Wednesday, I saw him drive into Holly's apartment complex.

"I don't remember seeing Harry on Wednesday, but I rarely see him when I'm working out."

I didn't tell her about the note I'd found in Holly's shoe. I wanted to think about who might have written it. I described the other photographs. "Holly and Sheldon Snodgrass sat together at one party."

"You're kidding."

I realized talking too much about Sheldon might hamper my efforts to lure Meredith to his Thursday night bash. I switched to Ned. "I saw several pictures of Holly with Ned Barclay."

"Sounds like a better match."

"He obviously adored Holly. She seemed fond of him, too."

"What did Sam say about the pictures?"

"That police are questioning the men about their relationships with Holly. One of them could be her baby's father. And her killer."

"She had a baby?"

"She gave birth a few months ago and placed the child for adoption."

Meredith shook her head. "Poor Holly. She must have been miserable the last days of her life. Why would someone want to kill that girl? I'm glad Sam's on the case."

"Yes. I'm glad you asked him to the grill. I enjoyed seeing him. We'll see him again tonight."

"We will?"

"There's a gourmet tasting party. Chefs and restaurant owners show off their delicacies. The press even covers it."

"Sounds intriguing. Where's the party?"

"It's hosted by *Food, Fitness, and Euphoria*—the magazine. You know, Sheldon's magazine."

"Not Sheldon. Sheldon Snodgrass? Oh, please."

"Sam's going. He thought the party might be interesting...said he'd pick us up at seven."

"I can't believe I'm doing this. Snodgrass will probably serve eggplant eggnog. Should I come dressed like a pickle?" She scowled.

I looked at her with basset hound eyes.

"Oh, all right. I'll be ready." She sped up faster and faced forward. She didn't even laugh at her pickle joke. It was time to end my workout.

"I'm checking out for today. Thanks for listening. I'll see you tonight." I scampered toward the steps before she had time to come to her senses.

When I entered the locker room, Sarah Savoy was primping at one of the cubicles. Since I needed to cash a check at the bank before going to class, I slipped behind the door of my locker to change into a pantsuit. I left my jacket off to use deodorant. When I went to the primping station next to Sarah, I noticed her beautiful suede suit. I complimented her on the elegant outfit even though it smelled like she'd recently retrieved it from storage. She probably didn't wear suits very often.

"My cousin is here from Dallas. We're going to dinner at La Mansion and a play at the Majestic Theatre...girls' night out." She reached into her purse for Chanel moisturizer and makeup and patted them on. Her eyes were as startlingly blue as Pete Reeves'. Those two blonds would make the perfect pair for a beach commercial.

"Did the police question you about Holly?" I asked.

She lined her eyes. "Yep. I can't believe they didn't know about her boyfriends. When she joined the club a couple of years ago, she started dating every guy in sight...even Sheldon Snodgrass. That didn't last long." She brushed on mascara. "When Holly dated guys from the club, it really chapped Harry Thorne."

"Really? Why should that bother him?"

"Harry's a control freak." She thinned her lips to apply liner. "I'm surprised he didn't drive her crazy. Who Holly or I dated was none of his business."

"What did he do when she dated them?" Sarah probably knew more than anybody about club members and staff.

"He'd sashay by and make snide remarks. Harry used to hassle me the same way when I dated a member. What a creep."

"What did Holly do?"

"Ignored him like he didn't exist." She filled in her liner with lipstick.

I grabbed an opaque bottle, smoothed the club's moisturizer on my face and neck and waited for everything to dry before putting on my jacket. "Did you work here when Holly dated Mickey Shannon?"

"Sure did. Mickey dated everybody, including me. He's one gorgeous specimen, but I got tired of his stupid jokes. I became gradually unavailable—said I needed to prepare for classes—that kind of stuff." She smirked at me. "He wouldn't have liked being flipped off. He's got a terrible temper."

"How long did Holly date him?" I hoped my questions sounded like casual gossip, not an interrogation. To prolong dressing, I sprayed more deodorant and blew at my armpits.

"A couple of months." She set her makeup with powder. "They got pretty cozy before Ned Barclay showed up." Sarah apparently liked to gossip.

"Can you imagine preferring Ned over Mickey Shannon?" she said. "Well, Holly did. Mickey didn't appreciate it one bit, but I guess he concluded he didn't have much choice."

No wonder Mickey enjoyed intimidating Ned in the weight room. He was getting even. "Did Holly date Ned for a long time?" I began applying makeup.

"Yes. I thought they might get married, but they never did. Holly disappeared for a few months. I didn't know whether they broke up or what." Sarah finished her makeup and started brushing her hair. "Ned still came to work out, wearing that sad, sweet face of his."

Did she know about Holly's pregnancy and adoption? I applied more mascara. "How long was Holly back at the club before we saw her at the pool?"

"Two or three days. She came to my aerobics class the morning of the pool accident looking weak and demoralized. I could tell she was struggling, so I stayed afterward to talk to her."

Sarah's aerobics class met from 9:00 to 10:00 a.m. Even though Holly lingered after class to talk, she still had time to stop by Harry's office before going to swim. Between 11:30 and noon, I spotted her floating in the pool. Maybe Sarah was the girl Meredith overheard arguing with Harry. If it was Sarah, she chose not to mention it.

"Holly told me she'd delivered a baby," she said. "She took Valium because she was depressed over giving up the child." She repacked her purse, looking despondent. Most women had trouble imagining how another woman could relinquish her baby. The pain of my own guilt soured my stomach. I felt the urge to defend Holly.

"Sometimes it's the only thing a person knows to do." I'd applied so much mascara, I couldn't afford to fog up. I blinked and swallowed.

She watched me. "Yes. Poor Holly." Sympathy softened her face. "Well, at least she's out of her misery."

I gathered my things. "I'll be getting in the pool for your water classes pretty soon. I'm sick of those treadmills." My buns felt like rocks.

"Great. I'll watch for you." She bustled out of the locker room, strutting like a fashion model.

All I had to look forward to was facing Dr. Carmody.

Eighteen

I didn't feel like eating lunch. I stopped by the bank, which made me late for Professor Carmody's class. He scowled at me as I tiptoed to an empty front row seat nearest the door and eased down on my concrete biscuits.

Wishing I'd wiped off excess makeup, I produced the most dazzling smile I could muster. He'd apparently never experienced having a student return after missing his first two classes. He raised his knife-like nose, sniffed the atmosphere and dissected me through thick bifocals as though weighing the significance of my return.

I checked him out. He appeared to be in his fifties. Since he was doughy above and below the belt and lacked upper body musculature, I surmised he valued eating over exercise. I wondered whether, after teaching Aspects of Aging, he'd change his lifestyle. I settled back to hear what he had to offer.

"We've discussed the elements of normal aging in the absence of disease and how the average lifespan increased due to improved medical care, antibiotics, sanitation and healthier lifestyles. The average life span is different from the maximum life span of approximately one hundred twenty years, which hasn't increased, so far as we know, over centuries." Students lounged over desks and peered at him from under droopy lids.

My hand shot up. "According to The National Center for Health Statistics, 'if major forms of cardiovascular disease were eliminated, human life expectancy could increase by almost ten years.' So, in addition to extending the average life span, couldn't scientists extend maximum life span by eliminating the major disease that kills people?"

Carmody opened his mouth but apparently couldn't get it in gear.

I continued. "We know the primary risk factors for heart disease: smoking, obesity, physical inactivity, high cholesterol, diabetes, high blood pressure..." His face got redder with each item I ticked off. He probably had three or four risk factors. Students waited for his response. When there was none, they flipped their heads toward me.

"We already reduce cardiovascular disease through diet and lifestyle changes. We control cholesterol, high blood pressure and diabetes with medication." Hopefully, Carmody's ruddy glow didn't indicate skyrocketing blood pressure. I was merely making observations. Students switched their attention to him.

"What you say is true, Miss...Miss..."

"Mundeen. Aggie Mundeen."

"Ah, yes. Agatha." He snorted. "I'm afraid your comments are simplistic."

I didn't care for his choice of words.

"You're not considering Programmed Theories," he droned. "Mr. Izumi died at one hundred twenty because his immune system failed. His hormones could have failed, or his cells could have stopped dividing. Error Theorists think external forces damaged his cells and organs so they could no longer function adequately, like wear and tear, and..." Students slumped while he babbled repetitive information.

While he blah-blahed through theories, I had another thought. When he stopped to breathe, I expressed it. "How can gerontologists separate Program Theories from Error Theories? Even if 'clocks' that determine aging and death are genetically predisposed, can't they be altered by good diet and exercise, or thrown off course by disease or error?" Carmody's bird face expanded like somebody had attached it to a bicycle pump. My classmates perked up.

"Which reminds me," I chirped. "What about those biomarkers? Have geneticists pinpointed what they are? Why don't scientists determine how genetics, disease and 'errors' affect biomarkers?" I eagerly awaited his response.

He pursed his lips and blew out a lot of air. "Scientists are trying to identify biomarkers in cells, tissues and organs but haven't pinpointed them yet. They only recently finished mapping human genes."

He didn't have to shout. I merely expressed questions triggered by the reading material. Weren't students supposed to be inquisitive?

One girl giggled, intensifying Carmody's exasperation. Since I hadn't achieved perfect attendance, I opted to become silent. Besides, I felt weirdly lightheaded. My stomach rumbled. I grew dizzy. I couldn't concentrate. Some disturbance had invaded my brain.

He started blubbering about fruit flies. He said scientists had found evidence of genes in fruit flies that appeared to be related to aging. How strange was that? I pictured aging fruit flies with gray wings flitting around. I snickered. They buzzed around in slow motion, bumping into each other. I giggled and slapped my hand over my mouth.

Carmody glared at me through segmented lenses. Bug-eyed. Like a fruit fly.

He yakked about longevity genes in mice. He said somebody had isolated mice genes to gain knowledge about human aging. He used a crock of big words, but I thought it was dumb to relate mice genes to humans. He mumbled something about "death genes" in nematodes, which disoriented me. Nematodes were stupid worms. I pictured an army of worms wriggling along in unison—"Ne-ma-tode. Ne-ma-tode..." I burst out in uncontrollable giggles.

He fixed me with an angry stare, probably trying to activate my death genes. I leaned forward over my desk and leered menacingly to activate his death genes first.

Far back in my mind, fuzzy words about antioxidants danced

around. Was he scared to talk about 'em? I couldn't remember what I'd read, but whatever Flabface said about 'em, I was ready to take him on.

When he stopped blathering, I presumed class was over. When I had trouble standing up, I decided not to ask Carbuncle to share his notes for classes I'd missed. Instead, I bathed him with a syrupy smile of southern appreciation. He swayed menacingly in my direction. Bug Eye Carbuncle should focus on lowering his blood pressure.

"Miss Mundeen. Have you considered dropping this class?"

What a silly thing to say. "Of course not," I giggled. I'd read a ton of material. I had to learn how to avoid aging. How to locate and care for my biomarkers.

Blowing him a mushy kiss, I wiggled my fingers "Bye" and bumped a desk on the way out.

Nineteen

I didn't remember driving home. Evidently, I toppled into bed and must have conked out because when Meredith called to ask what I was wearing to Sheldon's bash, I had barely an hour to get dressed. My recollection was hazy about disrupting Carbuncle's...Carmody's class. I couldn't remember a lick of what anybody had said.

My memory was hazy about an article produced by the Alzheimer's Association. I remembered something about foods that helped brain function. I thought I'd better review the article before eating out, especially at Sheldon's. I found it in my file under Brain Food.

The Alzheimer group reported that certain foods, especially dark-skinned fruits and vegetables, might have protective, preventive effects against Alzheimer's and dementia. The top five fruits were prunes, raisins, blueberries, blackberries and strawberries. Leading vegetables were kale, spinach, Brussels sprouts, alfalfa sprouts and broccoli florets. The article also recommended cold water fish that contained omega 3 fatty acids: halibut, mackerel, salmon, trout and tuna. Considering the recent state of my brain function, I planned to search for the items at Sheldon's bash.

By the time Sam picked us up for the *Food, Fitness, and Euphoria* party, I felt great. Sitting in the backseat, I thought about the time he'd searched for Meredith's husband. He was mesmerized by her slim, statuesque elegance, even though he was old enough to be her father. With flawless features and thick blond hair, Meredith turned heads wherever she went.

Once Sam recovered from the shock of meeting Meredith, he became rational and treated her like a younger sister. From then on, the three of us supported each other like siblings. When we found her husband, our discovery marked the end of Meredith's two-year marriage.

On the drive to Sheldon's house, he and Meredith were so grim that I had to chatter during the entire trip to sustain life in the car. I was relieved when Sam finally spoke.

He'd learned that Harry Thorne, after frequent bouts of vomiting, checked into the hospital Wednesday night. Sam planned to interview him on Friday. As for me, I was ready to party, even at Sheldon's house. I'd keep my eyes peeled for healthy delicacies and for clues to Holly's murder.

Meredith wore a slinky turquoise pantsuit with matching polished stone earrings that set off her light hair. My black pants and top were standard garb. I expected to see colorful folks at the party, but I preferred to fade into the background.

Sam had opted for a western cut jacket and slacks. He was easing into his version of Texas style dress. The brown suit complemented his doggy eyes. Purple dollops decorated his open-collared tan shirt. The blobs resembled eggplant, which seemed appropriate for Sheldon's party. I chose not to mention it.

Sheldon's habitat was a remodel on the fringes of the King William area, a sprawling mass of old homes which once housed San Antonio's elite. The next generation happily refurbished the spacious houses. We heard blaring, funky music as we approached the screen door. Sheldon stood just inside, wearing a silky outfit that looked like a cross between a clown suit and a red pepper. Meredith stalled on the porch and Sam tried to turn around, but I was ready. I looped my arms through their elbows and dragged them through the door Sheldon held open.

"I'm so glad you could come," Sheldon screeched above the music. He devoured Meredith and me with vigorously popping eyes. He led us to the bar where, in addition to recognizable drinks, vegetable and fruit drinks sprouted carrots, celery and mysterious protruding stalks. One glass had a sliced rutabaga pinched over the rim. I didn't want to think about what the glass contained. Meredith and I asked for red wine, and Sam requested a beer. It was safer to drink something bottled.

I didn't see Mindy, Knobs or Sarah, but Patricia Drexel flirted at full speed, honing in on attractive specimens. Pete, Mickey and Ned weren't there. Harry was apparently still recuperating at home.

A San Antonio *Flash-News* reporter circulated. I saw two others, one from *South Texas Newsletter* and one from *La Prensa*. The owner of a Blue Star art gallery milled through the crowd. Several men wore name tags indicating they represented San Antonio's best-known restaurants. A society columnist made rounds with her pad and pen, apparently scouting for notables. Photographers snapped pictures. Sheldon's party was a major event. He'd probably planned the bash for a year.

Feeling clammy and irritable, I decided to locate the powder room before I checked out Sheldon's food spread. When I saw beads hanging from a strip in front of a door down the hall, I concluded they marked one of Sheldon's bathrooms. I knocked through the beads, found the room unoccupied and entered. The medicine cabinet door was ajar, so I peeped in and saw more pills than I'd ever seen in one place. Some drugs were recognizable: antacids, gout pills, blood pressure pills and cardiac pills. For a fan of healthy eating, Sheldon sure took a lot of pills.

One bottle was so large, I picked it up. Valium. A huge cache of Valium. Holly had said she took Valium before getting in the pool. No. What she said was, "He gave me...I took Valium before I got into the pool." Who was "he?" Sheldon Snodgrass? Sarah had confirmed Holly dated him. Sheldon possessed enough drugs to treat everybody on the planet. Since he didn't mind telling people what to eat, he probably didn't mind dispensing pills.

I looked pale in the mirror, so I dabbed on lipstick and blush. When I left the bathroom, nobody was in the hall. The next room down looked like it might be Sheldon's bedroom, so I slipped in. His bureau stood against the left wall. I tiptoed toward the highboy to check photographs on top and was astonished to see four photos of Holly Holmgreen. I asked for forgiveness again before I moved closer. For each picture, she'd modeled a different Barbie Doll outfit. In the final photo, she wore baby doll pajamas that would make Barbie proud. Something protruded through the pajamas at her naval. I leaned closer and gagged when I recognized the tines of a pickle fork.

Close to the photos lay a small spiral notebook. Scrawled on the cover was, "Improving Holly." I was dying to know what Sheldon had written inside, but I heard footsteps. I snatched my hand off the notebook and bounded toward the hall, ready to ask whoever I encountered for directions to the bathroom. I found the hall vacant.

Returning to the party room, I saw the dining table was the center of attention. When I came up behind Sam and Meredith, they were evaluating food like lab workers checking amoeba.

Sam read the label by one platter: "Grilled Emu Fillet with Raspberry and Blackcurrant Sauce." The note added that emu, if not available, could be replaced with ostrich. I didn't think there were enough healthy raspberries to offset a tough bird.

Holding his plate and fork, Sam frowned at long strips of thinly sliced emu meat. "I thought Snodgrass was a vegetarian."

"He must make allowances for this event," Meredith said. She moved on to read about the next selection: "Australian Poached Rabbit with Bruschetta and Lemon." The note said the rabbit, boiled until tender, should be accompanied by Chardonnay and Chenin Blanc.

"It would take a lot of wine and bread to make me forget I'm ingesting a rabbit," Sam said.

"I overheard someone say Sheldon's in his Australian period," Meredith said.

That explained the selections. She slid to the next platter. "Stir-Fried Squid with Herbs and Spinach. Keep spirits high with a well-balanced Chardonnay. It's essential the squid be fresh and succulent."

"Which means," Sam said, "that you have to drink enough alcohol to tenderize the squid."

My stomach lurched. For some reason, I thought about Dr. Carmody. I might suggest to him that dining regularly with Sheldon Snodgrass could produce sufficient under-nutrition to extend his life span.

The woman next to me bit into a mini-sausage heavily swathed in cheese. She knitted her eyebrows and held up the remaining half of the delicacy for my inspection. We peered at the round, jelled pill stuffed into the middle of the sausage. "Does that look like Colace to you?" she whispered.

"Colace?"

"Colace. You know. Stool softener. Cheese is constipating."

Since my stomach had leapt into my throat, I could only nod. I slipped away, feigning interest in other food items. Gliding around the table, I pretended to view selections without reading any labels. When Sheldon grinned eagerly at me from across the room, I attempted to smile. He approached the other side of the table and aimed for the cheesecloth tent he'd created to cover the mysterious delicacy in the center.

He loomed behind the tent and raised his arms. I drifted closer to my side of the table, intrigued by the drama. Sheldon stood motionless, like he was preparing to conduct a symphony. The crowd grew quiet. Flashbulbs popped. With a flourish, Sheldon whooshed off the cheesecloth. There, on a mammoth platter, sat a huge upright pig with an apple in its mouth. That porker had probably weighed three hundred pounds on the hoof. Its feet, pointed forward, splayed in oblique directions. Heavy butcher twine trussed the stomach. I thought I saw something inside the cavity...a smaller animal?

Acid rolled into my throat. Before I knew what was happening, I tossed my cookies. Horrified but helpless, I stood there, aiming toward Sheldon's masterpiece. His guests scrambled backwards like crawdads. Sheldon stayed glued to his spot, eyes bulging like they were attached to metal springs. When I finally caught my breath, Meredith stood by my side with a wet cloth, wiping my face and forehead. "It's all right. It's all right. We'll get you out of here."

Feeling faint, I careened toward the table. Sheldon gasped and threw up his hands. I think he ripped his red suit.

Sam swooped me in his arms and charged for the door through a murky sea of astonished faces. Over his shoulder, I saw Sheldon smoldering at me. He was squinting so hard, his eyes receded in the sockets. His dark expression exuded pure hatred. Maybe the creep had killed Holly.

I felt lightheaded but better. I enjoyed the heck out of being in Sam's arms. When we got to his car, Meredith opened the back door and Sam slipped me in, ever so gently. He folded up his coat to position it behind my head. I resisted the urge to pull him in with me. It was a good thing I felt weak.

We rode quietly for a few blocks. "I'm feeling pretty normal now." I longed for a toothbrush.

After a few more blocks Sam spoke. "That was an abominable party. But you chose a pretty drastic way to get out of there, don't you think?"

I was nearly asleep, but I knew he was smiling.

Twenty

Friday morning I inched across the bed to grab the jangling phone. My pantsuit scratched against the spread. "Hullo," I croaked. My mouth was dry and nasty.

"Aggie, are you okay?" Meredith said. "You seemed all right when we took you home...just anxious to get to bed. You sure didn't want anything to eat."

"No. I mean, yes, I'm okay. I need to soak in a tub and drink water, lots and lots of water. Pure. Out of a bottle. I'm sorry I made a fool of myself and embarrassed you and Sam."

"You were sick. You should see a doctor."

I was unable to consume or process nutrients. My immune system was failing. I hadn't even reached middle age and my hormones were on the skids. Every cell in my body was approaching senescence. It might be too late for a doctor.

"I don't need a doctor. It's the club."

"The club?"

"Something at Fit and Firm makes me sick."

"It's that awful Tofu Temptations Grill. Just reading the menu makes me queasy."

"I thought there was something at the grill. I stopped eating there, but I keep getting sick."

"Could you be allergic to something? Creams? Sprays? Toilet water? Cleaning agents? Something in the towels?"

"Maybe. I'll try to figure out what the culprit is. I'm not going to exercise today."

"I should hope not. Members pack the place on Fridays anyway. Everybody's trying to burn enough calories to pig out over the weekend. I may go Saturday afternoon when it's not so busy. Sam didn't want to wake you, but he wants to know if you're all right. He says to call him if you need anything. Harry Thorne is home from the hospital, so Sam's going to visit him."

I thanked her and apologized again for messing up their evening. Now that she and Sam knew I was recovering, I could set my answering machine and not be disturbed.

Despite feeling disgustingly weak, I dragged myself out of bed and went to my computer to research "What to eat when you're ill and have to get better." Everything they recommended made me feel sick.

I thought about the bath salts from Grace's house. I could pour them in the water and relax in warmth. But I wasn't sure I'd be able to climb out of the tub afterwards. Easing into the shower, I washed my body and hair in slow motion. Flexing my arms, I was gratified to see my tumor muscles still bulged. To remind myself I'd fully recuperate, I put on workout clothes.

Remembering Sam's gentleness when he nestled me into the car after Sheldon's party, I contemplated how to reignite his concern without getting sick. To gain strength, I opened a can of Libby's fruit cocktail and nibbled.

The best cure for me was to find out who killed Holly. Although she and I were years apart in age, I felt her loss like my own. For some reason I couldn't quite fathom, I sensed our near-electrocution, her death and my illness were related.

Padding to the living room, I decided to research my symptoms online. Since I'd never suffered from food allergies, I focused on substances used at the club. In the locker room, opaque bottles with gold-topped atomizers were filled with toilet water, body cream and deodorant that smelled like perfume tempered with lemon. For jaccuzzi fans, there were tiny bags of bath salts.

Clicking through poisons, I chose Methanol, methyl alcohol,

since I'd heard about people dying from drinking moonshine—illegal, raw whiskey distilled from fermented wood. Producers used Methanol in paint varnish, paint remover, antifreeze and perfumes. If swallowed, inhaled or absorbed through the skin, the substance caused fatigue, headache, nausea, vertigo, pain, dizziness and vomiting—all the symptoms I'd experienced. Methanol metabolized into formaldehyde in the body, literally pickling its victim. If a person ingested enough of it, she went blind, into a coma and died. Either I hadn't absorbed enough methanol, or else I was one lucky duck.

Shuffling to the kitchen, I suddenly craved apple juice. Some scientists thought apple juice might prevent dementia. After I drank it, I wondered if wood from the apple tree could have dropped into the bottle and fermented into methanol.

I trudged back to my computer and read about potassium permanganate, a poisonous violet crystal compound that dissolves in water and looks like bath salts. Hustling to my bathroom, I gaped at the bag of violet bath crystals Boffo found, the ones Grace said to grab from him. I found a Ziploc bag in the kitchen, scurried back to the bathroom and, with tweezers, dropped the package of crystals into the Ziploc.

After stashing the stuff under my bed, I collapsed on the comforter. Were the bath crystals poison? Did Grace know? Could SAPD be right? Was she a psychopathic killer involved in the health club murder? I held my head. "Dear God, if Grace Livermore can murder people, the world's gone crazy. Grace Livermore can't be a killer. Tell me it's not true."

Bath crystals were common. Reading about poisons was making me paranoid.

Returning to my computer, I tried to remember other items I'd seen at Fit and Firm. The club provided towels and washcloths, so I searched detergents and fabric softeners. Cationic detergents, which were poisonous, were incorporated into ordinary detergents and softeners, but in amounts too diluted to be toxic. It would take a cup or more of fabric softener in a small bath or Jacuzzi to be lethal. The club's Jacuzzi was at least eight feet square, and I'd never been in it. I didn't think enough fabric softener could be concentrated in towels or washcloths to be lethal without making them noticeably limp.

So many common substances contained poisons. If a crazy person wanted to murder somebody, they could accomplish the deed at home, in a nursing home, hospital, beauty shop or health club—any facility that stocked cleaning products or toiletries. Judging from my symptoms, I feared such a person was after me. Although I'd survived, the junk that had invaded my system must have aged me. Who could guess my quest for fitness would cause premature aging...or death?

The club stocked other nasties a killer could use: alkalis, ammonia, naphthalene and rubbing alcohol. Tofu Temptations Grill stocked ingestible items, which in certain amounts, were poisonous: table salt, baking soda, potassium and calcium. People taking antidepressants could die from eating wine and cheese.

Live plants decorated the club. I hadn't even begun to research poisonous plants or pesticides. My gruesome discoveries had already given me plenty of ideas.

If I wanted my Dear Aggie readers to get in shape, I couldn't tell them about the plethora of poisonous substances at their health clubs. I might suggest they stay out of the hot tub and take their own toiletries since some people have allergic reactions to these items.

I plopped on my bed, stared at the ceiling and mulled over my options. Returning to the club was risky. Somebody wanted to poison me—probably the person who'd killed Holly. If I didn't find out fast who the killer was, he might bump me off using some other creative method. If he wasn't successful killing me, he could definitely disrupt my life. I'd waited a long time to start over. I didn't appreciate having my plans thwarted.

Suppose I told Sam everything I knew and hoped he found the health club killer before he discovered I was Lee's mother. If he found out, I'd probably lose him, have to forego using the club, be too angry and depressed to study and fail out of graduate school. I'd be alive but miserable.

I'd played it safe for a long time. Now I was ready to make things happen. After I weighed the possibilities, I knew what I had to do.

Twenty-One

When I woke up Saturday morning after a fitful night, it took me a few minutes to remember what I'd planned. Alternatives rushed through my brain. The risky option rammed its way to the front. My fateful day was about to begin.

I was determined to follow through with my scheme, but not eager to start. Meandering around my living room, I gazed at my impressionistic paintings. By painting points and swaths, artists invited viewers to mesh their imaginations with the artist's vision. Ordinarily I found their blurred scenes captivating. Happily adding my perception to theirs, I could feel breezes blowing and grasses swaying. Today I wanted the paintings packed with realism: I needed definitive pictures to help me proceed. Despite my prayers, God hadn't told me a thing.

Once I decided to expose Holly's killer, I thought sleuthing would be a lark: gathering clues, interviewing suspects, mimicking a perky journalist with secret Wonder Woman underwear. I never dreamed some idiot would try to poison me.

I plopped on my serape-striped sofa and caressed the rough fabric. I wanted to remember its scratchiness, its sturdiness against my skin. I rubbed my foot back and forth against the Tabriz rug, grateful for its softness and for the solid wood plank floor underneath. I wanted to come back here. Always.

For strength to carry out my plan, I padded to the kitchen and forced myself to eat a tuna sandwich topped with melted cheese, chewing each bite slowly so my stomach would accept the offering. To wash the food down, I sipped a glass of milk, packed with protein, good for building muscles and enhancing speed. So they said.

It was time to pack. My small gym bag was the perfect size. I tossed in my car keys, driver's license and a ten dollar bill in case of emergency. Like money would help.

By my computer desk, I found my small magnifying glass and dropped it into the bag. I planned to arrive at Fit and Firm in mid-afternoon when the locker room would be deserted. Before I left home, I wanted to hear Sam's voice. I dialed his line at the station.

"Hi. It's me."

"Aggie! You were really sick last night. Are you all right?"

His strong voice comforted me. I cleared my throat. "I'm okay. Meredith said you wanted to know if I needed anything, and I don't. I was just wondering whether SAPD has talked with Grace's children."

"Detective Sammis went to Enid, Oklahoma, to interview Kim. She didn't have much to say about Charlie Livermore...only that her father was alcoholic and his death was tragic. She said he didn't really want to go out that night, but because she and Grace were going to a birthday party, he and Linda went out for dinner."

"What did she say about her stepfather, George Ball?"

"That they loved him, especially Grace. His having a heart attack crushed everybody. She couldn't imagine why George would mix up his pills. She said she never touched them and was positive nobody else did."

"According to Sammis, Kim is a real Martha Stewart. While he was there, he started sneezing from fresh flowers she'd arranged all over the house." Sam laughed. "Her bathrooms smelled like perfume factories. She covered her countertops with perfumed soaps shaped like flowers and put bath crystals by the tub."

"Bath crystals?" My stomach flipped.

"That's what he said. Why?"

"I don't know. Soaps shaped like flowers seem the prefect touch for a Martha Stewart type. Did Sammis fly from Oklahoma to California?"

"No, he had work to finish here. He'll fly to LA tomorrow to interview Linda Livermore and George Ball's sons. Another SAPD detective learned something here, though, which may be more important."

"What?"

"Detective Green interviewed Grace's neighbor on the other side, Anna Holcomb. She's eighty-five and has an incredible memory. Anna said when she was sixty—she was positive about her age—Charlie Livermore got drunk and came after Anna's twelve-year-old granddaughter, Martha. Anna and her husband were still helping their son John raise his daughters, Martha and Lettie. When they found out what happened, the Holcomb men confronted Charlie Livermore. They told him if he came near either girl again, they'd kill him. Anna said Charlie had a reputation for chasing young girls when he got drunk."

I willed my tuna and cheese to stay down. "Did Grace know what Charlie had done?"

"Anna and her family concluded it was kinder not to tell her. But she could have known anyway."

Poor Martha Holcomb. Charlie's drunken advance could have affected her whole life. Poor Grace. If she knew what Charlie did, how did she feel when he died?

"They released Harry Thorne from the hospital and told him to rest at home," he said. "I'm going to see him today."

This was great news. I needed to check something in Harry's office and wouldn't have to worry about Sam's poking around the club and catching me.

"I guess you'll be resting today," he said.

"Um-hmm."

"I'll call you tomorrow. See how you're doing."

"Great." I hung up while I still possessed the fortitude to implement my plan. I had dawdled long enough. I reached under my bed for the package of bath crystals, slipped it into my gym bag and slung the bag into my Wagoneer.

It was too early for me to arrive at the club, so I decided to enjoy a leisurely drive past Fort Sam Houston. I meandered down Burr Road and looked out over the forty acres San Antonio had donated for the Army Post in 1870. The base employed thousands of military and civilian workers, which undoubtedly included a passel of smart, available men. I'd volunteered to help organize one of the parties they planned to give for the city's military and civilians.

The post hospital, Brooke Army Medical Center, rehabilitated thousands of men after every war. Since the post also had its own workout facility, the men had no reason to join Fit and Firm. Maybe I should mention to Harry if he offered military discounts, retired doctors and officers might join. I needed to expand my options. Once Sam found out what I was up to, I feared our relationship would be kaput.

I considered running an ad in the Ft. Sam Houston *News Leader*: "Patriotic grad student wants to meet eligible officer." I sounded like a groupie panting over a man in uniform. One aspect to consider was that officers were accustomed to giving orders, and I wasn't used to taking them. I'd revise the ad when my mind was less cluttered.

At 3:00 p.m. Saturday, I pulled into the club's parking garage wearing a T-shirt and tights and carrying a small gym bag like the ones members used when they came for quick workouts and intended to dress at home. My bag had another purpose.

As I expected, the women's locker room was empty. The area looked clean and elegant, swathed in calming blue and green walls. With perfectly arranged toiletries and towels, the rooms resembled a spa where nobody broke a sweat. I went to my primping station, swooped a bottle of each product into my bag and replaced them with random bottles from other stations. I checked to see that all products appeared undisturbed. Then I stuffed a couple of washcloths in my bag.

Once I pilfered those items, I scooted to the hot tub and scouted for purple bath crystals. I spotted them in a cellophane bag tied with a purple ribbon, perched on the ledge of the tub. Mindy, nearly submerged, inhabited the vat with her eyes closed. I tiptoed over and reached for the crystals. Just as I snatched them, she opened her eyes. "Hey! I was about to use those."

"My friend left them here," I lied.

She displaced a lot of water floundering after me. Before she could stand up, my protein kicked in and I skedaddled out of there.

I scrambled up the stairs, scooted past the administrative offices and skittered down the side of the basketball court to get close enough to the weight room to see who was there. Machine Mecca was packed. Mickey, Ned, Sheldon, Pete, Patricia and Sarah pumped iron. Even Knobs pushed and pulled a machine. As I whirled to leave, hoping nobody would spot me, several people glanced up. Their antennas were perpetually poised for possible encounters with members of the opposite sex.

As I retreated back past the basketball court and through the administrative corridor, I noticed that Harry Thorne's office door was closed. No light filtered underneath. I remembered Sam said he was going home.

A plainclothes police officer sauntered up and down the passageway, watching guys play basketball. Making a mental note to find a reasonably priced barber for the rookie police officers, I walked up to him and smiled. He checked out my T-shirt and tights.

"Hi," I said. "I'm Samantha Eggars. Detective Vanderhoven is visiting manager Harry Thorne at his home and asked me to bring them a photograph from Harry's office. Do you mind opening the door for me?"

"Well...uh, sure...if Sam..."

"Sam and I are old friends. I know he'll appreciate your helping him out." I batted my lashes and bathed him with a southern smile. He unlocked Harry's office. Before he could follow me inside, I reached between us to close the door. "It might take me a while to find the photo. Will you guard the door from outside?" I batted again for good measure, hoping I didn't develop a tic.

He grinned. "I'll stand guard."

I flew to Harry's desk and yanked out the photograph he'd tossed inside the drawer, the one showing the boxers and referee with the crowd behind them. When Harry had slung in the picture, I thought it symbolized his disgust with life at the gym. The next day it dawned on me that Harry didn't want me to see the photograph.

I hunched over the photo with my back to the door, slipped out my magnifying glass and passed it slowly over the boxing fans. Just as I thought, the small spectator in the front row whom I'd noticed before was a young girl about three years old. Somebody had dressed her like a Shirley Temple doll and propped her on a metal folding chair. I moved the magnifier over her face. She had big eyes and a head full of ringlets. I moved the glass to where her feet dangled a foot off the floor. She wore Mary Janes on her tiny feet—patent leather flats with straps across the instep. I'd bet the cost of a three-month membership the child was Holly Holmgreen. Even though Harry said he didn't have children, I'd wager a fat stock dividend that he and Holly were related.

Turning the photograph over, I read, "B's crash. H, 3." Underneath, someone had scribbled, "1975." "B" could be Harry's brother, Billy. "H" could be Holly. I'd have to decipher the rest when I wasn't in a rush.

The officer pounded on the door. Since I didn't have time to stash the photo in my bag, I raced to the door, slung it open and shoved the photo near his face. "Harry used to be a boxer." I batted my lashes. "He and Sam are reminiscing. Harry wants to show him this picture."

He smiled at me as though I were Mother Teresa. Hoping I looked pious, I returned his smile and scooted toward the steps, slipping the photograph into my bag with the other evidence. My feet itched ferociously. What did the connection between Holly and Harry Thorne have to do with her murder?

I bustled to level three to see if Meredith was on a treadmill. When I didn't find her, I decided to hustle away with my loot. I wasn't about to get trapped in the elevator with murder suspects or contraband, so I aimed for the stairs. I bounced down the steps with my right hand on the rail and my left clutching the bag to my chest. As I reached the landing and started to descend the flight to the first floor, I felt a shove. My evidence bag got away from me and tumbled down the stairs. Grabbing the rail with both hands, I managed to hold on most of the way down. I landed on my left side at the bottom of the stairs, hard. Shoving booty back into my bag, I craned to look up the stairs. A red sock and white tennis shoe disappeared from the landing where somebody had pushed me. Before I could determine whether the shoe belonged to a man or woman, the spectacle vanished.

Meredith appeared and tried to help me up. "What happened? Are you all right?"

"I think so." I stretched gingerly. "No broken bones. And I'm much too young for osteoporosis."

Pete Reeves, the trainer, materialized beside her. He scowled at me, then at my bag. "What made you fall?" He didn't seem particularly surprised that I'd sprawled down the stairs.

"I tripped over my own feet. Meredith can drive me home...Come on." I pulled her along, hoping Pete didn't notice her stunned expression. I didn't like the way he focused on my bag.

"What's going on?" Meredith whispered from the corner of her mouth.

"Can you drive me to the San Antonio Testing Laboratory? We need to learn about poisons."

Twenty-Two

"Poisons? We're going where? Aggie, did you hit your head? Are you dizzy?"

"Nope. I'm perfectly lucid."

My forehead did feel peculiar. I stretched my bangs down over the point of impact and discovered it hurt to touch my brow.

"Steven Eagleton is meeting us at the San Antonio Testing Laboratory. I found the lab in the yellow pages and called him on Friday...told him I had evidence somebody might be poisoning health club members."

Her mouth dropped open. "Your sickness is from poison? How do you know?"

"Because I stopped eating at Tofu Temptations Grill, but whenever I worked out at Fit and Firm, I felt terrible, sometimes right away, sometimes an hour or more later. I had headaches, perspired, felt flushed and became irritable and confused. I acted weird in Dr. Carmody's class. There's no telling what I said. You know how sick I was at Sheldon's party Thursday night. If food from the grill wasn't making me sick, the only other substances entering my body had to come from the locker room, most likely from toiletries. So I swiped a few bottles to have them analyzed."

Her eyes opened wider. "I used their sprays and creams, too. I remember feeling ill once. Since I always shower and change before going to Conrad's office, I decided to bring my own products."

"Good thing you did."

She furrowed her brow. "What about other people who use the club?"

"I don't know. I haven't figured that out yet." I wasn't ready to tell her I suspected the poison was intended primarily for me and was related to Holly's death.

"Do you think somebody poisoned bottles in the men's locker room, too?"

I thought about Harry Thorne's hospitalization. "I don't know. The same housekeeper cleans both areas between 2:00 and 3:00 p.m. when there's hardly anybody there. Anyone could switch poisoned bottles for regular bottles and put them on her cleaning tray. She could carry them back and forth without even knowing it." I knew what Meredith would say. I was ready.

"Surely, Aggie, you told Sam about this."

"He said to have the bottles analyzed, and when we obtained answers, he'd take the investigation from there." My ability to lie was downright amazing.

In my explanation to Meredith, I left out two things (besides the fact that somebody'd pushed me): my head throbbed from whapping it on the floor when I landed, and I'd agreed to pay extra to get the poison evaluation quickly, in case the lab felt compelled to report its findings to SAPD. I intended to go back to the health club armed with new knowledge and without interference from nosy police officers.

Meredith drove south on IH 35 and exited at South Laredo Street. We saw the San Antonio Testing Laboratory from the freeway. The backside of the building was painted with a replica of the solar system on a bright blue background. This establishment was definitely not a secret agency.

The yellow page ad said the lab could analyze metals, volatile and semi-volatile compounds, and had a microbiology lab to analyze bacteria and a wet chemistry lab. I wasn't sure what all that meant, but lab director Steve Eagleton had assured me his laboratory was adequate for testing the contents of Fit and Firm's bottles.

When Meredith got out of the car, I transferred Harry's boxing photograph and my magnifying glass from the evidence bag to my purse. I didn't want Eagleton speculating about why I possessed those items.

We rang the bell and Eagleton let us in. Tall and thin, like a clothespin with sandy hair, he pierced us with hazel eyes. He sized us up, giving Meredith a thorough perusal. He asked us a few questions before accepting my gym bag containing the bounty.

I told him since I repeatedly felt ill after working out at Fit and Firm, my SAPD friend suggested I have the club's toiletries analyzed. I intimated the detective had urged me to grab samples from the club on Saturday for immediate analysis. If they proved toxic or allergenic, police could notify the manager before the club opened Monday morning.

Naturally, I didn't reveal Sam's name or breathe a word about Holly Holmgreen. A *Flash-News* obituary had reported her death, but I figured Eagleton would immerse himself in studying test tubes and not connect our visit with her demise. Besides, she'd been run over, not poisoned. He led us to his office, a modest room that included a wooden desk, three serviceable chairs and a shelf against one wall covered with magazines, mysterious gadgets, reports and a bottle of Eco Toilet Sanitizer.

"Let's have a look at what you brought." He pulled on sterile gloves and lifted each item from the bag. Holding the perfume atomizer at arm's length, he sniffed and set the bottle on his desk without comment. His eyebrows peaked when he saw the bath crystals from Grace's house. When he found the second bag of crystals, he eyed me quizzically.

"I got them from two separate locations. Could you label one 'home' and one 'club?'"

He nodded, drew markers from his desk drawer and tagged the crystals as I instructed.

He seemed less interested in the washcloths, but he honed in on Fit and Firm's opaque bottles, which were supposedly filled with body lotion, body cream and hair spray. Holding them up, he studied the delivery plungers.

"These bottles are identical except the plungers have different sized holes to release substances. Some liquids are naturally thicker than others. Or something was added."

What poisons had I absorbed through those plastic tubes?

Eagleton squinted at words on the bottles. "The club's logo is clear, but labels describing contents are hard to read."

"Yes. Meredith and I discovered how easy it is to confuse products."

"Okay. Now that I know what you brought, let me give you a better idea of what we do here." Eagleton either wanted to show off the facility, evaluate us further or both. He led us to a room with a six-foot wide refrigerator with glass doors that housed trays filled with tubes of liquid. Did the tubes hold poisons I'd read about? On the countertop behind us, three machines, slightly larger than microwaves, occupied space to the left of a sink. Trays of empty test tubes sat to the right.

"This is where we analyze volatile compounds. If someone smells an unusual odor, we go to their business and use pumps to capture air from their facility. We bring the pumps here, liquefy the contents in water and measure the amount of substances in the liquid."

"So you change gases to liquids for analysis?" I asked.

"Or the reverse. We can also vaporize liquids to see if gases they produce are harmful."

"A substance doesn't have to smell bad to be poisonous, does it?"

"Not necessarily. Odors can be disguised by reducing them to liquids or combining them with other ingredients."

"Can you give us examples of volatile compounds?"

"They vaporize if exposed to air like gasoline, paint cleaners and some polish removers. If they get too hot, they catch fire."

My ears perked up. "The methanol used in paint varnish, paint remover and perfume is poisonous, correct?"

"You're right. We test for methanol in our GC/MS lab. I'll show you the lab in a minute."

I might learn how close I'd come to being pickled. He led us into another room where refrigerators stored more liquid-filled test tubes.

"We analyze semi-volatile compounds here, like naphthalene and pesticides. They don't catch fire, but they vaporize in air, so we keep them sealed and refrigerated."

He proceeded to the GC/MS lab. A machine covered a linear table that filled the long narrow room. "This is our quarter-million-dollar gadget, a gas chromatograph/mass spectrometer or GC/MS. The device can analyze over 250,000 substances, separating compounds according to size, shape and chemical properties. It identifies the class of a suspected chemical but can't tell us its exact makeup."

"Can it identify poisonous substances?"

"After GC separates the sample into components, MS can identify each substance."

"So you'll know for sure whether there's poison in each bottle I brought you?"

"Yes. We don't test for poisons per se. We test for specific substances which we know can be poisonous, like methanol, alcohol, potassium..."

"Potassium permanganate?"

"Yes. The substance that looks like your bath crystals."

Meredith turned pale. "Where did you get those?"

"By the hot tub at the club."

Eagleton made a U-turn and led us back to his office.

"I think it's the deodorant," I said. "I used it more than anything else."

"Then we'll start with that. We'll put your sample into GC/MS and distill it to fumes for analysis. If we find a toxic substance, we'll obtain a duplicate of the substance and run it through GC/MS for confirmation. The duplicate must be within ten percent variation of your sample or we repeat the test." Eagleton was all business when discussing data, but I thought he'd be a nice boss.

"When will you have results?"

"If the deodorant is poisonous, we'll know today and do a

confirmation test on Monday. If the deodorant is clean, and we need to test the other substances, we'll have answers by the middle of the week. We'll release the findings to you so you can inform the detective."

Perfect. I'd get the results. After all, I was the poison recipient. "If you find poison in the deodorant, will you also test both samples of bath crystals?"

"You bet." He seemed eager to get to work.

"I can't thank you enough." I handed him a card with my contact information.

"When I get a definitive answer that helps somebody, I really enjoy my job." He shook our hands and admonished us to drive carefully.

Meredith drove me back to the club to get my car, "I can't believe we're having samples tested for poison—that somebody is actually trying to poison you."

"It is hard to fathom. Maybe somebody accidentally mixed substances. It would be easy to do with all those identical opaque bottles."

"Right. Just like somebody accidentally dropped the radio in the pool. How did you know about potassium...whatever?"

"Internet research." I wasn't up for much discussion, even with my practical friend. Relief engulfing me made me feel giddy. My pounding head felt swollen, but getting definitive, scientific answers would make me feel better. When Meredith dropped me at my car, I drove home and collapsed into bed.

Twenty-Three

When I woke Sunday, my head throbbed from my hard landing on the stairs the day before. My sides felt like hammered meat. If I moved, I ached. When I lifted my Garfield nightshirt, purple bruises sprawled from my ribs to my knees where I'd bounced down the steps and hit the floor.

Sleuthing was becoming unpleasant. After a few subtle doses of poison, somebody apparently decided pushing me down the stairs was a quicker way to get rid of me. I must be getting close to uncovering information the killer didn't want me to have. The seriousness of my situation sank in. Somebody wanted me dead. I'd better step up my efforts to solve Holly's murder before her killer wiped me out.

I stood but felt woozy, so I eased down on the bed and reached to the chair for my warm-up pants. I tugged them on, waited a few seconds and tried to remain calm. I'd barely survived an attempt on my life.

Standing slowly, I slid one foot, then the other, to the bathroom. When I peeked in the mirror, I discovered that overnight I'd sprouted an egg. The bulge protruded straight out from my forehead, two inches above my left eye. The territory between the egg and my eye was red and puffy. My eye drooped into a sleazy wink. When I raised my arms up, I discovered I couldn't get my orange Garfield sleep shirt off over my head without smacking the egg.

In the cabinet under the sink, I found an old ice bag I'd

inherited from Aunt Novena, filled it with cold water and laid it gingerly on my head. The soft part of the bag sagged down over the protrusion. Pain prevented me from resting anything solid on my bump. I creaked to the kitchen to add ice to the bag. While I consumed hot tea and toast, I decided the best way to get my mind off my injuries was to figure out the connection between Holly Holmgreen and Harry Thorne.

After I finished breakfast, I retrieved the boxing photo from my purse, hobbled to the living room and placed the photo face down beside my computer. While the machine powered up, I lowered my aching carcass into the ergonomic chair and studied the inscription on the back of Harry's photograph, beginning with the scribbled date: 1975. Harry had said Billy was one of the last few soldiers killed in Saigon. My historical recall wasn't great, so I searched for "dates+Vietnam+war." One Web address looked promising: "A Vietnam War Timeline." I clicked it and scrolled down to the 1975 headline that read:

"Last Americans Evacuate As Saigon Falls to Communists."

A paragraph described how South Vietnamese President Duong Van Minh delivered an unconditional surrender to the Communists in the early hours of April 30. I shuddered, thinking of all the fine American soldiers and South Vietnamese people who died there before our country and theirs suffered a tragic, ignominious end to the war.

The final sentence of the paragraph caught my eye: "As remaining Americans evacuated Saigon, the last few US servicemen to die in Vietnam were killed when their helicopter crashed."

I yanked up Harry's photograph and squinted at his note: "B's crash. H, 3."

"B's crash" could mean the crash of Billy's helicopter. Billy Thorne could have been one of "the last few US servicemen to die" when his helicopter crashed in 1975. He would have been twenty-two years old when he died, just as Harry said. Everything fit together too well to be coincidental.

If Billy died in 1975 at age twenty-two, Harry would have been twenty-three, a year older. That meant Harry was born in 1952 and Billy in 1953. Harry would now be in his forties, the age I'd guessed.

What about the other item Harry scribbled, "H, 3?" When I'd moved my magnifying glass over the photo in Harry's office, I thought the child perched on the metal chair, dressed like Shirley Temple, resembled Holly Holmgreen. I reached in my purse for the magnifier and passed it again over the child's face. Her features were tiny and perfect in her doll-like face. Her huge eyes were exactly like Holly's.

I stared at the distinctive mass of curls springing from the child's head and remembered the wet ringlets plastered to Holly's head at the pool. I'd never forget the half-dry springy curls bouncing from the poor girl's head as she lay on the concrete near the parking garage.

The child in Harry's photograph, primly perched within ten feet of violence and sweat in the boxing ring, had to be Holly Holmgreen at age three. Harry's cryptic note, "B's crash. H, 3," indicated somebody took Holly's picture near the time of Billy Thorne's fatal helicopter crash. Why would Harry write a note linking Billy's death to Holly's age unless Billy and Holly were related?

The light dawned: Billy Thorne was Holly's father. Harry Thorne was her uncle. Either Holly had visited her Uncle Harry and grandfather, Arnold Thorne, at the boxing gym near the time Billy died, or she lived with them when Billy went to Vietnam. After Billy died, Arnold and Harry Thorne had raised her.

Where was Holly's mother? Why was Holly's last name Holmgreen instead of Thorne?

I couldn't answer those questions, but Holly's age in 1975 fit with what I surmised. If she was born in 1972, she would have been three years old in 1975. Had she lived, Holly would be in her twenties, which seemed to fit.

Uncle Harry Thorne, distraught with grief, would've submitted the bare minimum for Holly's obituary. I could verify her and Harry's ages by sneaking into the club's personnel records. Being the controlling type, Harry probably kept staff and club members' files in his private domain so he could check on people unobserved. Maybe I should sneak back into his office.

Suppose Billy got Holly's mother pregnant before he went to Vietnam. If he went overseas in 1972, Billy would have been nineteen years old. Military records would confirm his age. Billy's wife or girlfriend, Holly's mother, was probably between seventeen and nineteen.

When my head started working better, I'd try to evaluate the relationship between Harry and Holly. Why did neither acknowledge that Harry was her uncle?

My head pounded. My body was stiffening to the shape of the chair. If I tried to stretch, my side hurt. I squirmed to a different sitting position and decided to research more poisons. When I entered my symptoms—nausea, vomiting, flushing, weakness, sweating, irritability, and dizziness—a long list of toxic chemicals appeared on the page. At the top loomed an orange and black skull and crossbones. Just as I began to read, the doorbell rang. I pushed up from the chair, moaned and waited for my pain to pass and dizziness to stop. Barely ambulatory, I clung to the bag on my head, shuffled barefoot to the door and opened it.

Sam stood on the front stoop in khaki pants and a mustard and orange checked shirt.

Twenty-Four

Sam's colors were too much for a sick person.

At the sight of me, his brows shot up. "For God's sake, Agatha, what happened this time?"

When he called me Agatha, my head throbbed. I obviously couldn't tell him somebody pushed me down the gym's stairs. If I did, he'd tell me not to return to Fit and Firm.

"I fell down the stairs at the club. It's nothing. Just a little egg on my head. I'll be okay."

"You sure don't look okay. Here, let me see. Get that mushroom off your head."

He didn't have to remind me I didn't look my best. With my operational right arm, I gingerly removed the ice bag. Dampness had flattened the left side of my hair. He stepped closer, gently holding my shoulders as he leaned forward to evaluate my egg. When he peered through his bifocals, chin up, his lips nearly touched my nose. I would have liked a nose kiss, but he focused on my protrusion. "You could have a concussion. Are you having any trouble staying awake? Any sudden sleepiness? You should see a doctor."

"For a little bump on the head? I slept well all night. I feel normal this morning except for being more sore than usual." I wasn't aware of any other sensations until Sam cradled my shoulders. He led me to the sofa, sat me down gently and handed me my ice bag. While I repositioned it, he inspected me. I considered falling against him.

"If you feel any sudden drowsiness, or if that egg doesn't start shrinking real fast, you need a head x-ray." He took my hand and gazed into my eyes. "I'll drive you to the hospital." For the first time ever, I sensed he viewed me as more than a friend.

Feeling tingly and mellow, I understood, for the first time in my life, what motivated hypochondriacs. I smiled. My puffy eye closed into a wink.

This might be the perfect time to find out how much he knew about Harry. "Meredith told me Harry Thorne went home sick on Tuesday."

"That's right. One of the men I stationed at the health club told me about it."

I hoped he wasn't referring to the police officer I sweet talked into letting me invade Harry's office. If Sam found out about that little episode, he'd be furious.

"The officer said Thorne had a stomach bug," he said.

What had compelled Harry to rise from his sick bed Tuesday night and follow Grace and me to Las Tapitas?

"Thorne came back Wednesday morning but left again the same day."

Harry must have been desperate to get into Holly's apartment. Sam let go of my hand and shifted around to study my contusion.

"Around midnight on Wednesday," he said, "Harry's neighbor had to drive him to the hospital."

He leaned back to view my lump from a different angle. "They finally got his stomach settled down, but he was so dehydrated, they had to replace his fluids. He's back at home resting. Do you know Harry Thorne?"

"I went to see him after Holly's pool fiasco."

He frowned at me. He probably thought I should have told him about the incident. I made light of it. "Harry was positive the event was an accident. I think he hates to be wrong. He must have been devastated when Holly was murdered. Plus, think what the publicity could do to the club. Membership could be decimated."

It was difficult for me, the recent victim of a murder attempt, to be flippant, but I didn't want Sam to dwell on poor Holly and her baby. And I didn't want him considering the possibility that somebody had tried to kill me because of my link to Holly. To protect my past and to preserve Sam's interest, I had to solve this crime fast.

I failed to mention how Harry had glowered at me after I left his office, and I wasn't about to disclose that I'd spotted him near Holly's apartment. No way could I mention the little matter of my lying to the police officer to get into Harry's office and swipe the photograph. I was debating whether to tell him what I'd surmised about Harry and Holly's relationship when he stood and eyed me suspiciously.

"What else do you know about Harry Thorne?"

"Nothing much." I shrugged. "The day I went to his office, I glimpsed a photo of two guys boxing. A little girl among the spectators reminded me of Holly."

"Holly Holmgreen? Harry has a picture of her as a child? What's the connection between them?"

"I don't know." I shrugged. "Maybe the child wasn't Holly."

"Sounds like I need to pay Thorne another visit."

"Maybe so." I shrugged again. It was one shrug too many. Sam backed away and studied me. His eyes narrowed, causing a shock of peppered hair to flop onto his brow. I was afraid his considerable intelligence had kicked in.

"You fell down the steps? Yesterday? At the club? How did that happen?"

"I left something in my locker and returned Saturday to pick it up. My arms were overloaded and I tripped on the stairs." I refrained from shrugging.

"You went to the club Saturday? After being so sick Thursday night at Sheldon's house? What was so important that you felt compelled to retrieve it?"

"My curling iron."

His bullet-brown eyes pierced mine. If only he weren't a detective. Stalling for time to devise a more convincing answer, I gazed around the room and inadvertently glanced at my computer. Following my gaze, he snapped his eyes to the screen and marched toward it. The orange and black skull and crossbones were hard to miss.

"Poisons! You're researching poisons!" He whipped around and glared at me, eyes blazing.

"Your nausea, vomiting, weakness...that wasn't from Sheldon's food. You're being poisoned!" He turned white and stomped back to the sofa.

I was weak with relief that I'd turned Harry's boxing photo face down by the computer and that Sam hadn't picked it up. He tried not to jog me when he sat.

He grabbed both my hands. "What have you gotten yourself into, Aggie? You've got to tell me what's going on. Look. I've already lost Katy and Lee. We both lost Katy and Lee. I can't lose you, too."

He cared for me. He didn't want to lose me. If my body hadn't been a solid, suffering mass, I'd have melted right there on the couch. He didn't want me to die. I didn't want to die, either. I didn't even want to get old. Especially now that Sam cared.

My eyes filled. Actually, the large one got moist and the swollen one spilled over. He handed me a Kleenex.

"All right," I said. "I wasn't sure what was going on until Friday. Actually, I'm still not sure, but I think someone is putting poison in the club's toiletries."

His eyes widened to the edge of his tortoise frames as I proceeded to tell him how many times I'd been sick, where I thought the culprit had placed the poison, how anybody could have accessed the plastic bottles and how Sarah told me Holly had dated every guy at the club, including Mickey, Ned and Sheldon. I explained how I'd managed to infuriate all three of them, plus Patricia Drexel, Pete Reeves and probably Knobs and Mindy.

He seemed confused about Patricia, Pete, Knobs and Mindy. He stopped holding my hands, which was a shame. That was as close to him as I could get in my present condition.

"I need to check your locks." He sprang up and strode to my

front door. "You have a dead bolt. Good. And a peephole. Good. Don't open the door to anybody you don't know."

"I never do." I followed him around the living-dining room while he checked windows. "Sarah Savoy said Harry got upset whenever she or Holly dated club members and staff. I don't think Sarah likes Harry very much."

While he examined windows in my bedrooms and baths, I traipsed behind him and confessed to his back about snitching the club's toiletries and washcloths and taking them to the San Antonio Testing Laboratory. I didn't mention the bath crystals.

He inspected the door leading from the garage into the kitchen and my back door. "Your locks are secure, but you should lock your garage door, leave your car out and enter your house only from the front until we catch the bastard who's trying to poison you."

He returned to the living room and paced in a circle around the sofas. He paced faster and faster as though he feared being a step too late to prevent catastrophe. "I'll obtain the results from the lab." His face was red. "Then I will decide, with the department, what action to take."

Our conversation had lasted long enough that my egg felt smaller when I touched it. I didn't think the nasty bump would cause any serious trouble, except to remind me I was almost murdered.

Sam must have decided that scolding me wasn't productive. Having concluded I was not only lucid but aggravating, he remained in investigative mode, crisp and efficient. I'd never witnessed his aggressive detective personality first hand. Having been single for so long, I was rusty dealing with male pride. Once he announced he'd follow up with the lab, he didn't discuss poisons further.

He said he was researching Holly's adoption process to glean clues to who might have killed her. That revelation made my head throb harder.

He also told me that in order to counter bad publicity, Fit and Firm would proceed with plans to celebrate its tenth anniversary on

Monday. With extra people milling around the club, the event would be the perfect time for him to investigate without raising suspicion.

I kept quiet and let him talk. If he was going under cover, maybe he'd jettison his garish ties. He finally wound down and sat next to me. "We learned more from Grace's elderly neighbor, Anna."

My heart skipped. "The lady who said Charlie Livermore chased her granddaughter?"

"Yes. After Charlie died, Anna still lived next door to Grace when she married George Ball."

My head pulsated. I didn't want him to talk about Grace. It was pointless and cruel for SAPD to dig into her sad tragedies years after they happened. Couldn't he just put his arm around me? After all, I had crashed down the stairs. I sidled closer and tried to listen.

"Anna was still helping to raise her granddaughters, Martha and Lettie. When Grace married George, Lettie was twenty, a college junior. Martha, eighteen, had finished high school."

His eyes were liquid brown and luscious.

"Anna said that after Charlie Livermore tried to molest Martha, she developed problems. During her senior year in high school, she got pregnant."

"How sad." I removed my ice bag, sighed and leaned against him.

"Are you all right?" He put his arm around me, like a brother would sling an arm around a pesky sibling. Then he looked down and drew me closer.

"Um-hmm." I leaned my side under his shoulder and looked up. I trusted him; I knew so much about him. He knew so little about me.

We were close enough to kiss. I tossed the ice bag to the coffee table so it wouldn't drip on him, snuggled into the crevice of his arm and gazed up, inches from his face. "Does this information have something to do with my dear friend Grace?"

He shifted his position to accommodate the dead weight

sagging against him. "That's why I'm telling you about it. The two families were close, so when Martha's baby arrived, Grace's daughters couldn't wait to babysit. Linda was a student at San Antonio Community College and Kim was a high school junior. They took care of Martha's baby every chance they got."

"Grace told me that."

"Anna and her husband were getting old, and their son was weary of being a single parent for so long. So young Martha decided to place her baby for adoption."

"I know." I listened to his voice rumble in his chest. The soothing sound made me sleepy. If he'd just finish his long-winded story, he might kiss me.

"Martha made arrangements with a private adoption agency, but Linda and Kim begged their mother and George to adopt Martha's child. Grace and George almost agreed to it. Then George reneged. He wasn't the most energetic guy in the world, his health wasn't great and his boys were nearly grown. He didn't want to make new commitments. So, as she had originally planned, Martha placed her baby with Methodist Mission Home. Everybody was depressed over losing the infant. Shortly after that, George Ball suffered his fatal heart attack and everyone was devastated.

"Kim married her high school sweetheart and moved to Oklahoma. Linda shelved her pharmacy school plans, moved to California and opened a health food store near Patrick and Michael Ball's university."

I sat upright and stared. "Are you saying that because George Ball didn't want to adopt the neighbor's baby, Grace killed him?"

"No. That's a stretch. But lots of people were angry with George before he died. Suddenly. At age forty-eight."

I backed away from him. "Oh, for heaven's sake. George Ball didn't have any obligation to adopt Martha's baby. He was too old. Would you adopt a baby now?"

"Probably not."

"Well, see? This whole idea SAPD conceived about Grace Livermore being a killer is preposterous."

"Maybe it's preposterous, maybe not. Moseley will find out."

I stiffened ramrod straight. "Moseley? Elmore Moseley?"

"Yes. The man dating Grace. He's about to retire, but the captain talked him into taking one final case."

I jumped up and stared at him with both eyes bulging and my head about to explode. "You mean Elmore Moseley is dating Grace just to get information? That's despicable. The worst part is, she likes him. Grace actually likes him!"

He stood and reached for my arms. "He likes Grace, too. He said so. He's not going to hurt her. He's a perfect gentleman. If Grace had nothing to do with her husbands' deaths, she has nothing to worry about. Moseley will retire, and she'll never realize how they happened to meet."

My hands flew up. "Of course she'll know. Grace isn't a fool. She'll eventually find out. I'm not a fool, either." I yanked my chin up, which rattled my head. "It's time for you to leave." I backed away.

He looked stunned. "I never said you were a fool. Or Grace, either. Moseley's just doing his job. Like I'm doing mine."

"Oh. Is that what I am? Your job?"

"No, I didn't mean...You're not my job. You're...well, you're Aggie."

"It's Agatha," I huffed. I marched to the door, walking as straight as I could. It was hard to appear serious wearing a Garfield shirt and lime green warm-ups, barefoot, with wet hair drooping on one side, but I was.

He raised his hands as though he intended to speak but dropped them and backed toward the door. "You're going to rest now, aren't you?"

"Sure. I'm going to rest." I fumed at him while he crossed the threshold. Then I slammed the door, sniffing back angry tears.

Head pounding, I crumpled on the couch, miserable, and tried to collect myself. Sam and I could never be more than friends. We disagreed vehemently about Grace. He didn't realize that besides him and Meredith, Grace was my only real friend. I had to go back

150 Nancy G. West

to the club to ferret out the creep who'd tried to poison me and probably killed Holly. He would never understand that. He expected me to tell him everything and let him handle it.

I could never stop being curious, which drove him crazy. The police officer's pride that shielded him from hurt assured him he was always right. He was angry I didn't tell him about the poison. He could never stop probing and being officious.

He and I probably had hardening of the arteries. We'd lost too many brain cells to consider people and situations in a new light. After being whacked, my head probably couldn't even regenerate cells.

Sam was getting close to finding answers about Holly. His obsession with her would spur him to research the adoption of his daughter, Lee. He might contact Katy's obstetrician or track down the doctor who took over his practice. He might subpoena court records about Lee. Once he did that, odds were good that whatever bond we might have had would be quashed.

If I lived long enough to beat Izumi's 120-year record, I'd have to go it alone. Sniffling, I searched around for my Big Chief tablet. I cradled the pad in my lap and started to write, ignoring different-sized tears streaking down my face.

"Single white female. Mature graduate student. Curious..."

My words weren't coming out right. I sounded like an aging pervert. I started over:

"Single white female. Under forty. Avid health club member. Optimistic..."

I sounded like a pathetic physical specimen who was afraid she might die before she could get in shape.

This ad was getting way too personal. I gave up.

Twenty-Five

By Monday morning, the egg on my forehead had receded. When I covered the bruise around my eye with makeup, I looked almost normal. It was exhilarating knowing I could count on a settled stomach. My body pain had subsided to a generalized ache. When my feet began to itch, I knew I was well enough to return to Fit and Firm.

Sam called. "After I left yesterday, I paid Harry Thorne a visit."

"And?" I replied in a refrigerated voice as I padded into the kitchen.

"It seems Holly Holmgreen was Harry Thorne's niece. Harry's younger brother, Billy, was Holly's father. She was a baby when Billy died in Vietnam. Her mother, Billy's girlfriend, deposited the child with Harry and his father, Arnold, and cut out."

"Arnold owned the boxing gym?" I maintained a detached tone.

"Yes."

"If she was Harry's niece, why was her last name Holmgreen?" I peered into the refrigerator and retrieved a can of pineapple. The fruit had bromelain in it, a natural anti-inflammatory enzyme that encouraged healing.

"Holmgreen was Arnold's mother's maiden name. The men decided since their only choice was to raise the little girl next to a boxing gym, they should at least give her a different name to suggest a more illustrious past."

"Holly didn't know she was Harry Thorne's niece?" I cradled

the phone between my neck and shoulder, opened the can and poured pineapple, with its vitamins C and B1, into a bowl.

"Oh, she knew. She hated her parents for deserting her and transferred her contempt to Harry and Arnold. She despised life at the gym even more than they feared."

I remembered Holly's little girl clothes and baby-doll apartment. She'd tried to relive her childhood, imagining her life as she wished it had been. I took the bowl to the counter, grabbed a fork, perched on the barstool and stabbed a chunk. "What happened to Holly's mother?"

"She announced to Harry and Arnold she wanted nothing to do with Billy's baby. They could keep the child, but they'd never find her. Harry and Arnold looked for the woman for a solid year. Then they quit searching and legally adopted Holly."

"Most people would be grateful they took her in." I squeezed a bite of pineapple between my teeth and let the juice float in my mouth.

"Yes, but Holly loathed her environment and blamed Harry and Arnold. She looked demure, but Harry said she evolved into a wild child, especially during her teenage years. She seemed to improve once she lived in her own apartment, which Harry paid for. Harry talked her into joining the health club, where she could meet nice people and he could keep an eye on her. She agreed to join the club with the stipulation that nobody would know she was related to Harry."

"Poor Harry." My voice thawed before I could stop it.

"He only wanted to protect her."

I thought about the note I'd found in Holly's shoe. Harry probably wrote it. An expert in handwriting analysis could match the script against the scribbles on the back of Harry's boxing photo. I could ask Sam to take the notes to an SAPD expert, but I wasn't feeling cooperative. I concentrated on capturing another piece of pineapple.

Sam said Holly reviled Harry for being overprotective. "A couple of years ago, she started dating every man at the club, right under Harry's nose. He thought she did it to spite him."

That fit with what Sarah told me. I wondered if Holly got pregnant just to gall Harry. I paused before asking the next question. "Did Harry know Holly got pregnant and gave up her baby?"

"I don't know. He was in such torment over her death, I didn't have the heart to ask him."

Holly's baby was Harry's last chance to have a child as close as possible to his own offspring. What would he do when he discovered she'd relinquished the child? Explode and kill the ungrateful girl he tried to raise? I carried my bowl and spoon to the sink, suddenly feeling full. Continuous trauma had shrunk my stomach.

Holly had apparently changed so much that Harry hardly recognized the girl he adopted. She taunted and rejected him. Holly was probably the woman Meredith overheard arguing with Harry. Sarah had called Harry a control freak.

There was another possibility to consider. Maybe whoever killed Holly also tried to kill her uncle Harry. Was the "bug" that put Harry in the hospital the same poison that made me sick? Maybe somebody knew about Harry's and Holly's kinship and thought I'd discovered it. Who would care enough to murder me, as well as Holly and Harry?

I poured a glass of milk to soothe my stomach. I didn't discuss my thoughts with Sam. On information overload, I still percolated with anger over SAPD's sending Elmore to spy on Grace. I sipped.

"I'll question Harry more later," he said. "Right now, I just feel sorry for the poor guy. He's too miserable to go anywhere. He's got the club's ten year celebration scheduled on top of everything else."

I set my glass down. "When is it?"

"It's today. I'm not sure Harry can handle it. He said he might put his assistant in charge. I suggested to the assistant manager, a nervous fellow, that he remove the club's toiletries during the celebration."

"Are you going?" I tried to keep excitement out of my voice.

"Sometime during the day. By the way, I do have news I think you'll be glad to hear."

"What?" I wasn't eager for more of Sam's good news.

"Grace's third husband, Ray Peters, died of natural causes. He developed metastatic cancer and died at age sixty-two, six months after his diagnosis. His and Grace's children gathered at his bedside. He wanted them all there and was apparently content."

"Grace wasn't able to tell me about Ray's death. How did you find out?"

"She told Elmore."

Heat rose up the back of my neck. "Well, at least you know Grace isn't a murderer. Now you can leave her alone." Talking loud made my head throb.

He ignored the frost in my voice. "I'll call you with results from the testing lab when I get them. You're going to stay home and rest, right?"

"That's probably the best idea."

I clicked the phone off, set my glass in the sink and paced to the living room. I was glad Sam wasn't standing in front of me to witness my eager face. I rubbed my itching feet against the sofa. With Fit and Firm about to celebrate its ten year anniversary, and me full of pineapple with manganese and my enzymes producing energy at full throttle, staying home was out of the question.

Twenty-Six

I felt so much better that I longed to escape my habitat. The bump on my head had receded. With my bangs pulled down and makeup around my eye, I looked normal. The sun was shining on this mild Monday in January. The day was perfect to satisfy my curiosity with a little sleuthing.

Whenever I engaged in a life-changing event, I held my good-luck charm. I'd held the talisman before I turned in my first Dear Aggie column, before I left Chicago, before I bought my house, before I enrolled in graduate school and before I joined Fit and Firm. I kept the amulet in a fake, hollowed-out book in my bedroom bookcase. The tome, titled *An In-Depth History of the World*, looked like it had a thousand pages. Nobody ever picked up a book like that.

My good-luck charm was safe. The talisman wasn't actually a charm; it was my baby Lee's bracelet, the one they put on her arm in the hospital. "Lee Mary Mundeen. Girl. 7 lbs. 4 oz. 16 inches. Mother: Agatha Emory Mundeen." I'd clipped off the bracelet as soon as we left the hospital. I knew I had to give her up, but the bracelet would help to keep her near me.

I scurried to the bookcase, grabbed the book and opened it. Lee's bracelet was gone. How was that possible? Nobody knew about it. Nobody came in my bedroom. I crawled around the floor searching behind the bookcase and under the bed, groping behind furniture legs. Where could it be? I hadn't moved that bracelet. I never moved it.

Flying around the house, I rechecked windows and doors even though Sam had already inspected the locks. Everything was secure. Nobody could get in without leaving marks. I remembered the hairpin method I'd read about, sped to the front door and stared at the lock. The mechanism appeared normal. Had somebody picked it with a credit card?

A normal person would call Sam and have SAPD dust for prints, but then I'd have to tell him about Lee's bracelet, which was not an option. If I refused to tell him what was missing, he'd stake out my home, admonish me never to return to Fit and Firm and banish me to boredom land. Also out of the question.

Returning to the club was now urgent. Whoever took my baby's bracelet knew about my past. I suspected the murderer knew, which apparently made me a target.

Resigned, I put on my best workout clothes, a pink T-shirt and black Lycra-snug tights, fluffed my hair and headed for Fit and Firm. With the club full of people during the celebration, I'd blend with the crowd.

I drove past Fort Sam Houston, veered left on Dover Road and snaked through Terrell Hills, wondering when the murderer had entered my house. Anybody who saw me enter the club to exercise knew they had an hour, minimum, to search my bungalow before I returned.

Cruising through manicured neighborhoods, I admired various sized lots and homes. Small houses were costly and taxes were high, but residents happily paid them because of the Alamo Heights schools. One reason I'd chosen Burr Road was because the neighborhood was safe. Or so I thought.

Nobody besides me possessed a key to my house. I'd hidden an emergency key in the bushes by my front porch and told Grace about it. Although Sam had made me paranoid, I knew Grace would never enter my house without asking.

The club provided locker keys attached to safety pins. When members put valuables in lockers, they pinned the locker key to their shorts or swimsuits. I took the key with me to exercise, but somebody could have broken into my locker and pilfered my house keys.

I wound around Dover to Garraty and veered right, then left onto Vandiver Road. After a few blocks, I reached the old Austin Highway, not far from Fit and Firm. I parked in the club's garage and strode toward the entrance, determined to find the crazy psychopathic killer who'd swiped my baby's bracelet. Adrenaline pumped through me. When I saw the huge sign draped across the front of the building, my excitement mushroomed:

FIT AND FIRM HEALTH CLUB'S TEN-YEAR ANNIVERSARY!
NEW SPECIAL RATES!

The anniversary celebration was well timed. After Holly's death, Harry had told Sam the club lost members pretty fast. Someone had draped balloons around the entrance and on the check-in desk and tied them to chair backs in Tofu Temptations Grill. The staff had even decorated doors to the men and women's locker rooms and left them ajar so prospective members could tour the entire facility.

I was excited enough to think I could operate every machine in the place. I didn't see anybody I knew, but I smiled encouragingly at new people milling around. Getting in shape made you feel like everybody else should get with it. I was almost brave enough to scale the steps on the mountain climber. Instead, I walked forty minutes on the treadmill to ease my itching feet and tamp my zeal down to a manageable level.

After exercising, I went to the locker room to shower. With the suspicious bottles gone, I felt safe. The staff had done a good job of roping off bathrooms and changing areas to provide members with privacy. After folding my clothes in a locker, I wrapped myself in a club towel and headed through the passageway partitioned off for members' access to showers, nodding at a few women along the way. Outside the barrier, I heard visitors' voices.

When I reached the showers, I saw somebody had even tied

balloons to shower curtain rods. The area looked festive. I stepped into the shower, anticipating feeling fresh and invigorated, and turned on the water. Glancing down, I noticed a balloon on the floor. Was it leaking liquid or was water dripping from the shower?

My curtain cracked open. Somebody heaved in another balloon. When it hit the floor near the first balloon and burst, my feet started to burn. A horrible stench rose from the tile floor. My eyes stung. I gasped. Unable to breathe, I leaped from the shower, grabbed my towel and crashed into a woman careening out of the adjacent shower. With the asphyxiating odor engulfing me, I charged for the exit door. As people screamed and ran from the locker room, I thought I heard Harry Thorne bellowing orders.

We charged in a nude herd past the reception desk—women and men, in various sizes and stages of undress, barreling out the front door and crawling upward onto the sloping, grassy knoll next to the club. We got as far away as we could from the building and stopped to pant, sputter and cough...a wretched sound. Some people vomited. Others grabbed their throats or pressed hands against their eyes while they tried to cover their bodies.

Mindy stood a few feet away trying to hold a towel across her chest and another one in front of her pelvis while she coughed violently and shook, poor thing. Knobs quivered several feet from me. Bent over, she rubbed her eyes and held her throat without bothering to cover anything. Most of the women struggled to cover some part of their anatomy. I had grabbed only one towel, so every time I coughed, I had to readjust it.

Harry, Pete, Sarah and the other trainers tried to help people however they could. Staff members stood out from the rest of the herd, being fully clothed. I guessed they'd been too far from the stench to suffer symptoms. Male clients jumped up and down, holding their throats. They looked like huge naked grasshoppers.

We were quite a group: sixty to a hundred naked or nearly naked people, spread out over the grassy knoll within reading distance of the huge sign on the front of the building,

FIT AND FIRM HEALTH CLUB'S TEN-YEAR ANNIVERSARY!

We looked like a Roman orgy. Tires screeched on the freeway. I guessed motorists thought Fit and Firm was definitely a club to investigate.

I heard sirens and saw two fire trucks pull up. Firefighters reduced power on their hoses as much as they could and sprayed us. The spatter helped clear the noxious odor and washed the burning substance off our skin. We stuck our tongues out and let water run down our throats. Onlookers probably thought the San Antonio Fire Department was breaking up a nudist riot.

Sam ran up to me. "Oh, migod." He raced down the hill toward the EMS truck, yelling at technicians to haul up a stretcher. I realized the last time he'd seen me appear normal was in Tofu Temptations Grill three days earlier.

Two emergency technicians raced up with a stretcher. I crumpled on it, as thankful for the covering sheet as for a place to lie down. While I coughed and clutched the stretcher's sides, techs jostled me down the knoll toward the ambulance. I felt like I was galloping on the Body Trek. I bounced through a sea of inadequately covered bodies and flew past Mickey Shannon, naked as Adam, jumping up and down without a fig leaf. I would always remember him that way. From all his weight lifting, he probably looked better than Adam. He saw me and snarled.

We jounced past Ned Barclay clutching a towel in front of his groin. He saw me fly past and turned tomato red.

The technicians stopped to catch their breath before they hurled me into the ambulance. At that moment, I saw Sheldon Snodgrass wearing club towels wrapped around him like a toga. Engrossed in some sort of yoga move, he was oblivious to his surroundings. He seemed deep in meditation but karma made him aware of my presence. He spotted me, raised his arms and screeched. Fortunately, the techs shoved me into the truck before Sheldon's towels fell off.

Twenty-Seven

I wasn't on my leopard bedspread. My body lay on something hard and scratchy. I peered down through oxygen tubes taped to my nose and spotted white hospital sheets. Something weird had happened. I hoped the oxygen was destroying aging free radicals roaming inside my body. When I spied the plastic circle on my wrist, I remembered that somebody had stolen Lee's baby bracelet. Taped to my other hand was an IV tube.

Meredith laid her hand on top of my hospital bracelet. "Aggie. You're awake." She smiled. Her hair, usually perfectly groomed, resembled matted hay. Her clothes were wrinkled.

Sam, trying to avoid the IV, patted my other arm above the elbow. "Boy, Aggie, you really scared us this time. How do you feel?" The thatch of hair splattering his forehead was beyond recovery. When I looked at him, his somber eyes perked up. I remembered being furious with him, but I didn't feel angry anymore. What if I died and never saw him again?

"I feel okay." I sorted through memories, trying to figure out what was wrong with me, and remembered Sheldon's party. I was definitely not hungry, but my stomach felt settled. I'd apparently survived Sheldon's food euphoria. I hoped the purpose of the IV was merely to provide fluids.

I peeked up to see if the egg above my eye had returned. My forehead appeared normal, except for scraggly bangs thrust forward like a broom. When I coughed, my insides hurt down to my navel. My lungs felt like rusty buckets. I remembered the awful smell in the shower. When I tried to inhale, I couldn't get enough air in my lungs. I wheezed like an asthmatic—me, who was never allergic to anything. Having reduced breathing capacity scared me.

Meredith reached beside my bed for a metal canister with a plastic cup attached to the top. "Here. Dr. Sheeply said to use this when you woke up. He called it a nebulizer, an aerosol inhaler to open air passages in your lungs to help you breathe."

She pointed the cup toward my mouth. "Exhale as much as you can through your nose, put the mouthpiece into your mouth, past your front teeth, and close your lips around it. Take a slow deep breath while you press down on the container to spray medication into your mouth and lungs." Meredith would make a great nurse. I did exactly what she said.

"Hold your breath five to ten seconds." She checked her watch while I tried not to explode. "Now remove the cup and exhale slowly." When I exhaled, Sam exhaled with me.

I immediately felt better. "What is that stuff?"

"Albuterol," he said. "You can use it every four hours. If you need it again, Dr. Sheeply said to call the nurse."

Now I remembered technicians wheeling me into Methodist Hospital's emergency room with my eyes watering. Every time I'd taken a breath, my chest hurt. Somebody slapped an apparatus on my face. I heard the words "chest x-ray," "oximeter" and "blood gases," then blacked out.

"What day is it? How long have I been here?"

"The ambulance brought you in yesterday, Monday. You were here overnight." He looked like he'd been crumpled in a waiting room chair ever since I'd been admitted.

"What was that stuff in the club shower that smelled so bad?"

"Chlorine gas." He paled. "Somebody placed a balloon filled with ammonia on the shower floor, then threw in another balloon filled with Clorox. The creep who did it cut slits in both balloons. When they collided, Clorox mixed with ammonia to produce chlorine gas. The lab boys figured that out. Our team, in rubber suits and gas masks, stormed in as soon as they could to confiscate the balloons. Chlorine gas is extremely caustic—burns everything it contacts—eyes, skin, respiratory track. That's why you're receiving nasal oxygen...to counter effects of the gas."

I remembered panicking in the shower, unable to breathe and desperate to escape.

"Victims cough violently, can't breathe and are terrified," he said.

I remembered hearing wretched coughing sounds as the naked herd charged for the exit.

Everybody's eyes, throats and feet were burning. No wonder they gyrated on the grassy slope.

Sam held my upper arm with both hands, cradling my puny biceps and triceps in an effort to comfort me while avoiding my IV. "If your lungs had been seriously damaged, you could have suffered respiratory failure, had a heart attack and died."

When I tried to inhale, I coughed. My lungs were damaged. I couldn't breathe deeply like I was supposed to, to lengthen my life span. The gas had destroyed my cells: traumatic senescence. My vital parts had suffered so much wear and tear, Error Theorists could display my organs in their lab. What few hormones I had left were in hiding. Izumi's record was safe. I felt like I was a thousand years old. Maybe other club members actually died.

Meredith seemed to read my mind. "Since you ran the water, a lot of the mixture washed down the drain. Gas still rose up the sides of the shower, but because you jumped out fast and ran to fresh air, the effects weren't disastrous, thank heaven. The woman in the shower next to you didn't act as fast—she didn't see the balloon thrown in—but she wasn't as close to the gas, either. They kept her overnight for observation and released her this morning."

I sent up a quick prayer, thankful to be alive. "Was anybody else hospitalized?"

"No. They brought several people to the emergency room to be checked, but they're all okay."

Sam regained his composure. "Since the gas was partially enclosed by the shower, the damage was contained. Somebody also tossed a couple of balloons into the men's locker room, but no one was harmed."

With Sam back in efficiency mode, this seemed like a good time to ask why I was still in the hospital. He cleared his throat. "Dr. Sheeply wants to observe you and do a couple more tests. He'll be in after lunch."

I didn't like the expression on his face. "What tests?"

"He mentioned a chest x-ray and oximeter." Sam was usually very direct. I knew chest x-rays weren't a big deal. The oximeter thing must be the booger.

"Dr. Sheeply is a very kind man, a pulmonary disease specialist. Best there is. I checked around." He patted my hand.

I was grateful, but I didn't like the "diseases" designation. Aging progressed more slowly in the absence of disease.

At least Sam seemed to care about me, especially when I was incapacitated.

Meredith reported the health club would close for a week. Staff had told members that workers were repairing a gas leak.

Fit and Firm seemed doomed to suffer from lousy timing. Not only was their ten-year celebration ruined; they had to put off new prospects eager to join the club—all those people who witnessed the grassy slope dance. Maybe that was a good thing.

"Did you hear any more about Harry?" I asked.

"He's very despondent. We're keeping an eye on him."

Poor Harry. I decided not to mention I thought I'd heard Harry's voice not far from my shower.

Sam said once SAPD's lab teams removed traces of chemicals, he could investigate the club without members and staff hovering around. I felt a twinge of guilt for not telling him all I knew. My remorse didn't last long.

Meredith said she was relieved to forego working out for a week. Her coursework for American and British Literature was getting heavy. I couldn't process any more information. Until Dr. Sheeply came to discuss my condition, I just wanted to drowse.

*   *   *

When I woke up, Meredith and Sam were gone. Dr. Sheeply held my wrist to take my pulse. Tall enough to play college basketball, he had chiseled features and a high forehead, which undoubtedly housed a bundle of brains.

His kind eyes comforted me. I felt silly introducing myself to a man who was thoroughly acquainted with my innards, so I smiled meekly and waited.

"Your pulse rate has slowed, Ms. Mundeen. That's good. Let's see what happens when you inhale."

Cautiously, I sucked in air. Inhaling was easier than before, but I still coughed.

"Your heart rate is better than when you came to the emergency room. It approached one hundred sixty beats a minute when you arrived."

"Is my heart enlarged?"

"No."

"I know I inhaled chlorine gas. What, exactly, did the stuff do to me?"

"It irritated your lungs, made breathing difficult, made your eyes water and your throat burn. Chlorine gas acts like an acid, burning whatever it touches. If a person inhales enough gas, it attacks dry areas of the lungs, mixes with water and makes hydrochloric acid."

My heart skipped a beat.

"The results can be fatal. Since you escaped the gas quickly, irritation to your respiratory track was minimal."

"Then why am I getting oxygen?" I was worried about oxidative damage.

"To raise the oxygen level in your blood. When gas irritates your lungs and makes breathing difficult, the oxygen level in your blood decreases. Normal oxygen saturation is over ninety percent. Yours was seventy-eight percent when you came in. That's why I kept you for observation."

I perked up. If my oxygen saturation returned to normal, I might be all right.

"I want you to have another chest x-ray to check for fluid in your lungs and oximetry to measure your oxygen saturation."

There was that word. Oximetry. "Is that a bad test?"

"No. They put a monitoring device on your finger to measure the amount of oxygen in your blood. No big deal. If your tests are normal, which I expect they will be, you can go home this afternoon."

I was worried the chlorine gas had already damaged my cells and organs. "Did the gas cause my cells to stop dividing?"

"No."

"Didn't crosslink my proteins?"

"I don't think so." He checked his watch.

"Has my brain lost any cells? Can I grow synapses?"

"Your brain is fine. Your synapses are multiplying as we speak."

"Did my lungs lose breathing capacity?"

"No. You're breathing off the effects of the gas. Your lungs should be as good as before."

As good as before. That's what I wanted to hear. Sam was right. Dr. Sheeply was a jewel.

Twenty-Eight

A nurse appeared and stuck my index finger in the oximeter. When she finished, an orderly whisked in behind her and wheeled me to x-ray. I didn't mind going. This trip could be my ticket out of the hospital.

I had to consider the little matter that somebody had tried, again, to kill me. This maniac was determined. While the orderly pushed me back from x-ray, I lined up suspects in my head.

When we got to my room, Sam stood there looking like an eager puppy. "Boy, you look better. You've finished your tests?"

I'd almost forgiven him. He was just doing his job. "The tests were a cakewalk. Nothing to them. I'm ready to get out of here. I'm sick of being sick."

He grinned. "If Dr. Sheeply discharges you, I'll drive you home. I called the testing lab. They'd heard about the chlorine gas attack at Fit and Firm. When I told them we were investigating the contents of containers you took them as a related crime, they didn't quibble about giving SAPD the results."

"What did the analysis show?"

"Somebody put camphor in the spray deodorant bottle. When you sprayed under your arms, you got camphor poisoning through your skin." He patted my arm. I wished he'd wrap his arms around me.

"I've heard of camphor, but what, exactly, is it?"

"It comes from camphor trees that grow in Japan, China,

Formosa, Sumatra and Brazil. They use steam to distill it from fifty-year-old trees."

"Sounds exotic. Hard to get."

"Not really. Three-fourths of the camphor we produce in the United States is synthetic. We use it in plastics, lacquers, varnishes, explosives, pyrotechnics, moth repellents and cosmetics. Camphor is in Vicks VapoRub."

I remembered Aunt Novena's putting Vicks VapoRub on my chest and Campho-Phenique under my nose when I had a cold. "So camphor is easy to get?"

"Yes. Like ammonia and Clorox."

"How did camphor get into the club's deodorant?"

"The lab scientist said somebody crushed up a lot of mothballs, mixed them with liquid and put a hefty amount in the deodorant bottles."

"What symptoms does camphor cause?"

"Headache, flushing, sweating, nausea and vomiting, vertigo, mental confusion, irritability..."

"I experienced every one of those symptoms." I still didn't know what I'd said to Dr. Carmody. "I felt so terrible after eating, I thought the food was contaminated. But before lunch, after I worked out and showered, I used the deodorant."

He sat on the side of my bed. "Camphor acts within fifteen minutes to an hour after absorption through the skin. With sporadic use and various delivery amounts, I guess reaction time varies."

"When I got sick at Sheldon's party, camphor I'd absorbed earlier must have stayed in my system. Plus I couldn't avoid viewing his buffet table."

"If somebody gets a massive dose, they suffer seizures, respiratory failure, go into a coma and die." He looked stricken. He'd watched me stumble through various stages of destruction for days. My respiratory system really took a beating. I was thankful for every breath I took.

"What about the purple bath crystals?" I asked.

"They found a trace of potassium permanganate in the bag of crystals marked 'club,' but not enough to harm anybody. The cleanser they use to disinfect the hot tub contains diluted amounts of the compound. Whoever packaged the bath crystals could have accidentally mixed in a few particles of the cleaning solution."

"Employees who clean the locker room also package the bath crystals?"

"Yes. They scoop out measured amounts from a five-gallon container of crystals, wrap them in cellophane and put them by the hot tub."

"What about the crystals marked 'home'?"

"Plain old bath crystals. By the way, where did you get those?"

"I saw them by the hot tub and decided to swipe a second batch. I asked Mr. Eagleton to mark one bag 'home' to distinguish them."

I noted that my brain cells were percolating. Grace had not given me poisoned bath crystals.

My favorite nurse, Jenny, bounced in, smiling. "Looks like you're going home."

"Boy. They get those test results fast," Sam said.

"Dr. Sheeply asked them to rush the reports since she's here for observation. We always have patients needing beds."

Jenny helped me dress in clothes Meredith had brought from my house earlier. She found a wheelchair so Sam could push me downstairs.

My Tuesday Aspects of Aging class was already over. I would have to tell Dr. Carmody I'd been hospitalized Monday and Tuesday. I needed to concoct a plausible diagnosis so when I showed up Wednesday after missing two more days, he wouldn't respond with uncontrolled rage. If I told him somebody had tried to kill me, I didn't think he could take it. Instead of calling him, I would immerse myself in serious studying before I had to face him again.

Riding in Sam's car as we headed for home, I was euphoric watching kids running around and people mowing grass. The day, clear and bright, was about fifty degrees. Sun twinkled through leafless trees. I'd be sure to watch the sunset. The heavens would be streaked with pink, red and yellow—colors so vivid that, in a painting, they wouldn't look real. I wished Sam and I could watch the sunset together. When I smiled at him, he reached over to pat my hand. I wanted him to grab it. Instead, he cleared his throat. Since I was ambulatory, he was apparently back to business.

"Detective Sammis located George Ball's sons, Patrick and Michael, in California. Patrick is an accountant in San Francisco. Michael, a camera operator, goes on location with film crews. They confirmed Grace's story about their father's hunting trip. They said they couldn't imagine his doing it, but George must have mixed up his pills. They keep in touch with their stepsister, Linda Livermore, through her store manager."

I watched sunlight sparkle on the grass. "Detective Sammis met the boys and the store manager, Margie Carlyle, at Linda's Healthy Habitat store in LA. After Linda remodeled the store a few years back, she hired Margie. Linda added protein drinks and mineral supplements to the health foods, put in two treadmills facing the TV and added lounge chairs where people read health magazines."

"It sounds like Linda's store has been very successful." It seemed that everyone wanted to live a hundred and twenty years.

"Patrick and Michael worked there during college. They said Healthy Habitat financed a lot of their USC education. Margie Carlyle told Sammis that after customers' positive response to the remodeling, Linda decided to take a break. She announced she'd developed wanderlust, would be in and out and would contact Margie for messages. That occurred three years ago. Margie says Linda comes back to LA for a week or so to check on her stepbrothers and the store, then takes off."

I loved gazing at the horizon. Hospital rooms were so confining. "Do they know where Linda goes?"

"No, but in her back office, Sammis found catalogues from UT Pharmacy School and USC's School of Pharmacy."

"I guess she never discarded her dream."

"But why drop out of sight?" he said. "Sammis found out she gave up her LA apartment two years ago. The boys haven't heard from her for six months. Her cell phone number is inactive. They're worried. Sammis is checking the universities to see if she registered."

Sam's report was interesting, but I still thought SAPD was wasting a lot of money snooping around Grace's family just because her husbands died young.

"I talked with Harry Thorne again. He said a couple of years ago, Holly started dating every available male, didn't listen to anything Harry said and wouldn't give him the time of day. Her actions really hurt him."

"I'm sure they did. Poor Harry. He loved Holly, and she wouldn't even acknowledge he was her uncle." Her attitude must have distressed Harry on another level. The club represented his life's goal, and she made a mockery of his upscale, dignified establishment. Did her reaction turn Harry's love into hatred to the point where he flipped out and ran her over? I still wondered if he knew about the baby, his last chance to raise a child. I glanced at my nails. "When did Harry return to the club?"

"He felt pretty good Sunday when I left. He probably dropped in Monday morning."

I decided not to tell him just yet that I heard Harry bellowing on Monday, right after the creep tossed balloons in my shower.

When I popped up in Harry's office the day Holly nearly drowned, he might have thought she confided in me. Maybe he thought I influenced her to relinquish her baby. My relationship with Holly was too limited for me to influence her, but Harry didn't seem rational about his wayward niece. He might have followed me to Las Tapitas to confront me.

I didn't want to process any more information. I just wanted to meander through San Antonio with Sam forever and let crisp air hit me through the open window while the sun warmed my arm.

During my hospital stay, Sam had time to reflect and wanted to talk about it. "I've been thinking about those spray bottles, about whether the poison was meant for Holly. It's a question of timing."

"I wondered about that, too. The first day I experienced symptoms was the day Holly nearly drowned." I bit my lip and sneaked a glance at him.

He snapped his eyes at me. "Why didn't you tell me she nearly drowned, Agatha? I had to learn about it from officers who questioned the members and staff."

"I thought it was an accident."

"No, you didn't." He stared at the road.

"Well, I wasn't sure. I felt sorry for her, and I didn't want to discuss her misery. Then she was dead and it didn't seem to matter."

He whipped his eyes in my direction. "It mattered to the investigation."

"I guess I should have told you."

"You didn't tell me because you like to figure things out on your own. But murder is a little out of your field. Let professionals handle it."

I didn't want us to get angry. I just wanted to enjoy the weather and his company and being alive. I didn't look his way.

"Aggie, promise me you'll stay away from that club. They're going to open early, maybe on Friday. SAPD detoxed the building and scoured every inch of the premises for clues. It's clean, so the chief gave the go ahead. Harry's afraid if they stay closed any longer, they'll get so much bad publicity they'll lose prospective customers."

I wanted to say, "I'll promise to stay away from the health club if you promise to keep Elmore Moseley from snooping around Grace," but I didn't. I stretched my neck toward the window so he couldn't see how interested I was to learn when the club would reopen. I crossed my legs and rubbed one foot against the other.

"You're in danger, Aggie. I'm going to assign a patrol officer to watch you and your house. You're especially in danger at the club. Somebody killed Holly there and tried very hard to kill you."

He was back to know-it-all mode. Why couldn't he let me rest? I didn't blame him for getting worked up, but how could he solve everything? He didn't know nearly as much as I did about Holly or the suspects, and I wasn't going to tell him. He was dead wrong about Grace. I couldn't believe he let SAPD sic Elmore on her. Why should I do what Sam wanted? How could I make progress finding the killer if he had robo cop trailing me?

"Okay," I replied, as if I agreed with everything he said. "Let's think about what happened to Holly while I was poisoning myself with deodorant. The second day I got sick was the day she died. That was Tuesday. Maybe the killer tried to poison her but saw an unexpected opportunity to run her down."

"It's possible. Did you have symptoms again on Wednesday, after she died?"

I thought about it. Wednesday was the day I wormed my way into Holly's apartment. This wasn't a good time to remind him of that.

"I was a little queasy on Wednesday. As you know, I was terribly sick Thursday night at Sheldon's party. I recovered Friday. Saturday, I was...I fell down the stairs. Sunday, I recuperated. The egg...remember?"

He looked exasperated. Our schedule had been pretty hectic.

He pulled up in front of my house, inhaled, slowly let the air out and sat there. "The killer could have been after you all along."

"Or the killer could have targeted Holly, but after killing her, the murderer continued poisoning bottles to make it appear that the hit and run and the poison weren't related."

While he considered that possibility, another thought came to me. "What about Meredith? I saw her use the club's deodorant once, but she didn't get sick. Then she started bringing her own toiletries. Maybe she was the potential victim, but the killer didn't know she brought her own stuff." I had no idea whether the last part was true, but my idea sounded pretty good, so I kept talking. "I wonder if any of the men got sick."

He sighed. "No. Our officers questioned people at the club all during this investigation. The perp tossed balloons in the men's locker room, and men had to exit through the gas, but everybody escaped. No one reported any lingering illness."

He'd apparently forgotten about Harry's illness. I decided to let it ride. He got out, plodded around the car and escorted me to the door. I grubbed around for the key I'd hidden in the shrubs. As soon as we entered the foyer, he turned to face me.

"While investigating Holly's past, I learned something from the adoption agency. When Holly got pregnant, she did care about her child. She felt she couldn't keep it—she had issues in her life they wouldn't disclose to me—but she wanted to do the best she could for the child. She loved her baby and made the best decision she knew how to make."

I wasn't sure why he brought that up. He grasped my shoulders, bent down, kissed me on the cheek and wrapped me in a bear hug. Warmed by his embrace, I felt my irritation with him over Grace struggling against my attraction for him. I loved the smell of his aftershave. I decided to quit thinking and relaxed into the curve of his neck. I slipped my arms around his back and pressed him to me. I wasn't too weak to think about the splendid possibilities once I regained strength.

We hugged for several minutes, not moving. When Sam pulled away, he gazed into my eyes for a long time. Then he kissed me, pecked me on the nose, whirled and strode out the door.

Twenty-Nine

By the time Sam left, it was late Tuesday afternoon. I bathed, watched TV for a while, gobbled a couple of peanut butter and jelly sandwiches and daydreamed about him. Did his talking about Holly and hugging me mean he'd learned I was Lee's mother? He kissed me. Had he forgiven me? Maybe he was just apologizing for his anger when he caught me in Holly's apartment. I would have to wait and see.

I knew I should read material for Aspects of Aging. I absolutely had to attend Dr. Carmody's Wednesday class, but now that I was home, I could hardly keep my eyes open.

I checked inside *An In-Depth History of the World* for Lee's bracelet. My good-luck charm was still missing. Someone could have broken into my house while we attended Sheldon's party. I never saw Mickey, Pete, Ned, Sarah, Mindy or Knobs there. Harry was in the hospital. I had too many suspects to sort out. I crawled into bed, hoping to dream about Sam, and drifted off.

I dreamed about a second *Food, Fitness and Euphoria* party at Sheldon's house. More people packed his lair than the number who attended the real party. Guests gyrated to rock music, vibrating the floor and blocking my view of the dining table. As if on cue, dancers jostled backward in a uniform circle, leaving me an unobstructed view of a shrunken dining table centered in the room with the mammoth hog perched on top.

Mickey Shannon, wearing a cut-off tank top and very tight jeans, bounced around the disgusting animal in perfect time to the music, like a fighter sizing up his competition. The hog, stiff as a statue, resembled Harry Thorne. Its feet pointed in different directions. Its head was twisted around so its face craned back over its own shoulder.

Sheldon sidled up to me. "It's the first time I cooked a whole hog. I put it in my new trash can and stuffed ice around it. When I pulled the pig out, the creature was frozen with its feet sticking out. I worked for an hour just trying to straighten out the head." Giggling, he bopped off, twirling a string of sausages to the beat.

Mickey circled the stiff hog, monitoring its legs while trying to look the oinker in the eye. The boar began to move. The porker came alive, stood on its hind legs, sprang off the table and charged Mickey. They jabbed at each other and wrestled. Mickey got off some good punches since his arms were longer. The hog connected with his snout a couple of times, which grossed Mickey out.

They had hit the floor when Patricia Drexel appeared in low-rise jeans and a midriff top. She circled them, switching her body in time to the beat. Did she come to see if Mickey Shannon could wallop a hog? The circle of dancers surrounding them, dressed in tank tops and low risers, jigged in unison around the room.

I couldn't believe I was wearing low risers. I sucked in my stomach and slapped my hand over my navel.

When the music stopped abruptly, Mickey had a choke hold on the hog. He threw off the hog in a wild, aimless gesture. It hit Mindy and bounced off, crashed against Knobs and knocked her to the floor. Landing with its backside on her stomach, the hog returned to icy paralysis, its legs splayed skyward and its head swiveled back toward her terrified face.

Everyone froze. After seconds of silence, Professor Carmody glided in, a puff pastry on roller skates. He skidded to a stop and whipped his left skate sideways to the back of his right in perfect T-stop position. He held a baton high and directed invisible musicians who played tinkling strains of medieval music to cleanse the atmosphere.

Ned Barclay materialized at one side of the room. Dressed like a knight in gleaming armor, he parted the crowd. Holly Holmgreen floated in from the other side dressed like Guinevere. Pixie dust surrounded them and floated through the room's inhabitants, clothing them in thirteenth-century splendor.

I glanced down, pleased to see my chest artfully lifted with a tight corset and my navel covered with gauzy fabric that draped to the floor.

The music changed to a dignified waltz. Ned and Holly led the dancing, gazing into each other's eyes. A baby in antiquated swaddling clothes popped out between them, nestled on a tiny silk hassock. They smiled at their new attachment and kept on waltzing.

Sarah Savoy appeared at one side of the room, a snarl on her lips. A frighteningly beautiful medieval witch, wearing a cone hat with glittering streamers and a floor-length Prada coat, she raised a wand high above her head.

"Make sure," she hissed, "you're good parents. Bad parents will destroy the child!"

"Ohhhhhh," the crowd murmured, slithering back en masse from the elegant, fearsome creature.

Sarah shrieked at Holly and Ned. "A hex on you! You will be skewered by King Arthur." She flicked her wand and sprayed the room with evil black sparkle dust.

I woke up gasping for air.

Thirty

I was alone. The black night contributed to my fear. Then I remembered. Somewhere outside in the dark was the police officer Sam had assigned to watch my house. After the gas attack, Sam had instructed him to drive my car home. The clothes I'd put in a locker before the attack lay on top of my dresser. I'd throw them out later. After a while, I felt calm enough to drift to sleep without nightmares.

When I woke up Wednesday morning, I knew I had to get a grip. I must have sniffed too much oxygen up my nose, not to mention Albuterol. That stuff made me crazy. My brain cells were becoming senescent. I practiced deep breathing, brushed my teeth and drank water until I stopped coughing.

I tossed bacon in a skillet and beat three eggs with a fury. With my system free of camphor, ammonia and Clorox, I was starving. Brain food would help me hone in on the creep who was making my life miserable.

Sam and I had agreed that anyone could have substituted bottles filled with liquefied camphor for the club's deodorant bottles. I'd seen the cleaning woman move bottles between locker rooms. Maybe the killer asked the unsuspecting housekeeper to deliver toiletries to the women's dressing area. She'd probably re-supply the most accessible primping station first, which was the one I used. Members frequently asked her for refills. I remembered when Mason Jar obtained hair spray for Knobs.

I inhaled the odor of crackling bacon and salted my eggs.

If the murderer knew his victim's workout schedule, he could have employed another method to deliver poisoned bottles. He could have told a female club member that his wife or friend was out of deodorant and asked the naïve pawn to deliver it to the station he designated. Later, the killer would watch his intended victim. If she looked sick, the killer would know the poisoned bottles were well placed.

Several people saw Holly and me appear ill. Pete Reeves probably overheard me say I felt nauseated when I lingered to talk to Holly at Tofu Temptations Grill. Everybody who attended Sheldon's party certainly knew I was sick. Holly looked unhealthy the few times I saw her. Whoever wanted to kill Holly or me knew his poison was on target.

My eggs were superb. I'd forgotten how great food tasted. I consumed two pieces of toast, one with butter and one with apple butter. With my stomach full, I could study. Since I missed Carmody's Monday and Tuesday classes for two weeks and didn't want to be booted out, I had to get busy.

The syllabus said we would discuss heart disease. I recalled some scientists thought if they could eradicate heart disease, they could extend average life span by almost ten years. This was incredible news, yet Professor Carmody haughtily dismissed it. In addition to reading my notebook, I researched the subject online.

I studied all day, stopping only to devour a small peanut butter sandwich before I showered and dressed for the professor's Wednesday session of enlightenment.

I drove to University of the Holy Trinity and pranced into class smiling.

"How are you, Dr. Carmody?" I pronounced his name carefully. I was afraid I previously called him something else. His eyes widened. My reappearance apparently crushed his hopes.

"Flu bug." I slipped to my seat, hoping he was too stunned to uestion my absence. Sitting ramrod straight, I displayed strict control of my faculties in case my demeanor during our last class together had been less than decorous. I flipped through my notebook with intense interest.

Carmody rolled his eyes and looked toward heaven for help. "Today, we'll discuss heart disease, especially in women. Dr. Jenna Tranham, Director of the Women's Heart Health Institute, Southern University Medical Center, says cardiovascular disease accounts for nearly fifty percent of deaths in developed and developing countries. The risk of dying from heart disease is greater than the risk from AIDS and all forms of cancer combined."

He flicked me a sideways glance. I remembered Sam saying chlorine gas could have given me a heart attack.

"However, the doctor reports good news. Although more people in our aging population have heart disease, death rates from it are falling. In some cases, doctors can stop a heart attack in its tracks. They can treat heart rhythm problems and heart failure and give people with heart disease many more years of high quality life." He smiled at everyone in the room, avoiding eye contact with me.

"Dr. Tranham says the number of men who die from heart attacks decreased every year since 1979. But over the same time period, fatal heart attacks among women increased. Nearly one in two women dies of cardiovascular disease." He stared at me dead on.

That cinched it: I would resume exercising and adopt a healthy diet. I wasn't about to thrill Professor Carmody by dying. He didn't know my heart was strong enough to survive ingesting poison and careening down a flight of stairs. He covered some well-known facts and spent the remaining class time blah-blahing about statistics. By the time class ended, my mind had wandered to suspects at the health club.

I cranked up my Wagoneer and drove east on Hildebrand, thinking about my attempted murder in the shower. A woman could have tossed in balloons, but if the killer was a man, how did he enter the women's locker room without being noticed?

For the club's Ten Year Celebration, I remembered the staff left locker room doors ajar so prospective customers could tour the entire facility. They partitioned off changing areas and showers for members by constructing flimsy corridors—standing wood frames with fabric stapled on them. I'd heard visitors speaking through the fabric and felt uneasy walking unclothed to the shower with strangers clomping around on the other side. If somebody wanted to peek around the barrier, he could easily peel back a section of material.

I pictured the killer lurking unnoticed in the foyer among members and visitors, waiting until he saw me enter the locker room. He could pretend to tour the women's area, slip stealthily through the barrier and head for my shower.

I almost missed my turn onto Burr Road. I wheeled right at the last minute, thankful nobody was tailgating me.

If the culprit carried balloons, no one would notice. Balloons were everywhere. If someone saw him slip in or out of the partitioned area, he could say he got lost or was curious about the women's facilities. Harry Thorne could go anywhere without raising suspicion.

When I arrived home, I bounded inside to get my Big Chief tablet. I wanted to make a list of pros and cons for every suspect who could have killed Holly, starting with Harry Thorne. I placed it on the dining table and began to write.

Harry Thorne

Pros
Embarrassed by Holly.
Devastated by Holly.
Wanted kids (Holly's baby).
Had easy access.

Cons
Capable of killing niece?
Harry & car easy to identify.
Was sick when I was.
If caught, he disgraced his club.

Harry and Holly's history was so bizarre anything was possible.

I peered at my living room photos. When I'd perused photographs in Holly's apartment, I focused on the men I knew, but Holly had undoubtedly dated men I didn't know. I should have studied more faces in her pictures. Somebody captured on film could have been waiting in line at the celebration or working out somewhere in the club. I should have been more observant. I doubted I could riffle through Holly's apartment again. Sam had probably padlocked the door.

I thought about the men I knew. Holly had dated Mickey, Ned, Sheldon and probably Pete. I knew her involvement with the first three had ended in conflict. If Pete made her suffer using weight machines like he did me, she probably scratched him off her list as soon as she could grip her pencil. I didn't know enough about Pete to list pros and cons, but I thought his ego paralleled Mickey's. I knew he lacked patience. Maybe he was impatient with Holly, she flipped him off, and he killed her.

As for attempts on my life, I'd made all the men angry, so it was difficult to single one out. Since I believed Holly's murder was linked to attacks against me, and we had both associated with Sheldon, I decided to hone in on him. I picked up my pencil.

Sheldon was painfully serious about the magazine he edited, his knowledge of cuisine and his food choices. When I embarrassed him in front of San Antonio's culinary elite at a party he'd planned for a year, swarming with media, his hatred of me became intense. Not only did I ruin the most important event in his life by becoming ill at the sight of his delicacies, I might have hurt subscriptions to his prized magazine and jeopardized his livelihood.

Remembering his predatory attitude toward me in the elevator, I shivered. To comfort myself, I padded to the kitchen and ate a banana smeared with peanut butter. Did madness hide behind Sheldon's food fetish?

I thought about Holly. She was basically a sweet little thing, but she didn't strike me as a girl who became serious until she was forced to make a life-altering decision. Before she got pregnant, I pictured her as a delightful little waif who loved to dress up, party and date every available man. She worked Harry over because he and Arnold gave her whatever she wanted. I remembered how her closet overflowed with clothes.

I opened the refrigerator and poured myself a glass of milk.

Holly and Sheldon might have used drugs together, judging from Sheldon's supply. He would have hidden the bad stuff. If Sheldon were into drugs, he would have told Holly what to take, just like he told people what to eat. Once he became seriously controlling, I imagined Holly pirouetted out of the relationship. Sheldon, self-absorbed and positive he was always right, wouldn't have appreciated her independence.

I thought about the note in Holly's shoe. I'd assumed that Harry wrote it, but maybe it was Sheldon. Holly probably viewed her dates with him as a lark, whereas I doubted Sheldon took a light view of anything. Did he kill Holly for jilting him? Maybe she enraged him by dumping him at a previous Party of the Year. That could have done it.

I strode back to the dining table, reached for my Big Chief tablet and flipped to a clean page. Sheldon roared at me like an angry beast on the grassy slope outside Fit and Firm. Did he roar because I'd ruined his party or because he was shocked to see me alive?

Sheldon Snodgrass

Pros
Controlling food nut who failed to change Holly.

Holly probably ruined his party.

He gave Holly drugs. Did she threaten to tell?

Cons

Would he risk his magazine's reputation by killing somebody?

Sheldon's list was lopsided. I was suddenly exhausted from thinking about being murdered by the health club weirdo, assuming I didn't die first from heart disease.

To rest my mind, I flipped back to Carmody's notebook. For Thursday's class, he had scheduled "The Importance of Exercise," which wouldn't require much study. Pete, Mickey and Ned could write a dissertation on that subject. Unfortunately, one of them might be trying to kill me.

Thirty-One

First thing Thursday morning, I stuffed toast in my mouth and called Meredith. "Hey, I feel great. What are you doing tomorrow morning?"

"Gee...I don't know. What are you thinking?"

"I feel fabulous but fat. Want to work out? The club received clearance to reopen Friday morning. They're giving special discounts to the first two hundred people who show up."

"I can't believe you want to go back there. Does Sam know about this?"

"Not exactly. When he sees us there, he'll know we're fine. In the meantime, he has this patrol officer driving by and lurking outside my house to protect me. It's driving me crazy. I really need to work out. It'll be therapeutic after all the stress." I coughed.

"Agatha, you're impossible. Have you forgotten you almost got killed over there?"

"No, but whoever did it won't try that stunt again. No balloons. It'll take the creep a while to come up with something new. Just think, we might get a cheap six-month membership. This is our chance to maintain our workout routine. My body is just beginning to firm up."

The "firm" part wasn't exactly true. I hadn't eaten much except peanut butter for a week and was probably aging from malnutrition.

"Why don't we wait until the police find this crazy person and Holly's killer and then go back to the club?"

Meredith relied on logic. She couldn't help it. Sometimes her logic was really a pain. "Because we'll have to wait forever and pay full membership price."

"Yes, but..."

"Look. Police will be swarming the place. The balloon creep knows they're searching for him and so does Holly's killer. They're not about to try anything. This is the perfect time to go."

"Well, I don't know..."

"Okay. Think about this: We sign up and get the discount, then we leave. Or I find Sam or a police officer, tell him we're there, and we go ahead and work out."

"Well..."

"While you're thinking, let me tell you how we can slip past this cop and get to the club..."

I had deliberated about how to elude Sam's police officer and reach the club without being followed. It occurred to me Boffo might help, so I powered up my computer and searched through dog sites until I found "Earthdog Startup Training." It was exactly what I needed. I put my Big Chief tablet nearby to make notes. I clicked to a history of terrier/dachshund combinations like Boffo that explained how to train them to become good earthdogs. Boffo would have the opportunity to exhibit his proud heritage.

"Even an older dog," I read, "whose instincts have never been challenged, but lie beneath the surface waiting for that special moment to arrive, may prove to be the finest working terrier or dachshund in the kennel." There it was in black and white. Boffo had the chance to be a star.

The article described how to train a dog to develop his instinct to chase vermin through tunnels, route them out of burrows and capture them. It said the trainer should start by tantalizing the dog with a rat in a cage. "An adult dog, depending on the strength of his instincts, may easily accomplish cage training in one or two sessions." Boffo was about to fulfil his destiny. I steered my Wagoneer to the Austin Highway pet store and bought a laboratory rat, an 8" x8" x6" cage, rat food and doggie treats. The rat was kind of cute. I named him Addison. I took him home in his new cage, set it just outside my front door and threw in a few rat treats. My feet itched ferociously. After stuffing doggie treats in the pocket of my jeans, I bounced over to Grace's house and knocked on her door. "I hope I'm not bothering you."

"No. I'm trying to keep Boffo quiet so I can play the piano."

He flopped over my tennis shoe and growled, chewing the laces. I wondered if my insurance covered dog attacks. "If you put his leash on, I'll take him for a walk."

"Would you do that? That would be great."

"Sure. Before we go, I wonder if you have any clothes I can use for the military-civilian party at BAMC in March. I volunteered for the committee. We thought it might be fun to dress like people did during World War II. I know you were a child then, but I thought maybe you saved something from a relative."

"I kept a couple of items from Aunt Justa's war years. How about her boxy shoulder-padded jacket? I might even have one of her skirts."

"Perfect. Do you have one of those big hats they wore? The kind that covers your hair?"

"You bet. Aunt Justa kept a knitted snood women wore to keep their hair from tangling in machines when they worked in war production factories. She also had a big, floppy hat she called her 'nineteen forty-two' hat. You can use those. I don't have any shoes, though. I threw them out. Wait, I know. What about wearing Charlie's old Army boots? I saved a pair. I'll trap Boffo in the bathroom, and we'll have a look."

It was wonderful living next door to a pack rat. Grace dragged out boxes from the storage closet in the girls' old bedroom. We'd started rifling through containers when the doorbell rang. Grace answered the door and returned with Elmore Moseley carrying an armload of books.

"You know Elmore, don't you?"

"Yes." I managed to smile. "We met out front one day."

"Hello, again. I thought I ought to bring these back, Grace, before I take any more."

She smiled lovingly at the old sneak while she retrieved books from the top of his pile. "Elmore loves science. He's been enjoying the girls' collection."

My blood started to boil. SAPD had encouraged the old snoop to dig through her daughters' books? I wanted to throw them at him. It was smarter to see what titles he found so interesting: *Basic Chemistry; Plants and their Properties; Chemical Compounds in the Workplace; Fabrics with Panache: The History and Components of Textiles....*

"You're interested in science?" I smiled sweetly.

"Yes. As a business major, I studied only basic science. Now I'm satisfying my curiosity."

The old busybody.

"We have more books in the closet," Grace said.

"I have enough for now. I'm reading their research papers. With Linda studying chemistry, and Kim studying textiles for interior design, I'm learning a lot. It's a good thing they had the computer for writing papers."

"You have their computer?" I asked.

"I never use it," Grace said. "Elmore enjoys it, and I got the ugly machine out of this room."

I bet he enjoyed it, the meddlesome old coot.

"Let's think of something to do on Friday, maybe drive to the hill country." He winked at Grace. "I'll let myself out."

Cozy. Maybe Grace would get lucky and Elmore would tumble off a hill. The more I thought about Elmore's invasion, his pawing through books and documents that belonged to Grace's children, the madder I became at Sam.

After he left, Grace and I resumed sifting through her keepsake garments. Her clothes were exactly what I needed. Even Charlie's clunky boots fit me pretty well. The whole dowdy outfit was perfect.

Grace attached Boffo's leash, and he strained for the door.

"I'm going to let him sniff around our yards before we take off. After I bring him back, I'll take your clothes home and try them on, if it's all right."

"Sure. That's fine."

Grace was at the piano when we left. While she warmed up playing scales, I took Boffo around the outside of her backyard and took off his leash beside the fence. Just as I'd hoped, he wriggled under her fence and dug into his escape hole. Grace, oblivious to us, sang joyously.

When he burrowed into his cavity, I heard a varmint squeal. Grace was right: a rat lived in the underground hole. I scratched open the outlet in my yard and heard Boffo chasing the critter toward me through the tunnel. Poised at my end of the passage with a doggie treat, I leaned over the exit hole so my voice would carry inside.

"Addison alert. Addison alert," I called. The earthdog article said to repeat the same phrase to train the dog.

When the rat surfaced, I dropped the doggie treat. It almost hit Boffo on the head. He screeched to a halt, glanced at the escaping rat but went for the treat. He chomped and gazed at me lovingly while I re-attached his lease. We were bonding.

From there, the mutt and I sprinted to the front curb where he peed on my bush near the street. I used the opportunity to give him another treat and lengthen his leash. Then I ran him back toward the house where I'd stationed Addison in his cage, just outside my front door. Boffo sniffed and pointed his ears. He had spotted the quarry.

"Addison alert," I chirped.

Addison twitched, and Boffo lunged. When his nose was about four inches from Addison's cage, I yanked Boffo's leash taut. With his tongue hanging out, he sniffed and strained, circling his prey. The more he sniffed, the more excited he got. I gave his leash more slack. He barked louder, becoming more and more aggressive. Fortunately, Grace played and sang too loudly to hear him. Addison put his tiny feet over his eyes, balled up and rolled to the corner of his cage.

With the rat immobilized, Boffo appeared to lose interest. I'd attached a rope to Addison's cage and hidden it in the hedges, so I grabbed the end and gave the rope a yank to stir up Addison. "Addison alert. Addison alert."

When Addison rolled across the cage, Boffo went wild. I tightened his leash to keep him from biting the cage. When I yanked the rope again, Boffo strained harder against the leash and made frantic digging motions on my concrete porch. I let him bite the cage a couple of times, hoping Addison wouldn't die from fright. When I thought Boffo's feet might be getting a little sore from scraping cement, I tossed him a tidbit to distract him from the cage and pulled his leash toward the west side of my house. He bounded toward me. The pooch was getting the idea.

We charged around my house toward the back. When we stopped, he gazed at me, probably expecting another treat. I tossed him a stuffed mouse I'd purchased as a roommate for Addison. Boffo growled with glee, shook it, bit it a thousand times and wrestled the imposter to the ground. When he paused, panting, I flipped him another chewy morsel. He bathed me with grateful eyes. When I reached down to pet him, he rolled over so I could scratch his stomach. He had expended his aggressive behavior. Perfect.

I led him back to the street. We strolled down Burr Road at a respectable pace while I fumed over Elmore Moseley's sniffing through property that belonged to Grace's children.

After attacking, eating and running, Boffo panted hard. Every ten or twelve feet, he flipped around and lunged for my feet, but having nearly captured real prey, his heart wasn't in it. When I yanked his collar and chastised him, he resumed walking like a normal dog. By the time we got back to Grace's house, Boffo had logged in a month's worth of exercise.

"He might be pretty tired," I told Grace.

"It's good for him." When she gave him a dog cookie, I failed to mention he'd already consumed a handful. He burped and plopped in the corner.

Grace handed me her vintage clothes. "I loved playing the piano without Boffo jumping up and down, howling at me. Take him anytime you're going for a walk."

"Okay." I'd already planned to extend Boffo's exercise program. "By the way, I almost forgot. I hear there's a fabulous 8:00 a.m. breakfast concert at the Sunken Garden Theater in Brackenridge Park tomorrow morning. I can't go, but you and Elmore might enjoy it."

"We're both early risers. I'll give him a call. It's my turn to pay for something."

Thirty-Two

After romping with Boffo, I nourished myself with leftovers from the fridge. I brought Addison's cage inside and gave him water and a few treats. After I showered and flexed my arms in front of the mirror to check my tumors, I tried on Grace's clothes to make sure they fit.

While Meredith pondered whether to go to the club on Friday, I had to spend Thursday afternoon with Dr. Carmody at University of the Holy Trinity. When it was almost time for class, I dressed in a cotton sweater and faded jeans to look like a student, while I tried to remember what I'd read about exercise and aging.

I drove to the university and slid quietly to my seat. My mind was so full of plans, I didn't intend to contribute much to the discussion.

Carmody launched into the benefits of exercise. It was difficult to endure his proclamations with him in such lousy shape. My silence seemed to make him uneasy. Every now and then, he glared at me, probably expecting an interruption. Although stress and loathing emanated from his beady eyes, he was apparently resigned to endure me. He didn't have grounds to expel me. His satisfaction would come at the end of the semester when he would issue me the lowest grade possible.

He blabbed about muscle mass: "Without exercise, muscle mass declines twenty-two percent between ages thirty and seventy." I calculated that my puny biceps had already shrunk five and a half percent. If I made it to age seventy, without exercise I'd resemble spaghetti.

Carmody didn't look like he had any muscles. Soft and pliable, he appeared to be composed of tendons covered with rubber. My classmates gazed out the window.

"Exercise," he droned, "prevents losing muscle mass. Tufton University conducted a study where ninety-year-old residents of Nebraska's Hebrew Rehabilitation Center for the Aged increased leg muscle strength by one hundred seventy-five percent and muscle size by nine percent after only eight weeks of weightlifting." It appeared I'd have to return to Machine Mecca.

Carmody said bone loss could be prevented by eating foods rich in Calcium and Vitamin D: dairy products, dark green, leafy vegetables, salmon, which I loved, and tofu, which made me gag. Three students dozed.

He quoted *Getting Fit for Life*, an article from the National Institute of Health: "Lack of physical activity and not eating the right foods, taken together, are the second greatest underlying cause of death in the United States. Smoking is number one."

That assumed no one succeeded in bumping you off at the health club.

"Exercise helps older people feel better and enjoy life," he announced. "No one is too old or too out of shape to be more active." How could the bloated bird make that statement with a straight face?

He shot me a warning glance and launched into statistics: "A National Long-Term Care Survey reports disability among older Americans declined dramatically from nineteen eighty-nine through nineteen ninety-six, and the percentage continues to fall. Moreover, two hundred thousand fewer people live in nursing homes."

That was good news. I didn't want to escape being murdered at Fit and Firm just to register at the nursing home. He said many older people enjoyed a satisfying sex life, no matter their age. This combination of data reinforced my belief in a vitally important heath issue: Sam and I should get together.

To wake up the class, Carmody made us read, *What's Your*

Aging IQ? and take a test. It was simplistic, but I learned a few things: the fastest growing segment of the American population, people over age eighty-five, was expected to grow five times larger within the next fifty years. The Census Bureau predicted that by 2050, more than a million people in the U.S. would be over a hundred. I could look forward to being one of the younger members at Fit and Firm.

When Carmody repeated the obvious—keeping an active mind, eating well and staying physically active helped people remain alert—I could no longer remain silent. I knew I was on shaky ground, having endured only two weeks of the long spring semester.

I felt compelled to quote my findings from a Yale University's study: "If a person has passion...a cause, a purpose, that gets him or her up, out and going," I said, "that person stays young."

"You go, girl!" a student bellowed. "Ahl right!" another shouted.

One kid actually clapped.

While Dr. Carmody smoldered, I stood and turned to acknowledge their enthusiasm. As a gesture of courtesy, I attempted to contain my glee. My test grades would be too good for him to fail me. Carmody and I were fated to tolerate each other through May.

Age was teaching me patience. Nodding respectfully to my professor, I dashed out the door before the old curmudgeon exploded.

Thirty-Three

Having added Dr. Carmody to the growing list of people who'd like to see me dead, I hopped in my Wagoneer and drove off campus fast. My outburst was partially due to agitation about what I planned to do on Friday morning.

On the drive home, I tried to recall details of what had happened before and after the gas attack. I couldn't remember what preceded the chaos, except that I was pleased with the celebration, ready to shower and perturbed by the thin partitions protecting us from voyeurs. Once the gas erupted, I panicked and couldn't remember anything except that I'd heard Harry bellow. I saw Mindy and Knobs, a few instructors, and Sam, Mickey, Ned and Sheldon before techs hurled me into the ambulance.

When I arrived home, I threw my notebook from Dr. Carmody's class on the sofa, grabbed my Big Chief tablet and thought about Mickey Shannon. I pictured him enjoying Holly's delicate beauty contrasting with his masculinity. Consorting with Holly would accentuate his height, muscles and strength—everything he cherished. He wouldn't like it if Holly jilted him, especially when she chose Ned Barclay over him. Mickey would assume he controlled their relationship. I thought about the note in her shoe. I couldn't imagine Mickey writing he was "sorry to be possessive" or admitting that he "cared."

Mickey possessed a terrific ego, which was understandable since he was a drop-dead-gorgeous Irish-Greek god. But his ego would get tiresome. One could never seriously discuss anything, or disagree, or joke with him about his idiosyncrasies. His ego would block you like a concrete fullback. I doubted Holly really cared about that. She probably just got bored. When Ned came along, she found him an attractive new challenge.

Women flocked around Mickey. I doubted he'd ever suffered rejection. He was probably the one who decided when a liaison ended. I doodled on the page. Could a jilted Mickey be a dangerous Mickey, furious enough to kill? I ripped off my doodle page to start a fresh sheet.

Mickey Shannon

Pros
Hunk not used to rejection.
Could not control Holly.
Temper, temper.

Cons
If jailed as a murderer, has to give up women.

I put down the tablet and realized I was getting hungry.

Then I thought about Ned Barclay—dear, considerate, serious Ned. Sarah was probably right. Holly and Ned fell in love, and she became pregnant.

That's when she stopped going to the health club. It seemed to me Ned Barclay would love someone truly and consistently, forever. If Holly told Ned she was pregnant, he'd be overjoyed at the thought of their having a child. He'd want to marry her immediately to spare her embarrassment.

What if Holly didn't want to marry? Didn't want to be a mother? Maybe she was having too good a time, dating all the available men and wondering who she'd missed. Her attitude would have hurt Ned terribly. He might plead with her. What if he became controlling and demanded she marry him and have his child?

I thought about the note again: "Sorry to be possessive. I know you hate restrictions. It's just that I care." Those words sounded like something Ned would write.

The memory of what Holly said came back to me. She told me the baby's father had denied paternity. She thought DNA testing was useless because he was completely disinterested in fatherhood. That didn't sound like Ned Barclay.

I laid my tablet aside and tromped to the kitchen for a Coke. I popped popcorn in the microwave and put butter in a cup to melt.

The other possibility was that Holly had lied. Her sweetness and vulnerability made me feel sorry for her—sorry enough to convince me she spoke the truth. What if she were merely a flake who played around, a girl who didn't see any difference between men like Mickey, Sheldon, Ned, Pete or Harry Thorne because she didn't really care? Suppose deep down, she hated all men, beginning with her father, Billy, and continuing through her conflict with Harry and Arnold. I poured butter over the popcorn, blended it in with both hands and licked my fingers.

Suppose Ned pleaded with Holly, pushing her farther and farther away. I scooped popcorn into my mouth. Suppose she declared she'd never marry him. She'd give away their baby, and he'd never see his child. He might erupt. Pushed to the limit, Ned Barclay might, in a fit of anger and despair, run Holly over. I crunched popcorn, handful after handful, until the bowl was almost empty.

Saving a few juicy kernels, I carried the bowl to the sofa, cleaned my fingers with a napkin and picked up my tablet. Had Ned flipped out? Did he try to kill me because I tried to help Holly? Did he discover, somehow, that I'd also given up my child? Ned's hatred, like his sadness and embarrassment, ran very deep. I started writing:

Ned Barclay

Pros
Loved Holly but she flew the coop.

Holly gave up his baby.
Devastated, he flipped out.
Temper, temper.

Cons
Could he kill girl he loved?
Too sensitive to commit murder?

There was one sure way to find out who killed Holly and wanted me dead. I would confront the men with what I knew. If one of them was the killer, he'd make his move.

I scrounged in the bowl for the last of the popcorn. Sam wouldn't approve of my plan, but I didn't intend to tell him about it. When the club opened Friday morning, the regulars would be there including Sheldon, Ned, Mickey and Pete.

Mindy, Doorknobs, Patricia and Sarah might be there, too, although I couldn't imagine a motive the women would have for killing Holly. I knew Mindy, Doorknobs and Patricia didn't like me, and I could imagine Patricia Drexel giving me a shove down the stairs. It was harder to picture her as a murderer.

Harry Thorne would definitely be at the club. The other men would probably arrive early on Friday since they hadn't been able to exercise for days.

Sam said Harry had placed newspaper ads to reassure current and prospective members that Fit and Firm had reopened and was better than before. I'd have to confront the suspects before Sam showed up.

I finished the popcorn and carried my bowl to the kitchen. With the club offering discounts to the first people who signed up, the facility would be bustling with activity Friday. That would make my job easier.

Thirty-Four

By 8:00 a.m. Friday, I'd packed my satchel, a larger version of the gym bag I'd used to pilfer toiletries. Still in my nightclothes, I scurried to the hedges near the street, hid the bag and scooted back to my house. My Garfield sleep shirt fell six inches above my knees. I ruffled up my black hair until I looked thoroughly frowzy and waited for Sam's police officer snitch to cruise by. Before long, he came creeping along my curb in his patrol car, squinting at my bungalow like he was casing a nest of Columbian drug lords.

I ran out my back door, detoured toward Grace's property and hissed, "Addison alert, Addison alert," slurring the words together so they held meaning only for Boffo. I knew he'd burrow under her fence and scurry through the varmint tunnel. I tossed a doggie treat near his escape hole in my yard. He blasted out, grabbed the treat and followed me to the front yard.

I charged toward the officer's car screaming, "Help! Help! Somebody's after me!"

The officer screeched on his brakes, bounded from the car and barreled toward me.

"He's in the back. The perp is trying to get in the back," I shrieked, wide-eyed. "Addison alert. Addison alert," I mumbled.

The cop squinted, looking confused by my nonsensical words. Eyes wary, he yanked his pistol from the holster and streaked toward my house. Boffo charged after him, pounced on his shoe and growled up at him, expecting a treat. The cop tried to shake him off. "Damn dog."

"Don't shoot him. He's my neighbor's pet." Grace and Elmore were enjoying breakfast at the Sunken Garden.

"I hope the suspect doesn't escape through the front!" I'd left my front door wide open. "Addison Alert, Addison alert," I chirped. The officer, staring at me like I was a lunatic, hobbled to my house, struggling to shake Boffo off his shoe while he tried to close my front door.

I'd wrapped green string around the furry toy that happily cohabitated with Addison and had hidden the end of the string in shrubs near my door. While the officer tried to dislodge Boffo, I swooped down, murmuring sympathetic words, and surreptitiously yanked the string. Intoxicated with new vermin smell, Boffo bounced away to attack the furry imposter. While the officer locked my door, keeping one eye on the growling terrier, I flailed my arms and flew around to bolster his view of my dementia, passing close to the front hedges to check my hidden bag while I kept the officer in view.

Racing back toward the house, I swept low, grabbed the twine attached to the stuffed rat and gave it a couple more yanks to stimulate Boffo's aggressive behavior. Boffo growled so ferociously, the officer jumped six inches. Having secured my door, he was probably calculating whether the intruder would shoot him before Boffo attacked.

Having immobilized his prey, Boffo got bored. When the officer moved away from the door and sprinted around the side of the house, Boffo jumped to the challenge. He was back in the game. He charged after the cop and sprang onto his shoe. Clamping squatty legs around his captured vermin, he chomped his teeth into the cop's pant leg.

"Aggh!" He should have brought doggie treats. Cursing and stumbling, the police officer lurched around the side of my house with Boffo attached. He was making so much noise, an intruder could have taken off for the next county.

Boffo made me proud. Growling viciously, he wasn't about to relinquish his prey. He had mastered cage training and tunnel training and clung stubbornly to his captive. I thought he was ready for AKC's official Earthdog Test.

I smiled at the satisfying sight of pooch attached to the officer's leg, but I couldn't hang around for the finale. I scrambled back to the front yard, dove into my bag, grabbed Grace's frumpy oversized jacket and wrestled it over my head to cover my Garfield shirt. Crouching down, I wriggled the skirt Grace gave me up over the bottom of my nightshirt. Plastering the snood over my hair, I pushed stragglers inside and wrenched Aunt Justa's homely wide-brimmed hat over the top.

When the Ford Taurus approached and slowed near the police vehicle, I was digging for Charlie's boots. Clutching my bag with the boots still inside, I sprinted for the Ford and leaped in. Meredith stomped the gas pedal.

"Don't screech the tires," I yelled. "He'll hear you."

She backed off the pedal, drove thirty-four miles per hour to New Braunfels and turned right before either one of us exhaled.

Her black long-sleeved dress buttoned down the front to the calf-length hem. She wore thick hose and wide-heeled witchy shoes. A pillbox hat over a droopy black wig covered her light hair.

I started to laugh. "Where did you find that get-up?"

"I told Mom I was going to a costume party. She rummaged through my grandmother's trunk."

"I recognized your Taurus, but for a second after I jumped in, I thought I'd gotten in the wrong car."

"You look absolutely awful," she said. "Like a bag lady."

"I know. Check these brogans." I tugged on Charlie's heavy boots. I hoped I wouldn't have to run.

"They're gross."

"Did you get fake drivers' licenses," I asked, "in case the officer catches us? I'd hate for SAPD to find out who we are."

"No, I couldn't figure out how to pilfer licenses from senior citizens."

"That's okay. If another cop stops us before we make it to the club, you can say you left your license in another purse. He'll give you a ticket, but when you take your actual driver's license to court, you can say you were dressing for a costume party and forgot to put it in your purse. I'll tell him I don't drive. They really hate to pick on old people."

She exploded with laughter. "Agatha, I am amazed at the extent of your devious mind."

Frankly, I was, too. Sometimes you had to get creative. People put too much emphasis on aging. We'd outfoxed a young police officer, could probably outrun him and were having more fun than a couple of twelve-year-olds.

We made it to Fit and Firm and glided into a parking spot in the garage. Under our disguises, and under my Garfield sleep shirt, we wore workout clothes. My rolled-up leggings were killing me. We stripped down to T-shirts and rolled down our leggings. Underneath everything else, I had on a new swimsuit.

We pulled off the weird garb, dabbed on makeup and bustled toward the entrance. It was time to get serious. The frustrated officer had probably notified Sam, who would go to my house and tromp through every square inch of it to make sure I wasn't there and hadn't been abducted. Then he'd think about where I was and start fuming like a bull. I figured I had two hours, max, to confront the suspects before Sam showed up and spoiled everything.

Thirty-Five

When we approached the club's entrance, I saw somebody had removed the sign advertising the club's ten-year anniversary. In its place, they'd taped a sheet of paper to the glass door:

ATTENTION NEW AND RETURNING MEMBERS: Six Months
FIT AND FIRM Memberships
Half-Price for the first 200 people who sign up.

Meredith looked pleased. When we stepped inside, a dozen people stood in line. Waiting around could ruin my scheme. Fortunately, an employee behind the check-in desk broke everyone into two lines, one for new members and one for returnees. Eleven people moved to the other line, leaving only one person ahead of us. The club had our paperwork on file, and we already possessed club ID cards. Registering for the discount wouldn't take long.

While we waited, I peered across the lobby into Tofu Temptations Grill. The place opened for breakfast, but few people ate there. The room was empty except for one man who sat alone at a table studying the menu: Sheldon Snodgrass. If I could get past the grill without his seeing me, I could start exercising with Meredith, slip back downstairs before he left and corner him.

We checked in and registered for six month, half-price memberships.

"Isn't this great?" I asked Meredith.

As we passed Tofu Temptations Grill, I edged to Meredith's right side, putting her between Sheldon and me in case he glanced up. We climbed the steps to the third floor and picked two treadmills with the best view of the TV. I allowed time for us to program the machines and settle in before I announced I had to use the bathroom.

"Don't go to the ladies' locker room. Use the one on this floor."

We could see the door to the restroom by turning partway around. "Good idea. I'll wait until somebody else goes in so I won't be in there alone."

I knocked on the bathroom door, acted like I was talking to somebody inside, and entered. I stayed a few minutes, peeped out to make sure Meredith was engrossed in TV and sneaked down the stairs.

Sheldon still inhabited the grill. I walked slowly over to him and smiled sweetly. "Hi, Sheldon."

He lifted his fork and glared at me, eyes bulging. "What are you doing in this grill?" I heard a growl in his throat. "Did you decide to come ruin my breakfast?"

I didn't like the menacing way he held his fork. "I just wanted to say hello. The last time I saw you was...unfortunate."

"That's an understatement. Did you decide to come destroy a public eating place, too?"

This was apt to get ugly. I tried not to focus on what he devoured.

"I came to apologize for the way I acted at your party...you know, when I got sick." He growled again.

"I wanted to tell you the reporter from *La Prensa* told me later what a fabulous party you gave. You must have cleaned up quickly because she found the event awesome...the food...the people...everything!" His buggy eyes relaxed back into his head. He put his fork down.

Putting a finger to my lips, I rolled my eyes up. "Or was it the girl from *Flash-News?* Anyway, two different reporters raved to me about the party. Maybe they'll both write it up."

Sheldon licked his lips. "By the way, how are you feeling?"

"Better. Much better." I hung my head. "Sometimes I get depressed about Holly."

"Hmmm." He stuffed a mystery clump in his mouth.

"What's that you're eating? It looks really good."

"Soy and tofu pancakes drizzled with roasted honey," he mumbled, chomping.

"You have unique taste in food." Thank goodness I wasn't nauseated.

He nodded and continued ruminating.

"I guess Holly loved to eat exotic things, too?"

"Not really. She went for ordinary protein and salad...totally without imagination."

"After you dated her a while, surely you introduced her to some of the delicacies you love."

"I tried, but she just wanted to dance and party. She loved to be in the middle of lots of people. The only reason she ate at all was so she could keep moving."

"That must have disappointed you."

"Well, I've dealt with a lot of carnivores. They eat the same disgusting animal products...never branch out. That's why, in addition to vegetarian dishes, I highlight exotic meats for the misguided omnivores who attend my *Euphoria* parties."

I tried not to think about the hog.

"Holly did seem sort of rigid, uptight, like maybe she needed tranquilizers."

"I gave her some once so she'd relax, but she didn't like the feeling they gave her. Pills didn't change her eating habits, anyway."

"Then I guess she didn't use other drugs."

"Oh, no. I wouldn't allow it."

He apparently thought he'd controlled Holly. Temporarily.

"Why work out and eat healthy food," he masticated half a pancake, "if you're going to put junk in your body? I have two uncles who come over all the time, and I have to keep a whole stock of medicines for them. That's bad enough."

I molded my face into an image of sympathy. He concentrated on chewing.

"It's good to see you," I lied, backing away.

"Don't forget to remind the reporters about my party." He waved his fork with his mouth full of food.

I smiled encouragingly. He'd probably scour two publications for two months before he called the editors or confronted me.

He didn't appear to be sufficiently emotionally involved with Holly to have a motive to kill her. Either that or he was an accomplished liar. He was definitely more interested in food than people—a real cold fish. Of course, he could be acting nonchalant and biding his time while he hated me to the depths of his purified colon.

Even if Sheldon had tried to kill me, I knew I was safe from him for a while. He had to preserve me as his media contact.

Thirty-Six

It was time to check in with Meredith. I ran upstairs to the treadmills.

"Where did you go?" she said. "I was getting worried."

"My calves cramped, so I decided to find a police officer and tell him we're here, then go to the weight room. Want to go?"

"I've only done twenty minutes on the treadmill. In twenty-five more minutes, I'll do weights. Now that we're actually here, we might as well do everything."

"Okay. I'll finish the weight room circuit. If my calf muscles un-kink, I'll come back here and do cardio." My strategy was working. Meredith was happily occupied, leaving me free to implement my plans. I hoped to find Ned Barclay and Pete Reeves in the weight room.

As I scooted down one side of the basketball court on my way to Machine Mecca, I passed Mickey Shannon leaning over the water fountain. His leg muscles bulged all the way to his gluteus maximus.

"Hi." I made it a two-syllable word.

He straightened up, apparently surprised to see me. It looked like he started to scowl but produced a smile. Since he'd last seen me on a stretcher, and I'd weaseled out of his grasp a few days before that, he seemed confused about how to respond. Smiling provocatively, I batted my lashes.

"Sorry I was in such a rush the day you wanted to talk." I gazed skyward as though I had a revelation. Then I peered at him, wide-eyed, "Do you ever do laps in the pool?"

His pupils enlarged. "Sure." A grin spread across his face. "I'm going to do thirty minutes in Cardio Boot Camp, but we can swim after that."

I moved closer and traced a finger over his bicep. He flexed. "You're in great shape, Mickey. I'll see you at the pool in forty minutes." I turned to go and winked over my shoulder. I could practically hear him panting as I switched my body, not too fast, toward the weight room.

When I spotted Pete Reeves, he was helping a young blond operate a leg machine. His blue eyes were glued to her every move. I bet he didn't make her lie down on the floor and clamp weights on the ends of her bar.

I saw Ned at the back of the room. He was working on the stomach crunch machine and appeared accessible. He saw me coming and gasped. With his feet slapped onto the platform and his torso crunched over the bar, it was hard for him to escape. I planted myself in front of him.

"Hi, Ned. I'm awfully sorry about what happened with the leg extension machine."

He turned scarlet and did a dozen more crunches bobbing his head up and down, which made me dizzy but gave me the opportunity to talk. "I saw some beautiful pictures of you and Holly."

He popped up, surprised, and stared needles at me. "My relationship with Holly is none of your concern." He shifted out of the machine and walked to the angled, wide-grip pull down. He wrenched the bar down to his chest and started yanking the bar up and down so fast he made a human fan.

The pulley for working biceps was near him, so I picked up the handle, faced him and tugged it up to my chest. The faster he pulled his bar down, the faster I lifted my handle. It was a terrible stress on my puny muscles.

"Holly was my friend. She told me she cared for you, Ned. Very much."

Suspicion and anger flashed across his face. "Why would she

tell you that?" He released the wide grip pull down and strode to the seated bench press on the far side of the room. I scurried behind him, slipped onto the pectoralis fly next to him and scanned the instructions: "With arms at ninety-degree angles, touch elbows in front of chest." I strained to push my elbows inward. Not much happened. Didn't those yo-yos realize pectoral muscles were smothered by boobs?

While I puzzled the problems of anatomy, Ned dashed to the seated hamstring machine. I was afraid he was trying to complete the circuit and flee. Things were getting sticky. He might bolt before I could get anything out of him. I flew to the apparatus next to him, the leg extension machine. Realizing my colossal blunder, I zoomed to his other side, jumped on the back extension machine and assumed the preparatory position with my hands crossed demurely over my chest.

"Sarah Savoy told me you and Holly loved each other."

Ned gritted his teeth. Blood vessels pulsed against his temples. "I thought we did." He struggled to keep his voice low, grinding his words between clenched lips. "She was going to have my baby. That was my child Holly Holmgreen gave away!"

Ned had confirmed my suspicions. He was the father of Holly's baby. She had lied about her child's father denying paternity.

He pushed himself off the machine and stormed out of the room. He charged down the side of the basketball court. His shoulders shook with rage.

Thirty-Seven

I had needled Ned Barclay into a frenzy. I got zilch out of Sheldon, and it was time to meet Mickey. Swell. At least I hadn't bumped into Harry Thorne, which was just as well since I wasn't sure how to approach him. All I could do was forge ahead with the rest of my plan.

At least my timing looked good. Water aerobics had just ended. Sarah would return floater belts and water dumbbells to the equipment room. Mickey would be finishing Cardio Boot Camp, which would give me time to strip down to the swimsuit under my workout clothes.

I raced through the locker room to the storage room to catch Sarah. Sure enough, she was stacking water aerobics equipment on the racks and was about to lock up.

"Sarah, could you leave the room unlocked? Mickey and I want to work out in the pool. We might use a couple pieces of equipment. I'll lock up when we leave."

"Whoa." Sarah had a huge grin on her pretty face. "Don't get carried away and drown." She winked impishly. "Want me to put a 'Pool Closed' sign inside the locker room door?"

"Great idea." I returned her sneaky smile. "When we leave, I'll take the sign down."

"The equipment room's open. You guys have fun." She sauntered back to the ladies' locker room, laughing.

Dashing back to the locker room, I ripped off my workout clothes. My new suit was a bluish-green two-piece with a low-cut, uplifting top. I doubted I'd actually wear it in public. During the next stage of my plan, I'd have to be extremely careful or I might end up modeling my new swimsuit on a slab.

I fluffed my hair, put on lipstick and scampered to the pool, slowing my gait to a provocative swivel in case Mickey had already arrived. Climbing onto the diving board, I sat very straight—stomach in, chest out. I crossed my legs at the ankles and dangled my feet off to one side. Straightening both arms behind me on the board, I gazed with aplomb at the domed ceiling, mimicking the pose swimsuit models struck in magazines.

Mickey ambled in wearing red swim trunks. He'd lightly oiled his body, which made his muscles ripple seductively. He was one gorgeous hunk. He approached me, smiling like Tom Selleck, and planted his hands to either side of me on the board. Looking deep into my eyes, he kissed my cheek. He squared up and kissed me lightly on the lips. Just as his lips slid over my Adam's apple, I swallowed.

Putting my hands against his chest, I pushed gently, hoping my vocal chords could produce speech. "Sarah left the equipment room open," I gurgled, "so we can get a couple of floats for the pool."

"Whatever you want, sweetheart." He helped me off the board, which was fortunate since my knees wanted to buckle. He tickled my back as we walked toward the storage room. I had so much goose flesh, I must have looked like a plucked chicken.

As soon as we entered the room, I headed for the equipment rack, grabbed floating devices and flipped off the light switch.

"Ahl right!" In a leap, Mickey was behind me. I tensed, not sure what to expect. As he spun me around in the dark, I raised one knee, poised to inflict a soccer kick. Mickey nudged me up against the wall. Was he going to grab my throat and choke me? No. He was intent on some serious groping. Fortunately, I'd positioned two water noodles between us.

"Let's go in the water," I croaked. "We'll have more fun in the deserted pool, don't you think? Cool...comfortable..."

"I guess so," he panted. He put an arm around my shoulder so I couldn't escape, grabbed one of the noodles and nudged me, hip-to-hip, out the door. As we approached the pool, the underwater pool lights glared on. Mickey blinked. I spotted a black electric line in the water.

With all the force I could muster, I shoved him away from the edge. The tile was slick. Unfortunately, he crashed hard on his magnificent derriere. I marveled at his string of southern curse words as I scrambled back to the equipment room.

I grabbed the opaque club bottle I'd stashed outside the storage room door, yanked the top off, slipped the mace canister into my other hand, put my finger on the spray button and ran to the circuit box. "Hey!" I shouted.

The figure whirled around and lunged to flip the switch to electrify the line in the water. I aimed at her eyes and sprayed mace at Sarah Savoy.

Something popped out, flew from her face and tinkled when it hit the floor. While she sputtered, I grabbed an Aqua Belt off the rack, yanked her arms behind her back and tied them with the cinch strap. Unfortunately, I positioned myself in the cloud of mace and my eyes caught fire.

"What the...?" Sam appeared in the doorway wearing purple swim trunks, red socks, and beach sandals. Mickey dripped behind him, massaging his gluteus maximus. "I'll be doggoned."

Sam pulled handcuffs out of his swim trunks and snapped them on Sarah. "I believe you dropped your lenses, Miss Livermore. Linda, isn't it?"

"Sarah is really Grace's daughter? Linda?" The brown-haired, brown-eyed girl in Grace's photographs? I couldn't believe it.

"With bleached curly hair and blue contacts, no one pegged you as Linda Livermore, did they?" Sam said.

When I maced her, Linda's hard blue contact lenses had hit the floor.

"How did you know Sarah was Linda?" I asked Sam, fanning my eyes.

212 Nancy G. West

"Linda Livermore's trail led us from California back to San Antonio. Her leaving California fit with the timing of Sarah Savoy's employment here. We matched a picture of Linda her stepbrothers gave us with a photo of Sarah Savoy in the club records. The likeness was unmistakable. We thought Sarah's prints would match the ones on Linda's science books."

"Why would Linda Livermore kill Holly Holmgreen?"

"She wanted Holly's baby. Holly had promised to give her the child but refused to go through with it. Holly placed the baby with Methodist Mission Home, where it was quickly adopted. Ned Barclay told us what happened."

Linda bawled louder. Sam pressed her. "Grace and George wouldn't keep the neighbor's baby for you, would they, Linda? They wouldn't adopt the baby you loved. When George Ball reneged on you, you killed him."

My hands flew to my face. How could she do that? How could Grace's daughter kill the man Grace had married?

"They didn't want those babies," Linda sputtered. "Martha and Holly didn't even *want* their babies! Why wouldn't they let me keep them?" she wailed.

I was amazed that the congenial woman I knew as Sarah Savoy could look so evil. When Grace's daughter, Linda Livermore, transformed herself into Sarah Savoy, she finally got the movie star name she wanted. But the little girl Grace knew had disappeared years ago. I watched Sarah disintegrate into Linda Livermore's skin.

Sam retrieved a cell phone from his purple trunks and told headquarters to send two police officers to Fit and Firm Health Club on Austin Highway. "Looks like we have Holly Holmgreen's killer."

As Sam spoke, Harry Thorne lumbered up. "Sarah Savoy? That bubblehead killed my girl?" Harry's face reddened sideways to his ears.

I faced Harry. "Did you think I knew something about Holly? Is that why you followed me to Las Tapitas Tuesday night?"

Harry stared at the girl he knew as Sarah Savoy. The pain on his face was wrenching. He finally focused on me. "I thought you might know something about why Holly died. She and I had yelled at each other that morning. Before I could catch up with you outside the restaurant, I got sick. I've been sick ever since she died."

"Why did you go to Holly's apartment Wednesday afternoon?"

"I thought I might find something...some reason why somebody wanted to kill her. I'd written her a note. She thought I restricted her, but I just loved her. I wanted to see if she'd kept the note." He glared at Linda Livermore. "Why? Why?"

Harry, overwhelmed with grief and anger, could barely get words out. His eyes filled and he left. Trying to explain to him that Sarah wasn't even Sarah was a horrible prospect. Sam would have to untangle the whole sordid story for poor Harry Thorne.

I turned to Sam with tears streaming down my face. "Do you want Mickey and me to watch Linda while you change your clothes?" He looked very unprofessional. Somebody might snap his picture in that get-up.

"Not a chance. We're all staying right here in this room."

I told him I absolutely had to go to the locker room to wash my hands and flush out my eyes. Linda's eyes burned so much, Sam said I could bring back a wet towel to wipe the mace off her face. Once she felt better, Linda hissed at me not to touch her. "Too bad I couldn't kill you, too," she snarled.

"I don't see why you had to kill anybody," Sam said.

"That baby-faced brat deserved it! She stole every man I dated. Then she got pregnant with Ned and didn't even want the baby. She promised me I could have it. I paid for the doctor, the hospital, everything. Now I'll never have a baby!" Linda was sobbing so hard, she looked ten years older.

"Why not?" I whispered.

"I'm not married...and the gynecologist said..." She shot daggers at me. "It's none of your business what he said. You helped Holly. You liked Holly. You didn't even care what she did. You'd probably give your child away, too." She narrowed her eyes. "When you and I talked in the locker room, I thought that was exactly what you did." She reached in her pocket and flipped something toward me. It was Lee's baby bracelet.

Fortunately, I stood between her and Sam, with my back to him. I caught the bracelet midair and stuffed it down the front of my swimsuit. My heart was beating so hard, I feared it would blast Lee's bracelet out of there. Linda must have found it at my house. She must have stolen my house keys from my locker and let herself in.

Linda squinted her eyes into searing slits. "People like you and Holly deserve to die." She was deranged, but she was frighteningly perceptive. I dared not make eye contact with Sam.

Two SAPD officers strode into the equipment room. One had a chewed pant leg. He gawked at my swimsuit and stared at my face. I looked different with my hair combed, red eyes, and tears streaking down my face.

"Are you...?" He stared at my swimsuit again. "Aren't you the one who...?"

"Never mind, Stanish. Just escort Miss Livermore to the station. We'll get our questions answered in due time."

I tried to appear innocent, but I knew that Sam knew I'd befuddled his officer.

Stanish and the other officer put crime scene tape around the equipment room and escorted Linda Livermore out the door. Sam said he'd drive me home and headed for the men's locker room to change his clothes.

Mickey gaped at me. I think he was trying to decide which one of us should be angrier.

I wiped my eyes with a wet cloth. "If you promise not to grope me, I promise not to deck you near the swimming pool."

He looked at me for a long time before his face cracked. When he exploded with laughter, every woman who heard him probably praised heaven for the wonderful, deep-throated sound. Tiles probably shattered by the pool. I chuckled with him before I turned toward the women's locker room.

I would have to apologize to Ned Barclay another time. Right now, I wasn't up to it. As for Sheldon, he was probably planning his next meal.

Meredith ventured into the locker room. "Aggie, are you all right? I saw police escorting Sarah out of the club. It was her, Sarah Savoy? She's the one who killed Holly and tried to kill you?"

I nodded. "Sarah's real name is Linda Livermore, my neighbor Grace's daughter."

"Why on earth...?"

"Precious Holly Holmgreen stole all Linda's boyfriends. Sarah, who is really Linda, apparently decided Holly might be less competition if she suffered from a little poison. She noted which deodorant spray Holly used and put pulverized mothballs in the bottle. Made from Camphor, mothballs are poisonous. But I used more spray than Holly did, and it made me sick."

"Why did Linda want to kill Holly?"

"Linda apparently can't have children. When she learned Holly was going to give up her baby, she offered to pay Holly's medical expenses if Holly would give her the child. Holly agreed. Once the baby was born and Linda had paid for everything, Holly refused to go through with it. That's when Linda tried to electrocute her in the pool. When I showed up, Linda decided to help rescue her. She was so full of hatred, she rammed Holly with her car.

"Linda is irrational...demented. She concluded that because I sympathized with Holly, I must have given up a child, too. Maybe she thought Holly told me she'd reneged on her promise to give Linda her baby. Maybe she thought I'd figure out she killed Holly, so she came after me." I shrugged. "At least it's over and we're all right. And we have a six-month, half-price membership at Fit and Firm."

"Unbelievable. Unbelievable. Yes, we do. We can work out without wondering what will happen next. I don't know how you'll manage to help your friend Grace."

"I don't know, either."

I was glad Meredith didn't ask me what happened after I left her at the treadmill. We went to the locker room so I could change back into workout clothes, but my clothes were gone. Someone had swiped my pink T-shirt, leggings, and Adidas.

"I'll get your clothes from my car. The bag lady outfit."

I shoved my baby's wristband down to my waist. When Meredith returned, I pulled on the World War II garb with Charlie's boots, since they were the only shoes I had. When Meredith learned Sam was driving me home, she couldn't stop laughing.

Sam was waiting in the foyer. He looked more dignified in khakis than in swim trunks, even though his khakis were wrinkled.

"Why did you arrive in your swimsuit?" I asked him.

"I had an idea you might show up at the pool. I wanted to be ready for anything. I'm beginning to think like you, Aggie. Unfortunately." He looked me up and down but didn't comment on my attire.

Meredith stifled giggles as we walked her to her car. When Sam and I meandered to his vehicle, he didn't seem to notice he was walking with a refugee. His features looked frozen. I suspected I was about to hear a lecture.

Thirty-Eight

Sam got in the car and slammed the door. "Agatha, you could have gotten yourself killed. You skipped out of your house, deceived poor Stanish, made that dog practically rip his pants off and raced off to the health club to confront a killer. Are you crazy?"

I resented that. I was curious and imaginative, but I was definitely not crazy and he knew it. I had to defend myself.

"Look. I knew Sheldon, Ned, Mickey, and Pete better than you did. They all hated me. Well, Pete just disliked me. I thought he had pushed me down the stairs. Now I know it was Linda."

He shook his head and started the car.

"Anyway, I knew if I could make the men angry enough, the killer, whoever he was, would try again. I wasn't sure about Harry. It was hard to imagine him killing the child he'd helped raise, no matter how badly she'd hurt him. Anyway, the men were all suspects, even if Linda, Patricia, Mindy, and Knobs had easier access to the women's locker room."

"Who are Patricia, Mindy, and Knobs?"

I ignored his question. "I was pretty sure that whoever killed Holly also tried to kill me. So I tormented Sheldon. Then I infuriated Ned. I gave Mickey the opportunity to do me in after Cardio Boot Camp. Mickey probably bragged to everybody at camp we were meeting at the pool, which might have alerted another suspect I hadn't even considered."

He looked over with an "I told you so" look and shook his head again.

"Linda knew I was going swimming with Mickey. When she

went to the locker room, every woman there probably heard her tease me about it. I thought if I could be sure the equipment room housing the electrical panel stayed open, the person who tried to fry Holly in the water would be tempted to try again."

"Well, you were right about that." He drove so slowly, I was surprised people didn't honk. His hair had plopped so low on his brow, it almost touched his glasses. I guess he hadn't had time to get a haircut.

"Sometimes, Agatha, you wear me out."

"You want to know the whole story, don't you? I realized Sheldon was too self-absorbed to expend the effort to kill anybody. Poor Ned really loved Holly, even though she could never be as dedicated or as mature as he was. But he could never kill anyone. So that left Mickey, Pete, Harry, Sarah (who was actually Linda), Patricia, Mindy, and Knobs."

"Who are...?"

"None of the women liked me, but I didn't think they knew me well enough to want to kill me."

He sighed as he turned up Burr Road. I was pretty tired myself.

He stopped his car in front of my house, looked directly at me and grabbed my hand. "I care about you, Aggie."

I closed my eyes, gave thanks, and opened them. "I know. I care about you, too. I always have."

"We need to have dinner—a nice, relaxed dinner somewhere."

I gazed down at Grace's clothes. I didn't want to go on my first real date with Sam looking like a bag lady. I wanted to be sparkling clean, fresh and beautiful. And I needed to hide Lee's bracelet in a more secure niche. I already felt younger.

"I can't tell Grace yet," I said.

"No. I'm afraid there's more to it."

I withdrew my hand. "More?"

"Remember my telling you that Grace's first husband, Charlie Livermore, went after young girls when he got drunk?"

"Of course."

"Anna, the neighbor, told us she thought Charlie went after Linda, too."

"His own daughter?"

"I'm afraid so. Linda confided in Martha, Anna's granddaughter. That's probably what started all this. Charlie Livermore molested Linda. She couldn't tell her mother, Grace. She thought her only option was to kill Charlie."

"I thought he died in his car from the fire, after he'd passed out from alcohol."

"He did. Kim told us he didn't really want to go out that night. Linda talked him into putting on his wool and silk jacket and taking her to dinner."

"Wait. As for the jacket, wasn't it Kim and not Linda, who studied textiles?"

"Yes. That's why it was significant when we found Linda's prints all over that chapter of Kim's book, the chapter describing deadly fumes produced by burning wool and silk."

"Didn't you tell me that foam and plastic in burning car seats produce cyanide gas?"

"I did. Linda undoubtedly knew it, too. She augmented her chances of killing Charlie with the combination of his burning jacket, the car seats, alcohol, and cigarettes."

"You apparently obtained the girls' textbooks after Elmore Moseley weaseled them away from Grace." I huffed and looked out the window.

"Yes. Including Linda's books on chemistry, pharmacy, and toxicology, and her computer ear-marking her favorite toxicology sites. The full name of the school where Linda applied is the University of Texas School of Pharmacy and Toxicology."

"Toxicology. The study of drugs and poisons."

"And how they contribute to a person's aberrant behavior and death. Once we matched prints from Linda's California office with prints on the girls' books to make sure it was the same woman, we traced her whereabouts from California to San Antonio and went through Fit and Firm's employee records. We got more prints from

Sarah Savoy's club locker. Just as we thought, they matched Linda Livermore's prints."

"How could you ever prove Linda murdered Charlie Livermore, given the combination of alcohol, fire and cyanide gas produced by burning seats?"

"We couldn't. That's why the ME deemed Charlie's death accidental, even after an autopsy."

"Would the ME find anything different now if he exhumed Charlie's body?"

"No."

"So there's really no reason to tell Grace."

"I guess there's no reason."

"I heard you accuse Linda Livermore of killing George Ball when he reneged on his and Grace's plan to adopt Martha's baby. Were you just fishing?"

"Not really. I think Linda did kill George Ball. I think she switched his pills after he nixed the adoption. I know he was excited about going hunting, but he wasn't stupid. From what I learned about George, he would have carefully packed his pillbox. When he stayed up too late and drank too much, he got careless and didn't check his pills. So Linda got her revenge."

"She really is sick. How can I tell Grace her daughter is a serial poisoner?"

"You can't. We can't prove that Charlie Livermore's or George Ball's death were homicides. But we have a good chance of pinning Holly Holmgreen's death on Linda. I think we can also prove Linda attempted to poison club members. SAPD is searching her San Antonio apartment and LA office. I'm sure they'll find a trace of crushed mothballs and other poisonous substances marked with her fingerprints. They should also find physical evidence to tie her car to the one that hit Holly."

"That's bad enough. Poor Grace. We'll keep it to ourselves? That Linda killed Grace's two husbands?"

"We'll keep it to ourselves. But you have to admit SAPD was right to be suspicious of the way Grace's husbands kept dying."

I looked at my lap and nodded.

"You know, Elmore Moseley is the best person Grace could have to comfort her," he said.

"Why?"

"He's worked in this business a long time. He understands, as much as anybody can, why some people feel compelled to commit murder. He's comforted scores of victims' families. He'll know the best way to help Grace."

"Grace is bound to find out he's a veteran detective. The part about his snooping through the girls' things and suspecting Grace— maybe we could keep that to ourselves too."

"I think we can do that. I know Elmore will prefer to keep it quiet. He's awfully fond of Grace." He sighed. "I'll try my best to comfort Harry Thorne."

He gathered me in a hug. My emotions bounced from grieving for Grace and her daughter Kim to despising and pitying Linda Livermore; from feeling sorry for Holly and Ned and poor Harry, to loving Sam. I felt more wretched than a World War II refugee. I put my arms around his neck.

Had I really changed from the haphazard girl of eighteen he used to know? Steady and honorable, he deserved more than a girl like that. I was playful and curious, but I was pretty sure I'd managed to grow up. At least I recognized the differences in men. I'd learned to value qualities that mattered and to pray for guidance. I lifted my face to his and he kissed me.

People made mistakes. They suffered. They grew. Sam was just now learning to understand the pain women felt when they lost children, whatever the circumstances. For now, maybe that was enough.

He kissed me again before he eased me away.

"I have to go to headquarters. I need to make reports and question Linda about how she mashed and mixed mothballs to poison you and Holly. I have to make sure she didn't concoct an additional little scheme, like stashing her brew all over the club. Why don't I pick you up at seven?"

I smiled. "We won't go to Tofu Temptations Grill?"

"No. Not to Tofu Temptations Grill." He leaned over and kissed me, slower. Then he cupped my face in his hands. Before he got out of the car, he kissed me like he meant it.

When we walked up the sidewalk, Grace was standing on her porch. I crammed her aunt's hat further down on my head. When she saw us, she doubled over laughing and went inside, holding her hand over her mouth so we wouldn't hear. Before he followed her inside, Boffo barked and wagged his tail at me.

"I guess Grace wonders why I'm dressed like this."

Sam winked at me, and I felt young. "I'll see you at seven. I promise we won't go to Tofu Temptations Grill or anywhere near the health club."

He didn't make promises very often. But I knew for certain that he kept the ones he made.

Thirty-Nine

I had a new, pressing reason to stay young. I decided to drag out old columns to find Dear Aggie's best advice. I flipped through my file cabinet and checked categories: brain stimulation (chasing a killer took care of that), exercise (a fat file), diet (even fatter), workout clothes, hair products, skin products and makeup.

My brain had survived poison and accidents, I exercised regularly, and my diet had drastically improved once I learned to avoid Sheldon Snodgrass and Tofu Temptations Grill.

Since I had only a few hours before Sam picked me up, I decided to concentrate on skin, hair and makeup. I opened the skin file and grabbed a recent letter:

Dear Aggie,

Once I passed forty, my skin adopted a lusterless, close-to-ill look. I tried various makeup brands but they produced color blotches different from my natural hue and made me appear two-toned. I'm squeamish about facials. What do you recommend?

Pasty in Pittsburg

Dear Pasty,

I'm not big on massage products, but this one seems to work: handheld, battery-operated NuvoFace:

"Massaged over face and neck, NuvoFace micro-currents lift and tone within minutes, reducing lines and wrinkles and lifting neck, brows and jowls." The ad says to add Moisturizing Mist and Conductivity Cream, but I don't recommend it. You might get startling results.

Pink, stimulated and happy,
Aggie

I had used NuvoFace. I shoved new batteries into the gadget and ran the device up and down my face and neck. In the bathroom, I retrieved my Abundant Hair Shampoo and Abundant Conditioner. Once my face was bright pink, I concentrated on reading hair product labels.

The shampoo would strengthen my new hair and add body to my old hair. The conditioner included vitamin B6, amino acids and botanicals (which I hoped didn't include fertilizers). These products would increase my hair growth 125% in less than a month, making frequent haircuts mandatory. That was okay. I had time to get a haircut now that I wasn't solving a murder.

I showered, shampooed and conditioned. When I re-checked my files for makeup tips. I found this:

Dear Aggie,

I have fairly uniform features—big eyes, straight nose—but my ribbon-thin fish lips make me look cynical and mean. This unfortunate feature scares dating prospects. Any ideas?

Frustrated in Fresno with Fish Lips

Dear FF with FL,

You've probably considered having plastic surgery to

puff your lips. Aggie knows these things. Hold off. You're in luck. Try LipPuff. You apply it at bedtime and awake with "plump, firm, hydrated, SEXY lips." You're advised not to eat, drink or talk for awhile because your lips will plump continuously for hours. (Product advertisers accept no responsibility.) You might alert your doctor in case something else swells. Allow a full day for LipPuff to work before you go out. Your date will find you more appealing if you're able to speak.

Aggie

After writing FF with FL, I'd actually bought LipPuff and tried it. My lips puffed beautifully. I think my face also acquired a few bulges. It was hard to tell with my eyes swollen shut.

I'd had to write an alert and retraction for my Dear Aggie column. The newspaper was not happy since I took up space on a non-column day. They got a lot of reader reaction, though.

Sam was due in a couple of hours. My hair was fluffed and shining and my face was pink, either from NuvoFace or anticipation. I skipped the LipPuff. Sam had suffered enough trauma. Besides, I wanted everything to feel perfectly natural in case he decided to kiss me again.

Don't Miss Aggie's Next Adventure

DANG NEAR DEAD #2

A dude ranch disaster.

Aggie vacations with Sam and Meredith at a Hill Country dude
ranch with plans to advise her column readers how to stay young
and fresh in summer. Except for wranglers, dudes, heat, snakes
and poison ivy, what could go wrong?
When an expert rider is thrown from a horse and lies in a coma,
Aggie is convinced somebody caused the fall. Despite Sam's
warnings, she is determined to expose the assailant. She concocts
ingenious sleuthing methods that probe secrets of the ranch and
strain their dicey relationship. When she scatters a cabal of
cowboys, she finds that more than one hombre in the bunch would
like to see her permanently Home on the Range.

Mystery &Mayhem Short List
Chanticleer International Book Awards

"I love this character, Aggie Mundeen. West does such a good job of
making Aggie humorous, but with a brain."_Reviewer Jennifer Gott,
Houston, Texas

Second Edition

Aggie Returns to College

SMART, BUT DEAD #3

Academics can be murder.

Skirting forty and appalled by the prospect of descending into middle-age decrepitude, Aggie Mundeen blasts off to the local university to study the genetics of aging. She is doggedly determined to stay young.

Despite conflicts with her professor, she learns about the Human Genome Project and DNA. When she discovers a dead body, Detective Sam reminds her not to "help" with the investigation. But dangerously curious and programmed to prod, she races to solve the crime, winds up the prime suspect and is on target to become next campus corpse.

Mystery & Mayhem Short List
Chanticleer International Book Awards

"A tight mystery, an irrepressible heroine, and superb writing."
_Award-winning author James W. Ziskin

"Aggie's pluck, humor, intelligence and loving heart keep her young and make readers smile."
_Award-winning author Carolyn Hart

Destination Vacation: the San Antonio River Walk.

RIVER CITY DEAD #4

A vacation in paradise?

Aggie Mundeen, columnist and amateur sleuth, prepares for an idyllic weekend with her love interest, SAPD Detective Sam at a San Antonio River Walk hotel.

Single for years and pushing forty, she is jittery. She yearns for a weekend away from crime-a fiesta, not a fiasco. But Sam, already at the hotel, calls her. S omething is very wrong in their luxury suite. A surprise. Mischief. Murder.

Raven Award Mystery Winner

Killer Nashville Highlighted Book

"*River City Dead* is peppered with humor and wit and has a nice touch of romance in the plot. the Texas setting and use of Fiesta Week as background give distinctive flavor to this novel. This installment in the Aggie Mundeen series has all the elements of a great cozy mystery. Highly recommended." _Mystery Tribune

VISIT THE AUTHOR

Facebook

https://www.facebook.com/authorNancyG.West/

Website
https://www.nancygwest.com

Aggie's Blog
https://nancygwest.com/aggies-blog/

Nancy G. West

As she finished *Nine Days to Evil*, her novel of psychological suspense, a funny thing happened. A supporting character, Aggie Mundeen, with her wry sense of humor, entered West's consciousness and demanded she write a book about her...or maybe a series. The result, *Fit to Be Dead*, was Lefty Award Finalist for Best Humorous Mystery. The next Aggie Mundeen Mysteries, *Dang Near Dead*, *Smart, But Dead*, and *River City Dead*, won or were nominated for awards.

In West's novella, *The Plunge*, Aggie and Detective Sam are in a lakeside bungalow as the river rises and floods, exposing a suspicious drowning. This suspenseful mystery is based on West's experience in a flood and will likely lead to her next series, the Aggie Mundeen Lake Mysteries.

JOIN A PRIVATE CLUB

To receive special offers, updates and author insights, click subscribe below and enter your email address.

https://www.subscribepage.com/a1n3e1

CPSIA information can be obtained
at www.ICGtesting.com
Printed in the USA
BVHW040430280820
587480BV00010B/91